KILLING RICHARD DAWSON

A note from the publisher

Dear Reader,

If you enjoy riveting stories with engaging characters and strong writing, as I do, you'll love *Killing Richard Dawson*. A dark yet redeeming, funny thriller about love and death. It's Robin Baker's debut novel. It had me hooked from the very first chapter, and I couldn't put it down. It's a real *Story for Story Lovers*™.

If you haven't picked up a *Pantera Press* book before, you should know that simply by enjoying our books, you'll also be contributing to our unique approach: good books doing good things™.

We're passionate about discovering the next generation of well-loved Australian authors, and nurturing their writing careers. We've also given our business a strong 'profits for philanthropy' foundation, focussed on literacy, quality writing, the joys of reading and fostering debate.

Let me mention one program we're thrilled to support: *Let's Read*. It's already helping 100,000 pre-schoolers across Australia with the building blocks of learning how to read and write. We're excited that *Let's Read* now also operates in remote Indigenous communities in Far North Queensland, Cape York, and Torres Strait. *Let's Read* was developed by the *Centre for Community Child Health* and is being implemented in partnership with *The Smith Family*.

Simply buying this book will help us support these kids. Thank you.

Want to do more? If you visit www.PanteraPress.com/Donate you can personally donate to help *The Smith Family* expand *Let's Read*, find out more about this great program, and also more on the other programs *Pantera Press* supports.

Please enjoy *Killing Richard Dawson*. And for news about our other books, sample chapters, author interviews and much more, please visit our website: www.PanteraPress.com

Happy reading,

Alison Green

Killing Richard Dawson

ROBIN BAKER

PanteraPress
good books doing good things™

PanteraPress
good books doing good things™

First published in 2010 by Pantera Press Pty Limited
www. PanteraPress.com

A Cataloguing-in-Publication entry for this book is available from the National Library of
Australia.

ISBN 978-0-9807418-0-3

Editors: Glenda Downing and Pantera Press
Cover and internal design: Luke Causby, Blue Cork
Cover image of glass: © iStockphoto.com/Dusan Zidar
Author Photo by Robert Firth/ Acorn Photo Agency
Typesetting in Jason Text by Kirby Jones
Printed and bound in Australia by Griffin Press

Pantera Press policy is to use papers that are natural, renewable and recyclable products made from
wood grown in sustainable forests. The logging and manufacturing processes are expected to
conform to the environmental regulations of the country of origin.

For Lilian Little

"One faces the future with one's past."
Pearl S. Buck

"Friendship often ends in love;
but love in friendship – never."
Charles Caleb Colton

"I am scared that nothing is real."
Jostein Gaarder

ONE

Let me tell you something.

Don't get excited, it's nothing earth shattering. It just came to me and I thought I'd like to share it before I go.

I've been thinking about it a lot lately and I've come to this conclusion: the guy who said, 'It's better to have loved and lost than never to have loved at all', well, he really didn't have the slightest idea what the fuck he was talking about.

I know that sounds jaded and cynical, but it's true. How can it be better to have experienced the most wondrous joy you can imagine then have it torn away from you? How is it better to constantly feel hollow and empty, regularly finding yourself alone and sobbing, curled in a ball on the floor? Wouldn't it just be better to never experience love in the first place? That way, when you find yourself alone, you never knew what you missed out on so it doesn't seem quite as bad.

Because, believe me, you'll find yourself alone.

Is it really worth it? All the shit we go through, all the heartache and the suffering?

I'm sitting here wondering what happened. I'm trying to piece the whole thing together. I'm trying to figure where it all went wrong. Everything is just sailing along, then the slightest ripple and the whole thing capsizes. The smallest action and the world changes.

George is lying on the floor in front of me, doubled over with his hands clamped over his stomach. He is very pale and his lips are a strange bluish-purple colour that really doesn't suit him. I can see he is moving so he's not all the way dead yet. I should be happy that my best friend is still alive but really I can't feel anything. I am completely numb, in every way a person can be. I simply can't feel a thing. I just sit on this expensive grey blood-soaked couch and watch my best friend die.

George twitches again and his hands on his belly slip and blood squirts out and mixes with the already considerable pool spreading around him. He tries to close the hole in his belly with his fingers, pinching it between his thumb and forefinger, but it doesn't stop the blood pumping out.

He tries to roll onto his back and he almost makes it, but then utters a sharp barking cry and he falls back onto his side. I listen to him cry and can barely feel the tears rolling down my own face.

Funny how these little things bring up a whole storm of emotions. You can be dead to the world yet still cry over a cat lying on the side of the road. Funny how the mind works.

But I am glad George isn't dead. We've been through a lot together.

He tries again to roll onto his back and this time he is more successful. With one big push he makes it and crashes onto his back, panting. More blood erupts from his belly and he clasps his hands, red and wet and shiny and dripping, tighter over the hole between his sternum and his bellybutton. The blood is still pumping out of him with every beat of his heart. His shirt is soaked through and clings to his chest, which moves up and down as he breathes heavily through his mouth, up and down, and I can barely hear him over my own harsh gasps.

He swallows and a trickle of blood runs down his cheek. My own mouth is dry and when I run my tongue across my palate it's like licking sandpaper.

'What the fuck happened?' he asks me.

I've been wondering the same thing.

George groans again. His eyes are closed tight, his jaw is clenched and I can see the sweat running down his forehead. Judging by the pool of blood I'd say he didn't have much longer to live, which is not always a bad thing – being shot in the stomach isn't the nicest way to go.

Richard Dawson is dead. I know that now. I guess I've known it for a while but I've only just come to accept it. I had been hoping it wasn't so but now I see it's the truth and there's nothing I can do about it.

I guess it could have been worse. At least I wasn't there when it happened.

Actually, I haven't been there in quite a while.

All the memories of the people we've loved, the places we've been, the things that once meant something. We move along through this life and they fade away like stars in the dawn.

George's breath is coming in short little pants. He swallows again and I hear his throat click. I watch blood running down his cheek. This must mean that something inside him has ruptured and the blood is working its way up his throat and out his mouth.

'They're not coming back, are they?' he asks me.

I shake my head. 'I don't think so. Would you?'

George tries to laugh but coughs instead. The coughing tears through his chest and is replaced by sobs.

'Your guts aren't going to, like, fall out or anything, are they?' I ask.

George snorts and says, 'Dude.'

I tell him I'm sorry. For everything. I know that's not the best thing to say to someone who's just been shot in the stomach but it's all I can think of.

He speaks in a rush, holding his breath against the pain. 'Have you called an ambulance?' he asks.

I shake my head, no.

'Are you going to?'

'No.'

'Why not?'

'Because I think it's better this way.'

George licks his lips and leaves a red smear around the edge of his mouth. His face is a mix of colours: white skin, purple lips, red blood. His breathing slows and he seems to relax.

'Are you sure that's what you want?' he asks me.

'I think so, yes.'

He says, 'I can't remember much of what happened – it's all, like, a blur.'

I nod. 'Maybe you've lost too much blood and can't think properly.' I don't know how scientific this explanation is; I don't know the first thing about blood and brains and thinking.

He laughs again, just a single breath this time. It clearly hurts him to do this and his face bunches up and he inhales through clenched teeth. 'That might be it,' he says, but I don't know if he's joking or serious. After a moment, he asks, 'Can you help me?'

'What?'

'Help me remember. Fill in the blanks.'

'I'll try.'

'Tell me everything that happened.'

'Okay.'

I know this is going to hurt, going over the whole thing again. But hopefully it will convince George that dying really is the best solution.

I'm going to start at the start. Begin at the beginning.

I look down at George, his life running out of him through the hole in his stomach, and I try to think back to how it all started.

I think back to how it all went wrong.

It starts slowly but things speed up, so bear with me.

Ready.

Starting at the start.

Set.

Beginning at the beginning.

Go.

Two

My mother gave birth to me, back when I was a baby. I have grown a bit since then, which I guess is lucky for her. It was a good thing she spat me out when I was still small and not the size I am today.

It's not that I'm fat or anything; in fact I think I'm in quite good shape. But I'm a lot taller now than I was nineteen years ago.

I'll skip over a lot of this. Baby stories are one of those things you only pretend you're interested in. You sit through them if you have to and laugh at the appropriate cute moments, but really, you're wishing it were over. So I'll cut it short.

After I was born, I started to grow up.

I was an only child and what they say about only children is not true. I was never spoiled or given too much attention. When I went to playgroup I always waited my turn in line, just like everyone else. I never pushed or shoved, apart from once, when I got into a fight with Tommy McMurray. He started it, though. It was my turn on the swings and he pushed in front of me.

My mother used to ask me, why didn't I play with the other

children? Why did I always play games alone? I told her I liked it better that way, and that the other children were annoying. Although really, it was the other children who wouldn't play games with me. They would leave me out and pick on me and tease me and do all those other things kids do. I used to wonder why no one liked me, whether it was because I was too tall or too short or too fat or too thin or too stupid or what. Or maybe they were just scared of me, after what happened with Tommy McMurray. Maybe, every time they looked at me, they thought back to what happened to Tommy's face.

So instead of joining in with the other children, I would play alone. I would build cities out of blocks then pretend I was driving a little toy car around in them, watching all the people busy with their lives. They would be playing sport, walking their dogs, holding hands and having fun. Then, an earthquake would strike and the cities would be reduced to rubble.

I would sit by myself at the back of the classroom and draw pictures and think up stories about dogs and trees and other happy things. The people in the stories would go out and have picnics with their families and friends and they would laugh and sing, and I would sit and think about these perfect people and I would cry.

I was sitting in the back of the room one afternoon while all the other kids had gone outside to play. I had written a story about a bird and how it could fly anywhere, do anything, be totally free.

I hadn't actually written this story, of course. At this time, I couldn't read or write. So, instead, I had drawn a picture and had the story to go along with it all worked out in my head.

I had gotten to the part where the bird had met another bird so the first bird wasn't lonely anymore and I had started to cry without realising it. A boy came up to me and said, hello.

I looked at him through my tears and said, hello.

'Why are you crying?' he said.

I shook my head. I didn't know.

He looked at my picture and said, 'They're nice birds.'

I said, 'Thank you.'

He asked me if I was crying about the birds.

I didn't know. 'I guess so.'

'Why? Because they have wings and you don't?'

I didn't say anything, I just wiped my eyes with the back of my hand.

'Or is it because the bird has a friend, and you don't?'

I looked up at him. 'How did you know that?'

He smiled at me. 'Why else would you be sitting in the back of the classroom, alone and crying?'

I looked down again at the page, trying not to meet his eyes. He was awful smart.

He held his hand out. 'Hi, I'm George.'

I looked up again, expecting him to pull his hand away and laugh the moment I reached for it. But he looked at me levelly as I slowly extended my hand. He kept looking at me and didn't pull away.

We shook.

I told him it was nice to meet him. I went to introduce myself but he said, 'I know who you are.'

I smiled at him. He already knew my name.

He smiled back. 'Yeah, I did. And you don't need to cry anymore. I'll be your friend.'

'Really?'

'Really. Come on, let's go outside,' he said, and I followed him.

This was how George and I became best friends.

*   *   *

After that we did everything together. We built cities from blocks or sand and I would drive my toy car down the streets and look at the people and their friends and I would look at George and I wouldn't cry anymore. I would keep driving and waving at the people walking their dogs and I would be happy because I wasn't doing it alone. At the end of the day, when it was time to go home, there would be no earthquake to level the cities and everyone would get to live happily ever after.

George could always think of something to do. He would always have the best ideas for games when I couldn't think of anything.

After playgroup we would go into the trees at the edge of the park near my house and hunt for tigers. We carried guns made of twigs, or sometimes we hunted with only our bare hands. We would creep through the heart of the jungle and hunt the tigers, being careful to avoid booby traps set by tribes of head-hunting cannibals. When George thought we were getting close to our prey, we would crouch down and stay perfectly still, waiting for the tiger to show itself. Eventually it would give away its position and we would stand up and shoot it with our guns.

Sometimes there were no tigers and it didn't matter because we were too busy fighting a war. We would run through the forest, our faces streaked with mud, ducking as explosions and gunfire tore through the silence around us. We would take cover behind fallen logs and shoot hordes of soldiers as they tried to storm our position. Eventually the waves of enemy troops would cease and we would have won the war and saved the world.

On other days, when there were no animals to be hunted and no armies to kill, we would embark on more peaceful pursuits.

We would build boats out of leaves and sticks and sail them down the stream. We would lie on our backs and gaze up at the clouds, finding shapes and images in the sky. I was never bored when George was around. I never cried because I was lonely. This was one of the happiest times of my life.

One day, we were lying on our backs on the warm grass, staring up at the blue, blue sky, watching the birds dancing on the wind, and George asked me if I still wanted to be up there with them.

At first I didn't know what he was talking about. Then I remembered the picture I had drawn when we first met.

'Do you still want to fly?' he asked.

'I don't know. It was just a picture.'

'It must have meant something,' he told me, 'or you wouldn't have drawn it.'

'How do you know all this?'

He shrugged. 'I'm good at figuring stuff out.'

I agreed. He was usually right about stuff, too.

'So, it must mean something.'

I asked him if he was going to teach me to fly.

He smiled at me. 'Like the birds? No.' He watched the birds playing and said, 'One day I'll teach you to fly but not yet.'

I waited for him to say something else but he was silent. I didn't know if he was joking or serious or what, and I didn't want to ask. I liked it when George talked this way. He made it seem like the world was a wondrous place, full of excitement and mystery. I thought, as long as George was by my side, nothing could go wrong.

THREE

Psychologists, psychiatrists, defence lawyers, they all say the past is important.

The past follows us around. Our memories, those little scars we carry with us, they're some of the parts that make up the whole. The wounds left behind from when we were happy.

I've lived in the same place pretty much all my life, with just a few small changes. I lived with my parents and we got along pretty well; as well as can be expected, anyway. They didn't yell at me very much but they yelled at each other plenty. They were always fighting and the only time it was peaceful was when one of them was out.

When I was home alone with one of my parents we would have talks. They would tell me all about the world, and life, and what everything means and how I should act and what I should do and everything else they thought I needed to know. My mother would tell me one thing and my dad would tell me something else. I would never know whom to believe because their ideas were all so different, so eventually I stopped listening to them and started taking more notice of George. He seemed to have it all worked out.

My parents would complain to me about each other. My dad would tell me how my mother was lazy and all she did was sit around the house while he went out and worked and earned money to put food on the table, clothes on our backs and a roof over our heads. My mother would then tell me how hard she worked all day keeping the house clean and then how Dad was out all day doing god knows what and he never appreciated her. They continued to fight and bitch and moan up until the day my dad died.

My mother was never the same after that. At first she just complained to me about how he went out and left her right in the middle of everything and how she hoped he burned in hell but I thought she secretly missed him. Sometimes I would hear her crying late at night when I was in bed. If I got up to see what was wrong she would tell me she had something caught in her eye and not to worry about it and go back to sleep. So I did.

She started leaving me with babysitters, then with no one. She would go out, leaving me at home with the television, then come home noisy and drunk with some man who was always gone before I woke up. On these mornings I would sometimes hear my mother crying but I never knew why.

I only ever met one of these men. I was ten years old, nearly eleven, and my dad had been dead almost three years. My mother had been seeing this guy for about two weeks and she decided it was time to introduce me. She told me she had met him at a club one night and that he was very nice and I should be on my best behaviour. After school she dressed me up in a nice little suit and combed my hair and told me I had to act like a perfect little gentleman.

So this guy came around for dinner and, sure enough, I was nice and polite and said hello and please and thank you and excuse me and all those other things you have to say when you're being polite. When he arrived, we all stood at the front door while my mother introduced me.

He smiled down at me and said, 'Hi, it's nice to meet you.'

I tried to smile back up at him.

George had said this man might end up being my new dad. I told George I didn't want a new dad, I had liked the old one. George said the old dad was dead.

He held his hand out and I slowly placed my hand in his. His fingers closed around my hand and he shook it delicately, as if he might break it.

He said, 'My name's Donald.'

The first thing I thought of was Donald Duck and I tried not to laugh. He must have seen this because he said, 'Yeah, I know, it's a pretty funny name.'

My mother laughed nervously. 'Oh no, he wasn't laughing at you. Were you?'

I shook my head.

'It's okay, really,' Donald said. He looked down at me, smiling. 'Sometimes, I even laugh at myself.'

I smiled politely.

She laughed again. 'He's very quiet,' she explained. 'Please, come in.'

We all walked through to the main sitting room.

'Make yourself comfortable,' my mother instructed. 'I'll go get us a drink.' She walked through to the kitchen, leaving me alone with Donald.

There was a moment of silence.

Then another one.

And another.

Finally, Donald asked, 'So, do you like sports?'

I shrugged.

He smiled and nodded. 'You know, when I was your age, I used to play all sorts of sports. If it involved a ball, I used to play it.'

It was my turn to smile.

There was more silence.

Eventually my mother walked in carrying two drinks. She handed one to Donald, who smiled and nodded thanks. She sat down next to him. I noticed there was no drink for me.

Donald said to Mum, 'We were just discussing sports,' then to me, 'Weren't we?'

I shook my head, no.

Donald laughed quietly and took a drink. He turned to my mother. 'So, what's for dinner?'

We ate dinner and Donald told my mother all about his day and his job and his money and what was wrong with the world and his life. She had a couple more drinks and nodded as he spoke although her eyes glazed over and she stared at something over Donald's shoulder. Occasionally she covered a yawn with the back of her hand. One time, Donald asked her if she was okay, if she was tired. She told him it had just been a busy day, smiled, and had another drink.

I excused myself after I finished eating and went into my room to watch television. Before long I fell asleep but was woken by the sounds of muffled yelling. The little red numbers on my bedside clock said it was twenty past eleven. I couldn't make out what the voices were saying but they sounded angry.

Donald said, 'Bitch.'

Then my mother said something else.

Donald said, 'Dead' or 'Bed', I couldn't tell.

Then my mother yelled at him to get out, to get the hell out, then there were a few more yells, the sound of the front door slamming, and then silence.

I went back to sleep.

That was the only time I ever met one of my mother's boyfriends. After that incident she didn't have many more. I don't know if she ever saw Donald again. She didn't go out as much as she used to and she seemed quieter and more reserved. She stopped talking to people. George kept telling me that something was wrong but I never listened to him, I just thought she was sick or something.

We began to eat less and less and when we did eat it was either fast food or something barely recognisable she had cooked up herself. Towards the end she would hardly speak. She would rarely even acknowledge my presence. She was there physically but that's all.

One day I came home from school and I went into the kitchen to get a glass of milk. I pushed the door open and the first thing I noticed was the smell. It was a strange smell, almost spicy, and then I saw my mother was cleaning the oven. She was leaning on the open door with her head deep inside. I said hello but she didn't answer. I really hadn't expected a response; she didn't talk to me at all at this point.

I opened the fridge and took out the milk. There was a strange hissing noise coming from the oven and that smell seemed to be stronger.

I asked her if she needed any help.

There was no answer. She was probably angry with me for something.

I took the milk and went into the other room.

I thought maybe my mother wasn't sad anymore and the cloud had finally lifted from over her head. I thought maybe that's why she was working so hard to clean the oven and, even at dinnertime when she still hadn't come out of the kitchen, I didn't go in to disturb her in case I said something wrong and depressed her again. When she was still in the kitchen at bedtime, I was almost positive that, when I woke up, everything would be back the way it had been before she got sad.

Instead, when I woke up, she was still in the kitchen. The house was now filled with the smell coming from the oven and it was starting to make me feel sick. It also made me feel very sleepy and it was harder for me to wake up that morning than it usually was. If I didn't have my bedroom window open, I might not have woken up at all.

Then I figured it out.

The smell had put her to sleep.

She needed me to wake her up.

I walked through to the kitchen and, as I suspected, she was still sleeping with her head in the oven. I knelt down beside her and put my hand on her shoulder.

I asked, 'Mum?'

There was no response.

I shook her and spoke to her again, louder this time.

Still nothing.

This time I shook her almost as hard as I could. She slid out of the oven and rolled onto the floor, her head banging the cupboard door on the way down. She still didn't move, not even when I yelled into her ear or poured water on her face.

Eventually I came to the conclusion she might be dead.

I had never seen a dead person before, I wasn't home when my dad died, but at first I felt nothing at all. I decided I'd better call an ambulance.

I remember I didn't cry.

I picked up the telephone and dialled the number.

'Hello?' a voice asked me. 'What is the nature of your emergency?'

I told him I thought my mother was dead.

He asked me for my address and, after a moment, he told me an ambulance was on its way.

I told him there was no need to rush. I didn't think she'd be going anywhere.

He asked me if I knew what happened.

I told him how she had slept to death. How she had been cleaning inside the oven and the smell had put her to sleep and now she couldn't wake up.

He asked me how long she had been sleeping.

I told him how I had come home from school and she was sleeping and how she had been sleeping all night and how she was still sleeping this morning.

Soon after that the ambulance arrived and some police came, too. I remember men put my mother on a trolley and wrapped her in white plastic. The police asked me questions and they wanted me to talk to a psychologist but I told them I was fine.

The men wheeled my mother out and that was the last time I ever saw her.

Four

I'm sitting here in the front room of my grandmother's house talking to the social worker. Part of the deal of me living with Gran is that every two weeks I have to meet with the social worker and talk about life and whatever's on my mind.

Actually, the social worker was coming here anyway to check on my gran, but the government decided to use her for me as well, to save them sending two people.

The sun is streaming through the front windows and gives the room a warm and inviting look. On the walls there are photos of me when I was a baby. There are pictures of my mother when she was a baby. There are also pictures of someone else when they were a baby, but I don't know who.

The social worker is sitting on the couch opposite from me with her leather satchel open on the floor beside her. She has a clipboard on her lap and is writing something down.

She looks up at me and smiles, as if she's being paid enough to actually care.

'So, everything is going okay? There haven't been any dramas or anything?'

I shake my head. 'Nope. Everything's great.'

'Nothing you need to tell me?'

'Nope.'

She writes something else down.

We've been having these heart-to-heart talks for eight years now. That's how long it's been since Mum killed herself and that's how long I've been living with Gran. Since Gran is old, she needs someone to look after her. Since I was young and homeless, the government thought it would be in our best interests if we lived together. That way, I get a house and she gets someone to look after her. We both get welfare and it all works out quite nicely. We even get our own social worker.

She comes around for an hour every two weeks and talks about whatever. The first half is dedicated to Gran: how she's feeling, her medication, all that other stuff to do with old people. The second half is mine. This is where I get to sit down and talk about anything I like.

At first, when I was younger and we hardly knew each other, I never talked. It's hard to pour your heart out to a complete stranger, especially one who is being paid to offer you advice and sympathy. So, our time together went by and I would sit and she would ask me questions and I would answer them half-heartedly. Then the hour would be up and she would leave.

But as I got older I gradually started to open up. We're friends now, or at least as much as you can be with someone in that position. And these days we don't just talk about me. She tells me what's going on in her life and it's just like watching a fortnightly soap opera. I tell her what I'm feeling, she tells me what's going on in her life and in the lives of her other assignments. She calls the people she looks after 'assignments', and I can see her telling one of these people all about me.

So much for confidentiality.

Part of the reason she was assigned to me is because she's young. When we first met she was still in training and they had given my gran to her because she was old and would be good practice. Then I had come into the picture and she had taken me on too. They thought I was depressed and possibly suicidal, having lost my father when I was eight and seeing my mother commit suicide when I was eleven. Having someone not a lot older than me seemed like a good idea as she could be a friend as well as a social worker, someone I could relate to.

'Did you do anything on the weekend?' she asks.

'Not really. It was a pretty quiet one.'

'Me too. I had a date but it didn't go so well.'

'That sucks.'

'Yeah. But you know what they say. Guys are like parking spots: all the good ones are taken and the rest are disabled.'

I clear my throat, not so subtly.

She laughs. 'Oh, except you, of course.'

'Thanks.'

The social worker and I share a very open relationship. After she'd first started coming I used to try to make her life hell. I'd confide in her all my deep dark secrets that didn't exist. I'd tell her about horrible thoughts I'd never had and terrible things I'd never done. I tried to scare her away but she just kept coming back and in a way I'm glad. She passed my tests and now she's here to stay.

She says, 'I can't find Mister Right. How can I find someone who doesn't exist? I've tried all the usual stuff. Nightclubs. Singles' bars. The internet. How else do people meet?' She sighs. 'How about you?'

'I can't find Mister Right, either.'

She laughs. 'You know what I mean.'

I nod. 'I go clubbing and places like that, but honestly, finding Miss Right isn't that important,' I lie. 'For now, I'm quite happy being by myself.'

She nods. 'Maybe you and I should just hook up and save ourselves the trouble?'

I don't know if she's joking so I smile and nod and say, 'Yeah, it'd be a lot easier that way.' This way the ball is back in her court.

She does what I expect her to do: she avoids my remark. 'But seriously,' she asks, 'don't you ever get lonely?'

I pause and pretend to consider this. 'Not really,' I lie again. 'I'll meet someone one day and until then I'm prepared to wait.'

She smiles. 'Easy as that, huh?'

'Easy as that. After all, one day I'm going to become a famous celebrity and the girls will be crawling all over me.'

She laughs and nods. 'Yeah, whatever.'

'Hey,' I tell her, 'you're not supposed to say that. You can't depress me or who knows what I'll do.'

She tells me she's sorry, but in a light-hearted way. After a moment her smile fades and she asks me, 'You wouldn't, would you?'

'Wouldn't what?'

'Do anything drastic,' she says. 'Like, kill yourself or anything.'

This is another one of those questions you can't honestly answer, especially to your social worker. If I say no, they might stop sending her. Or if I say no, then do actually kill myself, how will that make her feel? Or if I just come right out and say yes, I'm going to kill myself, she's bound to get all worried and our relationship will go all the way back to square one.

No, I'd prefer to just spring it on everyone one day.

Surprise!

So I tell her, 'I wouldn't dare. If I did, you'd kill me.'

She smiles at this but doesn't meet my gaze and her smile quickly fades. 'You would tell me though, wouldn't you? If you were considering doing anything like that?' She doesn't have much of a sense of humour about some things.

'Sure,' I tell her, 'why not? We're all friends here, and it's your job to keep me alive and happy and a productive member of society.'

You don't need to die to destroy yourself.

'Good,' she says, 'because a lot of people would miss you if you left.'

'Really? Like who?'

'Your gran would miss you,' she tells me.

'My gran doesn't even know I'm here. She wouldn't know if I went out and never came back.'

'I know she's a little...'

'Senile?'

'Well, yes, senile, but she's not that bad.'

'Yes, she is. Trust me.'

'Okay, well, maybe that was a bad example. But how about me? Don't forget me.'

'Here you go again with your professional friendship and funded concern.'

'No, really,' she tells me, 'I would miss you. I'd like to think that over the last eight years we've developed more than just a professional relationship. I'd like to think of us as friends.'

'Yeah, okay, but that's only two.'

'What about a girl?' she asks me. 'You sure there's no one special in that department?'

'Oh, look at the time,' I tell her. 'Shouldn't you be moving on?'

She gives me a look and says, 'Come on. You never tell me any of the juicy stuff.'

'I'm sorry,' I tell her, 'maybe next time.'

Five

I'm leaning against the bar looking out over the crowded dance floor. The room is thick with cigarette smoke. Strobe lights and coloured beams dart around in random patterns, making it hard to see anything clearly; it's like watching something through a shutter that's opening and closing very quickly. The music is so loud I wonder how the bartenders know what people are ordering. You don't hear the music so much as feel it; the constant *boom* of the bass deep inside your ribcage. The songs all sound the same and blend into each other, which I'm sure is a great compliment to the 'musicians'. The bar itself is covered with a long mat, wet with beer, and when I move my feet my shoes stick to the floor.

George is standing beside me, yelling into my ear, but I can't hear him over the music.

The room is so crowded I can't move my arm without bumping someone. People are standing around looking at each other because it's pointless trying to talk. A few of them are still trying and you can hear a mumble over the top of the thumping music. They soon give up and resume their silence.

The guys all stand at the bar while the girls dance in small groups. There are a couple of guys trying to dance, unsuccessfully. They're all wearing the same sort of clothes and the girls look like they have all been made on the same production line: blonde hair, blue eyes, slim figures – real-life Barbies. Of course there are exceptions, such as the brunettes and people like me.

The truth is, I can't fit into these stereotypes. I'd love to be one of those guys who looks good and always gets the girl, but I can't, no matter how hard I try.

And, believe me, I try.

I spend hours in front of the mirror trying to make myself look perfect. I wear nice clothes, have a good haircut, I don't smell. But I can't ever pick up a girl.

That's why I come to clubs like this one. It's not for the music or the atmosphere or the drugs or the alcohol. It's for the girls. It's for the blondes and the brunettes and the redheads and even those chicks with dyed fluorescent green or pink hair. It's for the tall ones and the short ones and the slim ones and the ones with long hair and the ones with short hair. It's for the ones with big tits and the ones with medium tits and for the pretty ones and the ones with nice smiles and ones that even glance at me.

You wouldn't say I was picky.

We are attracted to people who we think would produce good offspring. Guys like girls with big breasts and childbearing hips. Girls like guys with broad shoulders and strong jawbones. It's all about the physical characteristics we want to pass on to our young. So, really, personality doesn't have all that much to do with it. That's why the music in clubs is so loud.

I hang around these clubs trying to pick up one of the girls. So far, I haven't had any luck.

And I don't just mean tonight.

I mean, ever.

I come to these places all the time, looking my best, being my most charming, and not once have I managed to pick up a girl.

George is yelling at me but I still can't hear him.

And I don't just try this club, either. Other places I've tried include shopping centres, supermarkets, dentists, fast-food restaurants, malls, doctors' surgeries, cinemas, parks, hospital waiting rooms, zoos, fairs, food courts, veterinarians, abortion clinics, concert venues, music stores, cemeteries, movie rental stores, funeral parlours, liquor stores, pharmacies, bus stops; anywhere where there's people. Anyplace is a good place to try.

And, believe me, I try.

I look around the crowded room and I can't really make anyone out. The flashing lights and smoke combine to obscure my vision, and all the bodies moving quickly make it almost impossible for me to see anything.

'Fuck this,' I say to George, 'I'm going for a walk.'

George yells something back at me.

'What?' I yell.

He yells again.

I tell him I can't hear him.

He can't hear me either.

I hold up my hand and point my index and middle finger at the ground and move them back and forth, to signify that I am going for a walk. I then point at myself, to confirm who I'm talking about, then I do the finger motion again.

He nods and gives me the thumbs up.

I turn and begin to fight my way through the crowd. Everyone keeps dancing, off in their own little worlds, as if I'm not there, trying to push past them. People are crashing into me, pushing me back and forth, some are almost tripping over me, but they still don't look around, they just keep dancing.

It's almost like I'm invisible.

The urge to reproduce comes from the hypothalamus, that tiny little pea inside your head that causes so much trouble. You see someone you like and it signals the pituitary gland, which then informs the sex organs by releasing the luteinising hormone. These produce oestrogen, progesterone and testosterone. Then, before you know it, you feel light-headed, your heart pounds. You're in love.

I keep walking through the crowd, pushing people away, using my elbows to fight my way through. I can see the door up ahead that leads to a corridor, which leads to the bathrooms. I don't need to go but there's always a queue, which is a good place to meet people.

First, the man sees the woman. She meets his criteria for a possible partner, and the heart starts to speed up. He walks over to her and says, Hi.

Finally I'm through the door and I'm in a long corridor that's dimly lit from small bulbs in the ceiling. As expected, the girls' line is long but sadly there is no line for the gents and a couple of guys ahead of me walk straight in. This gives me no plausible excuse to stand around outside.

There's no mating season or courting rituals for humans. The originality of the guy's approach scores points. Women also find physical attractiveness significant, but not as much as guys. For women, social criteria are important, as they want a male who will provide for the offspring and be a stable, long-term mate. Guys want sex.

Of course, this is all very theoretical. I wouldn't want to make it seem like I have all the answers. There's no right or wrong here.

Reluctantly I walk inside the bathroom. It's a typical male bathroom, with urinals, a couple of stalls and a wall with sinks and a mirror. I go to the urinal and piss even though I don't really need to because you can't go into a bathroom and not do anything as it makes people suspicious. I wash my hands and leave.

The female line has grown in the time I've been inside, which would have been three minutes, tops. Again I marvel at how lucky I am to be a guy.

I leave the corridor and am relieved to discover the music has become slightly quieter. I can now hear people screaming over the top of it but their words are still indecipherable.

I start to walk back across the dance floor and am immediately battered from both sides as people dance around me, as if I'm not even there.

I accidentally jab someone especially hard with my elbow and I instinctively turn to apologise.

Standing in front of me is a girl, my height, with long blonde hair and blue eyes. She's wearing a blue dress with what appears to be some sort of ocean print on it, with little pictures of fish and coral, and it brings out the colour in her eyes.

I tell her I'm sorry.

She yells, 'That's okay.'

I say I really didn't mean to hit her like that.

'Really, it's okay,' she yells. 'Really.'

I smile and try to laugh, and I tell her how hard it is to walk in these places, with people pushing you around all the time.

She nods understandingly.

'Honestly,' I tell her, 'it feels like people can't even see me. They just bump right into me.'

She smiles falsely.

I yell at her if she's been here before.

'A couple of times,' she yells at me.

I ask her if she likes it.

Looking around the room, she says, 'It's alright.'

'Listen,' I tell her, 'I'm feeling really bad about hitting you like that, would you let me buy you a drink to make up for it?' I offer to buy one because women are attracted to money and power.

She shakes her head, no. 'Don't worry about it.'

I nod.

There's a pause and she takes this opportunity to turn away from me and go back to the dance floor. I'm so close to scoring here, I'm this close, and I can't let her slip away so easily. Before she can make the complete turn, I ask, 'Do you like dancing?'

She slowly turns back to face me and I can't quite make out the expression on her face because of the lights but I'm sure she's happy I didn't let her get away. I know she wants me to pursue her; why else would she be flirting with me like this?

'Yes,' she says, 'I do.'

'What else do you like?'

'All sorts of things.'

I struggle to think of something. 'Do you like…?' I stop, unable to think of anything.

She looks at me and says, 'Yeah.'

I nod my head and say, 'Cool.' After a beat, I smoothly ask, 'Are you sure you don't want that drink? You haven't changed your mind?'

She shakes her head again, 'No, thanks.'

I nod, like it's nothing, to show her how cool I am.

'So where do you go to school?' I ask.

'I don't. I'm finished.'

'Oh, really? So where do you work?'

'At a supermarket.'

'Wow, that'd be pretty cool, huh?'

She shrugs. 'I guess.'

I wait for her to ask me, but she doesn't, so I volunteer the information. I tell her I'm still at school, university actually.

She nods. I can tell she's impressed.

'So,' I ask, 'what's your name?'

'Why?'

'So I know what to call you?'

She says something I can't hear over the music. It doesn't sound like a name though.

I sense I may be losing her so I tell her she has nice shoes.

'Thanks,' she says.

'And I like your dress, too. It brings out your eyes.'

She smiles and says nothing.

I go in for the kill. 'Are you sure you don't want a drink? Final offer…' I don't act too eager, because women find men more attractive if they act disinterested. Apparently.

She shakes her head.

'Alright, suit yourself…,' I tell her.

I turn and start to walk away, knowing any second she's going to put her hand on my shoulder and turn me around.

When she doesn't, I figure she might be shy or something. I'm still deciding whether to ask for her phone number or to just give her mine. When I turn around, she's gone. It may just be the low lighting and the smoke but I can't see her anywhere. I look around frantically, jumping in place to see over the people but everyone looks the same. She could have easily slipped into the crowd and be long gone by now.

Dejectedly I continue my journey back to the bar where George is waiting for me. He yells something to me but I can't hear him and I don't care enough to ask him to repeat it. I'm still thinking about the girl and what could have happened. I am picturing going out with her, meeting her parents, having dinner with them, becoming one of the family.

The bartender ignores me, taking orders from people further down. I have to open my wallet and hold the money out before he notices me.

I order a double bourbon and Coke and he brings it over.

I stand beside George, who is drinking the same, and we resume what we were doing before I went on my little adventure. We stand and watch the crowds moving around, drinking our drinks, not talking. I don't tell George what happened; I'm guessing he already knows because of the way I'm acting. The only time I drink a double B&C is when I've been shot down, crashed and burned. He knows better than to talk to me when I'm feeling like this.

So we stand there, drinking our drinks, listening to all the different songs that sound exactly the same.

When he thinks I've calmed down enough he asks me what happened.

I tell him everything and he nods his head.

He tells me not to worry about it. He says, 'It's not like they're interested in who you are. All they care about is what you look like and how much money you have. It's the same with you. All you care about is what they look like.'

'So?'

'So it doesn't matter what you say to her. The first time she sees you, she's already made up her mind. It's just the way things happen.'

I nod. 'You're probably right.'

'You're looking for fate in a nightclub.'

'I know. Plenty more fish in the sea.'

'That's right.'

'Let's get out of here.' He gulps down the rest of his B&C and I do the same. We fight our way across the dance floor, towards the glowing exit sign.

We get out of the way of the dancers then George bends down to tie his shoelace. While I'm waiting for him I notice the girl I was talking to, standing just ahead of us, putting her coat on. I kneel down and say to George, 'That's her. That's the girl.'

He looks up and says, 'Not bad. But you could do better.'

As I watch, a guy comes out of the shadows and for a moment I think I'm looking in a mirror. He puts his arm around her waist and she smiles at him.

I tell George what a bitch she is.

'Let it go, man,' he tells me. 'Try again. Plenty more…'

'I know, I know,' I cut him off. 'Plenty more fish in the sea.'

'Exactly.'

The guy keeps his arm around her and they walk together towards the door. He leans forward and holds the door open, she walks out and exits my life forever.

Six

The first time I met Fatty Mel was at the university cafeteria. It was at the beginning of the year, when things were still new and exciting and the novelty hadn't worn off yet. I was sitting at a table by myself, eating a cardboard container full of fries. It cost only $1.50 so I thought, why not? I had an hour to wait until my next lecture so I was relaxing at the table and looking out the window.

I notice Mel when she first walks in. She is about my height and quite pretty. She goes over to the counter and buys a salad sandwich. I had considered getting one of those but they cost $2.00, which was a bit over my student budget. She then walks into the main area of the cafeteria, looks around, sees me sitting by myself. She starts to walk over.

I immediately pretend I haven't noticed her and resume looking out the window. I eat another chip.

A moment later, I feel her standing near me. I still don't look around.

'Hi,' she says.

I look around, pretending to be slightly startled, and say, 'Hi.'

She smiles. 'Do you mind if I sit with you? I don't much feel like sitting by myself.'

This is when I look around and realise the cafeteria is completely deserted, except for the staff at the counter, and me, eating my French fries.

'Uh, no, go ahead,' I say. 'Be my guest.'

'Thanks,' she says, and sits down next to me. She holds her hand out. 'Hi, I'm Melinda Evans.'

I reach over, shake her hand and introduce myself.

She smiles. 'Nice to meet you.'

'Same.'

'So, what are you studying?'

I tell her.

She raises her eyebrows. 'That's pretty cool. Do you like it?'

'It's alright. What about you, what are you studying?'

She screws her face up and says, 'Teaching.'

She laughs when I ask her how she likes it.

'It gives me something to do, at least,' she tells me.

'What else do you do, apart from come here?'

She shrugs. 'I dunno. Just the usual stuff, I guess.'

'Do you work?'

'Yeah, I work at a supermarket. How about you?'

'No, I'm unemployed.'

'Oh, okay.'

There's a pause.

'Do you like the supermarket?' I ask.

'It's okay.'

Another pause. I eat another fry.

'What else do you do?' she asks.

I tell her I like to go to clubs and places like that. Hang out with friends. The usual.

'I go to those places sometimes.'

'Would you like a French fry?' I ask, holding out the container.

She says, 'Thank you,' and takes one. She says, 'You're Mister Generous.'

That's one of Mel's little sayings, Mister Whoever.

That was our first conversation. After that, we would see each other around the campus and we would always say hello. Occasionally we would stop and talk, and sometimes we would meet each other in the cafeteria or the tavern. It became a tradition for us to have lunch together that one day a week, where she would have a salad sandwich and I would have a container of French fries.

We would tell each other what we did on the weekend, how our social lives were going, things like that. Her life was much more interesting than mine. She would tell me about any dates she went on, her work, any clubs she went to, or anything else she did. By comparison my life seemed incredibly dull – all I did was go to university and hang out with George.

But although Mel did all this cool stuff, she never seemed entirely happy.

But, when I thought about it, who was?

The reason I call her Fatty Mel is because one day she asked me if I thought she was fat.

I was sitting in the university tavern drinking a bourbon and Coke, passing the time until my next lecture, watching a couple of guys playing pool.

There were a couple of babes sitting down the bar from me, also watching the game. I was sitting casually, coolly drinking my drink, hoping they'd notice me, but they didn't.

Melinda walked in and came across to the bar.

'Hey, sexy,' she said jokingly. 'How's things?'

I said hello and told her things were good.

She swung her bag onto the floor and took a step back. 'What do you think of my dress?' she asked.

I told her it's nice.

'Really?' she asked, testing me again.

'Yeah,' I said. 'I've always liked that dress.'

She gave me a look and said, 'It's new. I only got it yesterday.'

I laughed. Trying to cover myself, I said, 'Yeah, I know, I was just being silly.'

She didn't buy it. 'Sure,' she said. 'But, really, what do you think?'

I looked at it for a moment, pretending to consider. 'I like it. Really.'

'Really?'

'Really.'

'Do you think it makes me look fat?'

Of course, I realised this was a trick question. I'd already failed one test, so I had better not fail this one too. I decided to try a different approach.

I told her it made her look like a whale.

She gave me another look and said, 'Thanks very much. You're being Mister Mean today.'

That was how it started. It came to be our little tradition. When we met up, instead of saying hello, we would exchange abuse. From that day on, every time I saw Mel, I would ask questions like, 'Have you been gaining weight?' or, 'Mel, what have you been eating?' She would then make some comment about my clothes, or my hair. But we were joking so it was alright.

* * *

I'm at a club one night standing in line at the toilets. This particular club doesn't have one long urinal, it has little separate ones, and there are only four of them. Four urinals in the entire club.

So I'm standing in line and the guy in the line next to me leans over and he says, 'Do you know what this is?'

I tell him it's a fucking disgrace, having to wait.

'No. Well, it is, but no. Not the situation. This…' He holds something in his hand. I hadn't noticed him holding it before because I was looking at his face and I'm pretty drunk.

I look down at the object. I tell him it's nice.

'Yeah, I know it's nice,' he says, 'but that wasn't the question. The question was, do you know what it is?'

I look at the object a moment longer, my eyes fighting for focus. 'It's a doll.'

'Yes,' he tells me, 'it's a doll. But it's not an ordinary doll.'

'No?'

'No.'

I wait for him to continue. He doesn't. I ask him why it's not an ordinary doll.

'Because this doll is special.'

'Why is it special?'

'Because.'

And that's all he says.

I turn and resume looking at the back of the guy ahead of me. Eventually he moves and I step up to the urinal. The doll guy steps up beside me.

I'm almost ready to go when I realise I'm holding my left thumb in my right hand so I quickly make the necessary changes.

Tonight, I'm Mister Pissed-As-Hell.

'So do you want to know why the doll is so special?' he asks me.

I look over at him, holding himself in one hand, the doll in the other. He looks back at me, his drunken gaze trying to centre on my face.

'Sure,' I say.

'Are you sure?' he slurs.

'Yes,' I slur back.

'Because,' he tells me, 'the doll is blessed.'

I look at him a moment longer, then feel a smile crawl across my face. I start to laugh, quietly at first, then building. Suddenly there are tears streaming down my cheeks and I'm laughing so hard I'm pissing all over the walls.

I expect him to be mad at me, but when I squint in his direction, through the tears and the drunken haze, I see he is laughing, too.

I don't know what the people behind us are thinking.

I don't know if I'm pissing into the urinal, into a different urinal, or onto the floor.

I don't know if the doll guy knows why I'm laughing or if he's just too drunk to care.

Eventually, I get myself under control and readjust my aim. I apologise to the guy beside me.

I say, 'So, the doll is…'

'Blessed?'

'Yeah, blessed.'

'That's right,' he slurs.

I ask him who blessed it.

'I can't tell you, man,' he informs me. 'It's, like, a secret, you know?'

'Yeah, man, that's cool,' I tell him. 'I completely understand.'

'I mean, I would tell you, you know, but it's, like, a secret, you know?'

'I know.'

I've always loved drunken conversations with complete strangers.

I ask him what the blessed doll does.

'What do you mean?'

'Doesn't it do anything special?'

He laughs to himself. 'Yeah, it sure does,' he says.

I ask him, 'What?'

He looks down, realises he's finished, puts himself away, then zips himself up. I do the same.

'What?' I ask, as we're walking down the line towards the washbasins.

'What?' I ask, as we're washing our hands.

'What?' I ask, as we're leaving the bathroom.

'What?' he asks. He's forgotten our conversation.

'What does the blessed doll do?' I remind him.

'You want to know what it does?' He looks around, making sure no one else is listening. I lean in towards him, waiting for the answer.

'You have to promise not to tell anyone,' he says, 'because it's, like, a secret, you know?'

'Yeah, man, I promise.'

'Promise?'

'Promise.'

'Okay,' he says, then looks around again. He leans closer to me, still gripping the blessed doll in one hand. 'This is the truth, I'm not lying. The doll helps me pick up girls.'

I stop. 'What did you say?'

'I said, it helps me pick up girls.'

'How does it do that?'

'I told you, man, it's blessed.'

'Fuck off,' I say jokingly, convinced he's lying but believing every word.

The doll guy, he says, 'It's true, man, I swear it.'

'No, it's not true.'

'It is.'

'It's not. You're just making fun of me because I'm drunk.'

'I'm not, man, I'm being serious.' He starts laughing again and I can't help but join in.

'Prove it.'

'What?'

I say again, 'Prove it.'

'Aww, I dunno man, that's asking a lot.'

'How can you expect me to believe you if you won't demonstrate the powers of the blessed doll?'

He stops and thinks for a moment. 'Okay,' he says, 'I'll demonstrate.' He looks around the dance floor, then over at the bar, and says, 'Pick one.'

'Pick one what?'

'A girl. Pick a girl.'

'Okay,' I say, scanning the room. I point. 'How about her?'

He looks. 'Nah, it won't work.'

'Why not?'

'Because she's blonde.'

'So?'

'The doll only works on girls with the same colour hair. Today, the doll has brown hair which means it will only work on brunettes. Understand?'

'So you can only pick up brunettes?'

'If I want a blonde, I'll dye the doll's hair.'

'Oh.'

'So pick a brunette.'

I look around for one that looks really snobby, one that would never go for him in a million years.

'Her,' I say, pointing.

He tries to follow the direction of my waving finger but we're both too drunk. Finally he sees the one I've picked.

'Okay,' he says, 'wait here.'

He conceals the doll down the front of his trousers then walks over to her and starts talking. They talk for maybe five minutes then she walks away. The doll guy walks back over to me.

'Looks like you bombed out.'

'Nope,' he says, smiling. 'She's going to get her coat. We're leaving. See? I told you it works. The doll is blessed.'

I'm too stunned to say anything. I can't believe it.

'Anyway, man,' he says, 'I gotta get going. It was nice meeting you.'

'You too,' I say, still stunned.

'Cool,' he says. 'By the way, I'm Beau. Beau Branson.'

I'm about to tell him my name when he sees the girl coming out of the cloakroom. He says, 'Looks like it's time for me to be going. I'll see you around.'

'Sure,' I say as he walks off to meet the girl. He smiles at her and puts his arm around her waist.

They leave.

Beau Branson is one of the most interesting people I've ever met.

Another night, another club. There's an absolute babe working the bar and I'm feverishly trying to get her attention. I'm trying to order a B&C but I'm also trying to start a conversation with her in hopes of getting a phone number or at least a name. There is also a guy working the bar so I'm trying to get the babe's attention but not his, so every time he looks my way, I avoid making eye contact and hide my money so he doesn't approach me.

George and Beau are here with me. Beau is off chatting to some girls on the other side of the room. George is standing beside me, also wanting a drink. He's telling me to forget the babe and just talk to the guy because we're getting desperate. I tell him to be patient.

'Yeah, well while you're being patient, I'm going to take a piss. I'll be back.'

I nod and he walks off.

Eventually the babe finishes serving, and looks my way. I hold the money out casually and look at the bottles behind the bar to show her how I just want a drink and am not really interested in her. She walks over.

'What can I get you?' she asks.

I look up at her, as if just noticing her presence.

'Hi,' I say. I order the drinks.

'Sure,' she says and pours the bourbon.

I hand her the money and ask her how long she's been working here.

'Almost a year now.'

'Do you like it?'

'Yeah, it's pretty cool. You get to meet a lot of people.' She smiles and says, 'A lot of cute guys, too.'

I laugh. 'Yeah, I bet.'

I'm about to continue when this guy slams into the bar beside me as if he'd been running across the room. He leans over in front of me and says to the babe, 'Hey, Nick wants a shot of tequila.'

'Sure,' she says and pours the shot.

I tap the guy on the shoulder. He turns and looks at me.

'Excuse me,' I say, 'I was in the middle of a conversation.'

'I'm sorry, dude, but Nick really needs a drink.'

The babe walks back over carrying a small tray with the shot, a slice of lemon and a little dish of salt.

'Thanks,' the guy says, and pays her.

He licks his hand, puts a pinch of salt on it, licks it off, drinks the drink, slams the glass down and jams the piece of lemon into his mouth. He sucks on it, then eats all the flesh and spits the peel back onto the tray. I watch it sail through the air.

He shakes his head back and forth rapidly, as if trying to clear his head, and stumbles backwards. I catch him before he falls and he turns around.

'I thought you said the drink was for Nick.'

'It was,' he says, 'and Nick enjoyed it thoroughly.' He looks at my confused expression and smiles. 'Ah. Nick has confused you. It's simple. Nick is me.'

'You're Nick?'

'Yes. Nick is me.'

'Why do you speak like that?'

'Nick doesn't know. Nick thinks it's more interesting this way.'

'Alright,' I say. 'Whatever makes you happy.'

He laughs. 'It does, dude, it does.' He extends his hand. 'Nick McCarr.'

'Hi,' I say, shaking his hand.

'Come,' he says, 'Nick has a table. We can sit.'

I shrug and say, 'Sure, why not?'

I follow him over to a table at the side of the room. On the way I see Beau and I point to our new table. He nods and turns back to the girls.

There is already someone sitting there and the table itself is covered with empty glasses. Nick sits down and I follow his lead, placing George's drink down on the table but holding onto mine.

Nick leans over the table and says to me, 'This is Nick's friend, Jesus.'

I pause for a moment. I look down at my drink. I'm pretty sure I haven't had that many.

'Excuse me?' I say.

The friend leans over and says, 'Jesus. My grandfather was Mexican. It's pronounced Hey-soos, but this dimwit thinks it's funnier the other way.'

'Oh. Okay.'

'So why are you here on this fine evening?' Nick McCarr asks me.

I shrug and have a drink. 'I dunno, there wasn't much else going on, so we decided to come down here.'

'We?' Jesus asks.

As if on cue, Beau sits down beside me.

'Hi,' he says, 'I'm Beau Branson.'

I lean over to him and ask what he was doing with the girls.

He lifts his shirt up and shows me the doll tucked into the front of his pants. Its hair is auburn. He cocks his thumb behind him, and I look, and there is a girl with auburn hair standing with a group. Every now and then she looks at Beau, smiles and blushes. I look back at Beau.

He smiles at me but says nothing.

I say, loud enough for them to hear, 'This is Nick and Jesus.'

'Jesus?' Beau says. 'Let me tell you, you're not what I was expecting.'

Beau has a strange way of being friendly.

Jesus just smiles at him like he's heard it a thousand times and says the same thing he said to me. Beau nods and apologises and I know he has no intention of ever calling him Hey-soos.

'Oh, thanks,' Beau says, noticing George's B&C sitting on the table. He picks it up and drinks it. He winces with the taste, slams the glass down and looks at me, pleased.

'So do you guys go to uni together?' Nick asks.

'No,' Beau says, 'I met him in a bathroom one night.'

'Really?' Jesus asks.

'Yeah,' Beau says, and I already know where this is heading. 'I was showing him my… well, it's kinda personal.'

Beau looks at me and smiles.

What a bastard.

'Oh, I see,' Jesus says knowingly, smiling.

Nick says, 'Nick has known Jesus for only a few weeks. We met while we were dropping out of uni.'

'I thought you were Nick?' Beau interrupts.

I tell him I'll explain later.

'Sorry,' Beau says to Nick, 'but I have no idea what you're talking about, my friend, but I am sure of one thing: I need another drink. Excuse me.'

He stands up and walks off in the general direction of the bar, saying hello to a few girls as he passes.

'And Nick needs to take a piss. He'll be right back,' Nick says, and leaves.

I'm sitting here alone with Jesus.

There is a moment of silence.

I take a drink and look around the bar. It's still early and the real crowds haven't arrived yet.

For some reason this moment is far more awkward than it should be.

Finally, Jesus says, 'So you guys met in a bathroom, huh?'

I smile. 'Something like that. It's not what you're thinking, though.'

'It never is,' he replies and has another drink.

I laugh lightly, as if amused. I ask, 'So you didn't like uni?'

'It wasn't what I was expecting,' he tells me. 'Now I work in a supermarket, which is much easier. Nick digs trenches all day.' He says, 'Beau seems cool. You look happy together.'

I feel I should straighten this thing out before it gets out of control. 'Listen,' I say, 'Beau and I are just friends, that's all.'

Jesus smiles. 'So you're not a couple, then?'

'No, of course not.' I say this strongly, to show I'm being serious, but not too strongly, so he doesn't think I'm some sort of insensitive, gay-hating homophobe. I tell him I don't think of Beau that way.

'So do you have a girlfriend?' Jesus asks.

'No.'

'A boyfriend?'

'No.'

Jesus nods. 'Me neither,' he says. 'I'm single, too.'

'Oh.'

He's about to ask something else when Nick returns to the table.

'Wow,' he says, 'the line in there is incredible. Nick had to wait for ages.'

'We noticed,' Jesus says.

Nick laughs and sits down. He says something I don't hear to Jesus, who laughs. They keep talking and I start to get bored. I look around the room, watching the crowds move.

A few minutes later, a hand grabs my shoulder and Beau says, 'Come on, man, we gotta go.'

'What?'

'Look,' he says, cocking a thumb back over his shoulder. 'You see them?'

I look. A group of girls are standing around by the door with their jackets slung over their arms. One of them has auburn hair.

'What about them?' I ask.

'What do you think? Come on, let's go.'

I stand up. 'I just need to find someone,' I say, thinking of George.

'No, man, we don't have time for that. We gotta go now.'

'Hold on a second.'

I turn to Jesus and Nick. I tell them I have to go, and it was nice meeting them.

'Sure, you too,' Nick says.

Jesus says, 'See you around.'

'Gotta go, gotta go,' Beau is repeating into my ear.

To Beau, I say, 'Wait, let me look for him. Give me a couple of minutes. I can't leave without him.'

'Alright, suit yourself,' he says, and walks off.

I search for George upstairs, then in the dance area. Eventually I find him downstairs standing at a bar. I tell him about Beau and that we're leaving. He nods and follows me through the crowd, back towards the entrance.

I don't see Beau anywhere. I look around again, double checking, triple checking, but he is nowhere.

At the door I ask the bouncers if they've seen a loud guy with a doll stuck down his pants leaving with a large group of girls.

They say no.

I walk out into the car park and see if I can find him. There are a few groups standing around but they're all talking quietly to themselves and I can't hear Beau's voice echoing through the parking lot. He must have gone.

I've been abandoned. Again.

George says, 'Let's go.'

We get in the car and drive home.

I wake up at half past ten in the morning and I try to get back to sleep, but it's no use. I resign myself to getting up at this unholy hour and stumble out of bed, my eyes still stinging and crusty. I walk out into the family room and Gran is sitting on the couch, staring at the wall.

'Hi,' I say.

She doesn't say anything.

I make myself a cup of coffee.

Gran laughs. There's one single hoot, followed by a stream of little cackles. The whole thing is finished in less than two seconds and it takes me a moment to determine if I really heard it.

I take my coffee and sit down in the armchair opposite from her. She doesn't so much as acknowledge my presence and continues to stare at the wall.

I run my hand through my hair, which is sticking up at crazy angles. It feels coarse and dry and I consider changing conditioner.

I take a drink and study my nails. They are smooth and short and clean but there are flecks of something under my thumbnail. I look up and Gran is staring at me.

Not speaking, just staring.

I meet her gaze. I can't tell what she's thinking; she's looking at me blankly and I wonder if she knows who I am.

She keeps staring.

Staring.

Staring.

Finally, I say, 'What?'

'What do you want for your birthday?' she asks.

'What?'

'What do you want for your birthday?' she asks again.

I tell her it's not my birthday.

'But what do you want for it? When it comes.'

I tell her my birthday is months away.

'Really?'

'Yes. I think so. What day is it today?'

'I don't know.'

'Well, I'm pretty sure it's not today.'

There's more silence and she keeps staring at me.

I take another drink.

I ask her what she did last night.

'Nothing,' she says. 'I watched television.'

'What did you watch?'

She sighs. 'I don't remember.'

'Oh. Was it good?'

'I don't remember. I think so.'

I nod slowly. I say, 'Cool.'

Pause.

She asks, 'Where did you go last night?'

'I went...' Pause. 'I'm not sure. I... don't remember.'

'Were you drunk?'

'No. I don't think so.'

'Good.'

I ask myself, where was I last night?

I look down at the strange stains on my thumbnail. The inside of my wrist is a rainbow of ink, stamps from clubs, none of which I recognise.

I quickly drink the rest of my coffee and get up. The cup slips out of my hand and rolls under the chair. I bend down to pick it up and Gran starts scratching my head.

'Good doggie,' she says, scratching wildly. 'That's a good dog.'

I don't know if she's joking, so I decide I'd better not say anything, because if she thinks the dog is talking to her she might have a heart attack and I'd be forced to get a job.

I stay on my hands and knees for a moment then pick up the cup. I start to crawl off, and she scratches my back as I pass, telling me what a good dog I am.

I get behind her and stand up. I put the cup on the table and walk back to the armchair.

Gran is staring at the wall again, having forgotten the whole incident.

As I sit down, she asks, 'Would you like a chocolate?'

I tell her no, thanks.

'Are you sure? Go on, have a chocolate.'

'No, thanks, really. I'm fine.'

She starts to laugh, cackles that gradually get louder, and in a moment she's laughing hysterically, saying, 'I'm not going to give you a chocolate.'

'Okay, Gran,' I tell her.

'You can't have one.'

'Fine.'

'I'll give you a dog biscuit.'

'Uh huh.'

'That's what you can have. A dog biscuit. Would you like that?'

She keeps laughing, cackling about dog biscuits, then stops and resumes staring at the wall.

The social worker thinks there's nothing wrong with Gran.

I disagree.

Seven

Everyone's life has a turning point. Something happens that changes the way they look at the world. For me, it was when I saw an angel.

If I'd never seen her, everything would have been different.

My life was on auto-pilot. I'd go to university, I'd go to clubs, I'd go out with my friends.

Repeat.

That was all there was to it. There was no excitement. There was no change. There was no interest. Everything was planned and I knew exactly where I'd be at any time of the day, any day of the week.

It was an endless circle. I'd be at home, I'd look after Gran, I'd meet with the social worker.

Repeat.

Occasionally there'd be something special. I'd go to a party. I'd go somewhere I hadn't been before. I'd meet someone new. Mostly I was treading water, staying afloat but going nowhere. Everything else was the same, day after day.

Repeat.

People crave something new. They need it. Otherwise they settle into routine, and nothing drains passion like routine.

So every now and then, something happens.

Things get spiced up a little.

It was a perfect night. The day had been warm and the ground was still retaining the heat. Even though it was late, it wasn't cold. The sky was clear and lit up with a billion stars, like pinpricks of light through a sheet of depthless black.

George and I had spent the day at the beach. Initially we had gone to the popular areas, where all the beautiful people go, but after my repeated attempts to pick up a girl had failed we decided to go someplace else. We walked along the beach on the firm sand at the water's edge, talking about life and girls and other important issues, or, at least what you think is important, before what's still to come.

We walked as far as we could before the beach gave way to cliffs, and I stood at the top of the jagged rocks, looking down into the churning sea below. The waves crashed into the cliffs, sending cold spray into my face, the salt stinging my eyes.

Was I crying?

The wind whipped around me, rocking me back and forth, and any second I may have slipped.

I wondered what the hell the point of it all was.

I took a step forward and balanced with my toes hanging over the edge of the precipice. The sea boiled below me and lapped angrily at the rock face.

Was I suicidal?

George sat on the rock beside me. I knew that, if anything happened, he'd let me go. He was a true friend and he wouldn't stand in the way.

We stayed there and talked about our lives.

I stood, watching the ocean eat away at the rocks, then looking up at the point where the sea gave way to the sky, then above that, at nothing, and I stood that way for a long time.

The next thing I know, I'm sitting further back from the edge. The darkness has arrived and extinguished the sun. George is gone.

The sky is clear and I watch the stars for an eternity before climbing down off the rocks and walking back along the beach.

In the darkness, with the people gone, the noise of the sea seems amplified a hundred times. I feel small and alone.

I walk along the beach, the white sand warm under the soft night sky.

At first I think I am dreaming.

She is lying on the beach ahead of me, her arms folded behind her head, looking up at the stars. As I get closer she doesn't move and I wonder if she is dead.

I debate whether to speak to her or leave her alone. I stand for a moment and watch her and she doesn't move, so I think I should check on her and make sure she is okay.

I walk up to her and say, 'Hello.'

There's no response.

'Hello?' I say it louder this time.

She turns her head and looks at me and my heart skips. With all the colour drained out of the world, with all the people gone and the only noise coming from the sea lapping against the shore, the place seems dead.

I ask her if she is okay.

'I'm fine,' she says. Her voice is like liquid and I imagine it being one with the sea.

I tell her I was walking along the beach and I saw her lying there and she wasn't moving and I didn't know if she was alright or not.

'I'm alright,' she tells me, sitting up. 'How are you?'

'I'm okay.'

'You sure?'

'Yeah. Why would you think I wasn't?'

'Why are you all alone on a beach at two o'clock in the morning?' she asks.

'Why are you?'

She smiles and her face lights up and even in the darkness I know it's the most beautiful thing I have ever seen.

'Do you like the beach?' she asks.

'Yeah. It's peaceful, I guess.'

She says, 'I love watching the stars.'

'You only come to the beach at night?'

'Most of the time,' she says. 'Things take on different meanings at night.' She looks back up into space. 'It makes me wish I could fly. To not be restrained.'

'I have a friend who once told me he's going to teach me to fly.'

'That's great.'

'You don't think it's stupid?'

'I wish I had a friend like that. My friends are all serious and straight. None of them has any imagination. They all exchanged magic for truth a long time ago and now they're boring and dead.'

'Dead?'

'Inside, anyway.' She asks, 'When your friend teaches you to fly, will you teach me?'

'I will.'

She nods.

I ask, 'Why do you like stars so much?'

'I don't know,' she says. 'I mean, it's just a big, black nothing with a few white dots in it. I could draw that with some crayons. But it's something more, you know? I can't describe it, it's something you have to feel.'

I don't remember the last time I felt anything.

I say, 'I think I know what you mean.'

She asks me, 'Have you ever seen a shooting star?'

'No.'

'The beach is a good place to see them, there's no streetlights or buildings or anything.' She pats the sand beside her. 'There's bound to be one, sooner or later.'

I take a step towards her, where she indicated. My heart is thumping so hard it hurts, though I know it's just my hypothalamus kicking in. I lie on my back beside her, close, but not too close.

'Keep watching,' she says, 'and you'll see one.'

We lie there looking up at the black sky, the water rushing up the sand but retreating before it meets us. The night is completely still, the only noise coming from the waves.

This moment seems too perfect to be real. I wonder again if I am dreaming.

'Look,' she says, grabbing my arm. With her other hand she points to the sky. 'There's one.'

I follow her finger and there's a faint white stripe amidst the stars. It fades from view in a matter of seconds. This simple sight does something to me and I realise this is one of those moments that I will remember for the rest of my life.

I'm Mister Enchanted.

'Wow,' I say.

'It's magical, isn't it?' she says. 'I could lie here all night.'

We do.

At daybreak, as the first of the early morning joggers arrive, we decide it's time to go home.

We stand in the cool dawn air and the gulls sing overhead.

I say, 'What's your name?'

She says, 'Jade.'

She turns and starts to walk across the beach, towards the dunes. I watch her go for a moment, wanting to call out, needing to have one final interaction before the perfect night is over. As usual I can't think of anything so I turn and slowly walk away.

'Hey,' she calls.

I turn around, my heart thumping again.

'Why were you on the beach last night?' she asks.

I smile. I tell her it doesn't matter anymore.

'Okay,' she says, slightly puzzled, but smiling nonetheless. 'See you.'

She starts walking again and disappears over the dunes. My legs give out and I fall to the sand, overwhelmed.

I have been saved by an angel and, for the first time I can remember, it seems like there might be a reason after all.

Eight

Rewind back to when I was younger.

I'm ten years old and my mother is still alive. We're sitting on the couch in silence, watching television. There's a show on, and in it, the woman is having a baby.

I ask my mother, 'How did that baby get inside the woman?'

She doesn't say anything for a while. Eventually, she says, 'It grew inside her.'

'Yuck,' I say. 'Is that where I came from?'

'Yes,' she says. 'You came from inside my tummy.'

'Oh. Did it hurt?'

'When you came out it did.'

'Oh. So how did I get in there in the first place?'

'Your dad put you there.'

'Oh. How?'

She pauses again, for even longer this time. I think she isn't going to answer at all, but then she turns to me and says, 'I think we need to have a talk.' Then adds, to herself, 'Shit.'

When she has finished explaining, I think two things: (1) Eww, gross, I'm never going to do that, ever; and (2) Why didn't I think of that? It just seemed so obvious and yet I never guessed it.

I ask, 'So how do you choose if it's a boy or a girl?'

'You don't,' she says. 'God chooses. It's a surprise. Don't they teach this in school?'

'God chooses? But what if he gives you the wrong one?'

'He doesn't give you the wrong one. He gives everyone what they deserve. That's why I got you.'

'So God watches us from heaven?'

'Yes.'

'On, like, a big television?'

'God doesn't need a television.'

'Then how does he watch us?'

'I don't know. Maybe through our souls? He just does, okay?'

'What's a soul?'

She sighs but it's more like a groan. 'It's inside you. It's what makes you, you.'

'So God watches us and then he decides whether to give you a boy or a girl?'

'Yes.'

'So what did you do to deserve me?'

'I ask myself that every day.'

'Do you know?'

'No. You'll have to ask God when you meet him.'

'When will I meet him?'

'When you die and go to heaven,' she says, bored with the discussion.

'Is that where Dad is? In heaven?'

'Maybe.'

'You don't know for sure?'

'Nobody knows for sure. You either go to heaven or hell, depending on if you be good or not.'

'What's hell?'

'Hell is the place where all the bad people go when they die.'

'What happens there?'

'They get punished for all the bad things they've done when they were alive.'

'How long do they stay there for?'

'Forever.'

'Even if they only did something little? Like something that was bad, but not really bad?'

'I don't know. I guess so. But you just have to be good when you're alive, and that way, when you die, you'll go to heaven instead of hell.'

'What if someone does something bad but then the rules change? Do they still go to hell?'

'I don't know.'

'Or what if someone is made to do something bad, even when they don't want to?'

'I don't know.'

'What if it's an accident? What happens then?'

'I don't know. Listen, just be good and you won't go to hell, okay?'

'Oh, I get it. It's like when you tell me not to eat any cookies before dinner or I'll get a spanking? Right? That's the same thing?'

'Sort of, yeah.'

'Okay,' I say. 'Well, it sounds pretty fucked up to me.'

We had a goldfish that swam around in a little bowl on a stand. The bowl had blue and green pebbles in the bottom, with a plastic plant stuck in the middle. The fish was called Goldie and he was all gold, except for a small black patch on his head. I would sit and watch Goldie swim around his bowl, trying to make patterns out of his movements.

One day I reached into the bowl and tried to grab him. He swam out of my grasp and it took almost a minute before my fist closed around him. I was careful not to squeeze too hard. I lifted him out of the water and carried him over to the table where I had my instruments all arranged.

I placed him down on a mat and let him go, and he instantly started to flop around, trying to find his way back to the fishbowl. I put my hand on him again and made him lie still. I removed my finger and he began to convulse again.

I picked up the pin that lay beside the mat and, holding it between my thumb and forefinger, slowly pushed it through Goldie's body. His body tensed up and curved and his little mouth opened and closed, opened and closed. The pin came out the other side of Goldie and into the mat, holding him in place.

His scales reflected the fire from the lighter.

The water on his body began to sizzle as I brought the lighter closer and he tried to move away but he was pinned in place. I moved the flame up and down his body. Goldie's scales turned black. I let the flame linger at his head and soon his eyes turned black too and funny liquid began to leak from them.

The lighter was getting hot so I put it down. I watched Goldie for a moment; he wasn't squirming anymore but his mouth was still opening and closing, over and over, but slower now.

I held him still with one hand and with the other, brought the knife up and pressed it against the meaty section below his head, between the gills. I pressed harder and the sharp edge of the knife slid into his body. Blood began to trickle out of him and onto the mat. I drew the knife along the underside of his body and it caught on something so I had to saw through whatever it was. Eventually I got to the tail and the knife pulled away, with small black and pink tubes stuck to the blade.

I let him go to see if he would flop around anymore but he didn't.

I opened the incision further with my fingers and looked inside. I put my index finger deep into the hole and curled it up, like a hook. I then pulled everything inside out.

Goldie's interior was filled with little mushy things. There were more tubes and pipes and guts and stuff and they were warm and gooey. Some of them stuck to my fingers and I had to wipe my hand along the mat to get them off.

I removed the pin and waited for Goldie to start jumping around again.

He didn't.

He lay completely still, not even his mouth moved anymore.

I sat and watched him.

After a while I put him in the toilet and flushed him down, sending him away with all the other shit. I was disappointed because I had not seen him go to heaven.

I had expected something more to happen with Goldie. There was no ghost, or spirit, or soul. There was just meat and blood inside of him and that's all.

Death was just something that happened. It wasn't pretty or magical but it wasn't sad or evil either. It just was.

So why does killing someone make you a bad person? It's not like death wasn't going to happen eventually anyway.

I had killed a goldfish. Did that make me bad? Would I go to hell for this?

I doubted it. I didn't see Goldie's soul sitting amongst his organs, so I doubt he even had one.

And if he didn't, chances are I didn't, either.

And if I didn't, then did anyone else?

Inside, Goldie was just like the rest of us. Just flesh and bone.

My mother didn't even notice Goldie was gone.

For a while I had dreams about Goldie coming back. I would wake up, convinced he would be in my bed, or on the pillow beside me. Sometimes I would have to get up and check the empty fishbowl to see if he was there.

He never was.

Sometimes I would stand in the bathroom, looking down into the toilet. I would watch the water, waiting for Goldie to come swimming up. I would wait for a ripple, a bubble, anything.

The water was always still.

Wherever Goldie had gone, he wasn't coming back.

I had killed him and now he was gone forever.

He was gone and no one had noticed.

He was gone and no one cared.

Would it be like that when I died?

The more I thought about it, the less it all seemed to matter.

Nine

I'm flicking through the telephone directory, trying to find Jade's number.

I really, really want to call her, but have no idea what I'd say if I did. She'd ask where I got her number, then I'd have to go through how I tracked her down, which would probably freak her out and convince her I'm some sort of crazy stalker.

What if she doesn't know who I am? What if she meets guys on the beach every night? What would happen if I called her and introduced myself and she said, 'Who?'

Even if she did remember me, what would we talk about? She'd ask why I called and I would have no reason. Before I called, I'd have to come up with some sort of story.

I keep flicking through the phone book, searching for her name.

This is all the social worker's fault. She's the one making me do this.

I get to what I think is the right page, and run my fingers down the list of names, looking for the right one. I find it.

Hold on.

Let's rewind.

*　*　*

As always, the social worker is late. Ten minutes after her supposed arrival time, I hear her little wreck of a car pull into the driveway. I get up and go out to meet her. She comes stumbling up the driveway, her arms loaded with papers and files, and as she passes, she says, 'Here, can you take some of these for me?' and unloads them onto me.

We go inside and she takes her usual place on the couch in the front room and I drop her stuff onto the seat beside her.

'Thanks,' she says, and begins to sort through the files.

'Rough day?'

'You could say that,' she says. 'One of my assignments died this morning.'

'I'm sorry. What happened?'

'She just died. She was really old.' She shuffles through her papers. 'She was, like, ninety-three years old and last night she just went to bed and never woke up again.'

I tell her that's really sad but I'm not feeling anything at all.

'Yeah,' the social worker says, 'she was really nice, too. It wouldn't have bothered me so much if she was a bitch.'

We do the usual routine: we get up and walk into the family room, where Gran is sitting, staring blankly at the television.

In the kitchen, the dishes are piled up in the sink. I set this up every night before the social worker comes, so she can see all the leftovers and know that Gran is actually eating.

All week, whenever I eat anything, I never throw away the leftovers. I keep them in the fridge and then the night before the social worker's visit, I put them all on the plates. This creates the illusion that Gran is eating. My week's leftovers look the same as the remains of a meal for two people. It works out a lot cheaper this way than actually feeding her.

The social worker goes over and kneels down in front of Gran. 'How are you today?' she asks.

'I'm fine, thanks,' Gran says. 'How are you?'

'Good,' the social worker replies. 'Do you know who I am?'

'No,' Gran says, 'but I always like meeting new people.'

The social worker asks Gran this every time she comes, and every time, Gran says the same thing. Although the social worker has come every two weeks for the last eight years, Gran still doesn't know who she is.

The social worker smiles at her then stands and walks back over to me. 'She seems okay,' she says.

I nod and say, 'Yeah, she's fine.'

The social worker sighs and says, 'I'm sorry, I just can't do this today. All this death has brought me down.'

I tell her that's okay, and ask if she'd like a cup of coffee.

She smiles and says, 'That'd be great, thanks.'

I consider saying, 'While you're there, make me one, too', but I don't think she'd appreciate this today. Instead I make the coffee while she goes back into the front room, leaving Gran to stare at the television, which is not turned on.

The social worker thanks me as I hand her a cup. I sit in my usual chair across from her.

'So what's been going on with you?' she asks.

'Just the usual stuff,' I tell her.

'Nothing interesting at all?'

I decide to play along. 'Well, there was one thing...'

'What?' she asks, and sips her coffee. She looks down at it, then up at me suspiciously, and I'm flattered she thinks I'm devious enough to tamper with it.

'Well,' I say, 'I...'

'Go on,' she says, 'don't keep me in suspense.'

'I met... someone.'

She raises an eyebrow. 'Just someone, or someone... special?'

'At the moment, just someone, but I'm hoping it'll turn into something special.'

She smiles. 'And what's her name?'

'Jade.'

She repeats it to herself. 'That's very... exotic.'

'I know.'

'What's she like?'

'She's... amazing. Unlike anyone I've ever met.'

'Wow,' the social worker says, 'she really made quite an impression.'

I nod and smile, not wanting to tell her about what meeting Jade has done to me. I don't want her to know about me standing atop the cliffs, ready to step over the edge into the churning sea. I don't want her to know that the thought of this girl has made me choose life over death.

'So when did all this happen? When are you seeing her next?' the social worker asks.

'About five days ago,' I tell her. 'I didn't get a phone number or anything.'

'Look her up.'

'She said she goes to the beach all the time. She likes to look at the stars. I'll see her again.'

'You're going to leave it to chance? You're sure? You know this woman that died this morning? My assignment?'

'Yeah.'

'If there's one thing I've realised doing this job, it's that what they say is true: you should live every day like it's your last, because one day it will be. It's a total cliché but one day it's all going to be over, and you want to look back on it and smile and not regret all the mistakes you made.'

'Wow, that's beautiful,' I say. 'It's a load of shit, but it's beautiful.'

She gives me a sour look and says, 'You're going to look back on this chance you missed and hate yourself for it. You say you do already, so now here's an opportunity to do something right. Fix a mistake before you make it.'

For the rest of the social worker's visit, we just made small talk. She asked me the routine questions: how was university? Did I have enough money? How were my friends? Was I planning on killing myself any time soon? The usual stuff.

So here I am, flipping through the telephone directory. I already checked the internet.

I find what I hope is the right listing and I stare at it for a moment.

I slam the book closed and walk away.

A little while later I open the book again. I flip through until I find the page.

I reach for the telephone, dial the first three numbers and then hang up. I close my eyes for a moment, taking long, deep breaths, my heart thumping inside my chest.

I sit like that for a while.

I look back down at the page and dial again. This time I get all the way through, and I'm having a hard time holding the phone steady against my ear because I'm shaking so much.

The phone rings once, twice, three times and then there's a click as it's picked up.

A voice says, 'Hello?'

I hang up.

I pace back and forth in the front room, trying not to panic. I take deep breaths and cross my hands behind my head, trying to ward off the cramp that's tearing up my side. I've drunk several large glasses of water but my stomach is in knots and I can't sit still.

I stand in the bathroom and stare at myself in the mirror. I slap myself three times across the face, hard, then quickly storm out and pick up the telephone. I dial the number and press the receiver against my ear, my eyes clenched tightly closed.

Someone picks up on the fourth ring.

'Hello?'

'Hello,' I say, my heart thumping so hard I think it's going to burst from my chest.

'Hello?' the voice says again. 'Can I help you?'

It takes me a moment before I finally say, 'Is Jade there, please?'

'Excuse me?'

'Jade. Is she there? Can I speak to her, please?'

'I'm sorry, I think you have the wrong number.'

I'm silent for a moment. Then, 'Are you sure?' I ask if this is the number I dialled.

'Yes, it is, but there's no Jade here.'

'Are you sure?'

'Yes, I'm sure.'

I tell her I'm after Jade.

'There's no Jade here. Goodbye.'

'Wait,' I tell her. 'Listen, this is really important. I really need to speak to Jade. Please, could you just get Jade for me? It won't take long. Please. Hello?'

She's gone.

I listen to the broken connection for a moment then put the phone down.

I think this was the straw that broke the camel's back.

We build things up so much in our minds that when it doesn't happen, it seems like the end of the world.

There's only a certain amount a person can take before they snap. And me, I'm lying in a thousand pieces.

I imagine this is how people on life support must feel when the machine gets turned off. The only thing that keeps them going is taken away and they have no choice but to die.

I'm so pathetic. I still think this is as bad as it's going to get.

I head along the beach towards the cliffs, walking under a blanket of stars, the waves crashing soothingly against the shore. I sit on the cliff in the same spot, watching the ocean stretch out forever in the dark, unable to distinguish where it ends from where the sky begins. The wind tonight is much stronger than it was last time. It whistles around the cliff face and the ocean roars as it chews hungrily at the rocks, sending spray and water everywhere.

A storm is coming on the horizon and I'm seeing the moon in double, triple, as the tears stream down my face.

The wind blows in off the ocean, cold against the tears on my cheeks. I wipe them away with the back of my hand but they're replaced instantly.

I'm suddenly very tired. I'm tired of waiting for something to happen, for something to change. I'm tired of having nothing, of being nothing. I'm tired of wanting to be happy.

The cold wind whips my face, and when I touch my nose, it feels frozen.

I think of George, promising to teach me to fly. Maybe this is my big chance. All I need to do is take a single step forward.

If I stepped off this cliff, no one would notice I was gone. It would probably be the social worker in two weeks who would raise the alarm. And then she'd get a new assignment; another person to look after who is just as fucked up as me.

A single star sails across the sky.

I tell myself: one chance. One last chance. Don't give up yet. Fuck it.

I turn away from the cliff. I stumble sideways as the wind pushes me, wanting to take me down into the sea but I regain my footing in time.

And this decision changes everything. The slightest action can change the world.

The beach is deserted. I make my way to where I had met Jade. I lie on the sand, watching for shooting stars, replaying our conversation in my head, remembering the sound of her voice, her smell, her presence.

Mister Longing.

Behind me, Jade says, 'Hi'.

From nowhere, she appears, like magic.

From where I'm lying, she looks upside down.

Before, George told me, 'Don't attribute her with false power. She can't save you.'

'I know,' I told him.

George said, 'You're the only one who can do that.'

Here, now, on the beach, I sit up on the sand and Jade joins me.

We listen to the waves.

All the frustration and anger is still inside me but already it seems more subdued and muted. Just being around her is calming.

I ask her when things started getting so complicated.

She's silent and for a moment I don't think she's going to answer. Then she says, 'Did you know that the sun is so far away that it takes eight minutes for light to reach the earth? This means when you look at the sun, you're not seeing it where it is now, you're seeing it where it was eight minutes ago.'

'Yeah, I guess.'

'When you look at stars, other galaxies, you're seeing the light from where they were, millions of years ago. The deeper you look into space, the further back in time you're seeing. Theoretically, if you had a powerful enough telescope, you could see all the way back to the beginning of the universe.'

I nod.

'No matter how hard you try, you'll never see things as they are,' she says. 'By the time you figure something out, it's passed. When you finally see the light, we're already eight minutes further on.'

She stops for a moment and says, 'Well, maybe not eight minutes, but you get what I'm saying.'

The waves crash against the shore, oblivious of us. The world will keep moving, whether I'm here or not.

I tell her she looks up into the night sky and sees beauty and magic and wonder, but when I look up, all I see is emptiness. It's just a huge expanse of nothing and a lot of the time that's what it's like when I look inside myself. It's like there should be something inside of me, some sort of emotion or feeling, but there's just nothing there. I'm as empty as the night sky.

She says, 'Don't you ever feel happy?'

I shake my head. 'Mostly just nothing.'

Jade says, 'Do you know why you feel that way?'

'No,' I tell her. 'I guess I'm just...' I trail off, not knowing how to continue.

'Don't you have people who care about you? What about your friend who is going to teach you to fly.'

'He's the only one. The others are just... I dunno, I mean, they're around, but there's no connection, you know? They're the people I get drunk with.'

She nods in the darkness. 'Do you have an attachment to anyone else?'

I could lie here and say how I love everyone and show her how fun and exciting I am, but I don't. For some reason I want to be honest with her and tell her the truth, even though it's possible, and likely, it'll scare her away.

I say, 'No, I don't think so.'

She nods but doesn't say anything.

I ask her, 'Do you think people need other people to survive? Do you think you can... substitute? Compensate? Adapt? Why do we need other people in our lives? What is it about another person that makes us need them? Why do we get lonely? Why does it matter?'

There's a long pause.

She asks, 'Why don't you reach out more? Put yourself on the line? People who go that extra distance usually get what they want.'

I think for a moment, really think. Finally I tell her, 'If I put myself on the line again, and I lose out... I don't know if I could take it. If you put yourself, everything you have, on the line... that's a lot at stake. Especially when you don't have all that much left.'

This is what pulses inside me. A hollowness needing to be filled. A constant sense of longing, of wanting, of needing something, anything. A sense of purpose, of place, of direction, of meaning. I realise that I, like the universe, am filled with nothing.

I scratch at an ant crawling down my neck.

Jade says, 'People say that when you die, your whole life flashes before your eyes. That's only half true, because our life is flashing past, but not when you die. It's flashing past right now. We just don't realise it.'

We lie on the sand for a while and it's wonderful.

Then she tells me she needs to go. My heart breaks. We stand up and brush the sand off our clothes. I want to say something but can't.

She says, 'A few of us are going out next weekend, would you like to come?'

Calmly, I say, 'I'd love to.'

Mister Understatement.

'Great,' she says, smiling more naturally this time. 'Give me your number. I'll let you know what's happening.'

'Sure,' I say. I tell her my number and she keys it into her phone.

She says, 'Thanks. I'll call you in the next couple of days.'

I sit in the car and cry. Soon my breath becomes easier and it no longer hitches in my throat. The tears subside and I'm able to start the engine. I wipe the remaining tears away with the back of my hand, confused about where they came from, and drive home.

TEN

Fatty Mel looks at me like she's never seen me before, like I'm an alien from another world or something.

'What?' I ask.

'Large?'

'So?'

'What happened?'

I'm feeling so uplifted that I decide to spend the extra money and get a large serving of French fries. I'm smiling as I walk over to the table and sit down, putting my feet up on a vacant chair. Melinda has obviously noticed my extravagant spending and unusually buoyant mood.

'What do you mean, what happened? Aren't I allowed to be happy?'

'Not unless something has happened. You're never happy just for no reason.'

'There's always a first time.'

She sighs. 'Fine, if you don't want to tell me, that's okay. I understand.' She looks down at her sandwich and picks at it then sighs again.

I eat another chip and look around the empty cafeteria, ignoring her sarcasm.

She sighs again, louder this time.

'Oh, alright,' I say. 'Not that there's really much to tell.'

She looks at me, smiling like she knew it'd only be a matter of time before I broke and told her everything. 'Well if there's not much to tell, it won't take long then, will it? So come on, hurry up.'

'If you must know,' I tell her, 'it just so happens that this weekend I have a date.'

Her smile falters for a moment, then it's back. I know she's shocked and can't believe the news.

'Wow,' she says, 'that's really something. I can see why you're so elated. Congratulations.'

'Thanks. Though it's not technically a date. Just a group thing.'

'So who is she? Do I know her?'

'No, you don't. We met on the beach one night.'

'Really? What's her name?'

'Jade.'

She repeats it to herself. 'That's very… exotic.'

'I know.'

'So… tell me all the details.'

I tell her how I met Jade on the beach, twice, and how she invited me to go clubbing. I tell her how Jade called me yesterday and told me that on Saturday night, if I wanted to, I could come out with her and some of her friends.

Did I want to? she'd asked.

Sure, I'd said. I'd love to.

So that's what was happening, Saturday night we're going out.

I tell Mel she can come if she wants, but I'm thinking, please say no, please say no.

She laughs and says, 'Thanks for the offer, but I wouldn't want to intrude.'

'Alright,' I say, 'suit yourself.'

'Have a good time.'

'I will,' I say, smiling.

'She must be really something,' Fatty Mel says. 'I've never seen you like this before.'

'Never seen me like what?'

'Like this,' she says, waving her hand. 'Mister Happy. Mister Excited.'

I shrug. 'It's the first good thing that's happened to me in a long time.'

Mel says, 'Oh.' She says, 'I hope you have a good night, then.'

She stands up and tells me she has a tutorial and she'll call me later.

The look I'm going for is smart casual, like half dressed-up but half not. I want to appear sophisticated and well dressed, but still cool and casual. I want to look good, but not look like I spent hours achieving this look.

This is a lot harder than it sounds.

I stay home on Friday night to ensure I'm not tired the next day. I go to bed early, even though it takes hours to fall asleep, then get up late, so I'm completely relaxed and my skin is soft and smooth. I eat a large breakfast of fruit and cereal with lots of juice and water. I avoid coffee or sugar or anything that will add to my anxiety. I spend most of the day wandering around the house, too restless to do anything. When it gets later I shower, shave and get dressed. This last one is the hardest, and it takes me the better part of ninety minutes to decide what to wear.

I apply a dab or two of aftershave, have a breath mint then get in the car, my stomach still in knots.

I make it to the end of the street before I have to pull over and vomit onto the side of the road. Luckily there is no one around so I quickly get back into the car, take another breath mint and drive off.

We're meeting at a new club called Cosmic and when I get there I have to wait in line for almost forty minutes before being let in. When I finally enter I see the club is just one big room with a bar along the wall opposite the entry, the toilets on the right-hand wall and a raised platform for the DJ on the left. There's a large model of the solar system inside the domed roof. The sun is the only real source of light and the planets revolve around the sun on little tracks in the ceiling. Tiny little fairy lights are spread all over the roof, like stars, and they flicker on and off. The effect is hypnotic and I stand looking up at the fake planets revolving in the fake sky for a long time.

Looking through the crowd I spot George standing at the bar. I walk over to him and put a hand on his shoulder. He turns and says, 'Hey, man.'

I ask him why he's here.

'Just having a look,' he says, smiling. 'I haven't been here before. And you don't think I'd let you go through this alone, do you?'

'Thanks for the support,' I tell him. 'What do you think of the place?'

'It's alright. I guess it's the same as all the other clubs.'

'How long have you been here?'

'Not long,' is all he says.

George finishes his drink in one gulp. 'I'm going to take a piss. See you.'

I nod and say, 'Have a good night.'

'You too,' he calls back over his shoulder as he walks away.

I'm hoping Jade arrives soon. Now she's so close it feels like time has slowed, making the wait all the more difficult.

According to the planets on the ceiling I wait around for years but really it's only ten minutes.

I'm looking around and suddenly I see her walking through the crowd. My breath catches in my throat and my heart starts to thump. The room goes silent and everyone else disappears.

She walks in my direction but I don't know if she's seen me. Above her the sun burns brightly and I am the planets revolving around her.

My stomach is burning and knotted and I feel light-headed.

She looks my way, sees me standing there, and smiles. She walks over and says, 'Hi.'

I can't say anything back. The way the sun illuminates her from behind, creating a halo of light around her head, takes my breath away.

Mister Spellbound.

'Are you okay?' she asks, still smiling.

'Fine,' I manage to breathe. I force a smile. 'How are you?'

'I'm good, thanks,' she says. 'Have you been here long? Sorry to have kept you waiting.'

'That's okay,' I tell her. I'd wait a lot longer than ten minutes for her.

'This is a pretty cool club.'

'Yeah, it is.'

'Have you been here before?'

'No, never.'

She nods. 'Come on, I want you to meet some of my friends.'

She turns and walks back the way she came and I follow. The sea of people parts as she walks then closes again behind us.

We walk over to a small group standing below the DJ platform, three girls and two guys. The girls are pretty and under other circumstances I may have tried to pick one of them up, but when they're standing beside Jade, they are eclipsed. I regard the guys with a mixture of dread and suspicion and I'm suddenly aware that I don't know if Jade has a boyfriend. I instantly hate both of these guys, just in case either of them has the slightest interest in her.

Jade does the introductions but I can barely hear her because of the music and I know that even if I could hear her, I wouldn't remember any of their names anyway. As she points to each of them, I nod and say hi. They do the same to me.

I say to Jade, 'I can see why you chose this place.'

She smiles. 'It's not quite the same though, is it?'

I watch the third planet, a small blue-green globe, complete another revolution. Just watching this artificial galaxy reminds me how small I am in the whole scheme of things.

'The planets sure are fast,' I tell Jade. 'If we were on that Earth, we'd be, like, a hundred years older in just the time we've been here.'

She laughs and says, 'Sometimes it feels that way. It feels like things are going so fast, and there's not enough time to just enjoy the ride. We can't just stop and admire the scenery.'

She says, 'Some people are obsessed with the past. The past is just a story, it doesn't matter anymore. They're just watching repeats.'

She says, 'Other people are too concerned with tomorrow. They spend their whole life planning and organising for a day that may never come. Pretty soon, everyone runs out of tomorrows, then what have you got left? Nothing, because you spent your whole life looking forward and never actually did anything while there was still time.'

She says, 'People should just live now. The past and the future have their place and shouldn't rule people's lives. Now is all you have.'

We spend the next few hours dancing, drinking and trying to talk over the music. The others don't pay much attention to me and I don't care. As the hours creep by Jade is the only one who talks to me and that's all that matters.

She's a good dancer; her moves aren't extravagant, they're precise and rhythmic. I can't dance well at all but I can do enough so as not to embarrass myself.

Jade and I talk about nothing for a while and I relish every word.

I ask Jade if she wants a drink and she smiles and says she'll have some water.

I go over to the bar and order water for Jade and a B&C for me. I don't know how many I've had but I don't think I'm drunk so it's alright.

George is standing next to me at the bar and I ask him if he's having a good night.

'Yeah, not bad,' he says. 'You?'

'Really good. I think it's all going really well.'

'You sure?' he asks.

'Yeah. Why wouldn't I be?'

He nods behind me, as if indicating something. I turn to see.

There is a guy talking to Jade. My heart jumps.

'What are you going to do?' George asks me.

'I don't know. I'll think of something.'

I take a drink in each hand and walk back towards the pair. I stop beside them and hand Jade her water. I look at the guy and say, 'Hi.'

'Hi,' he says. 'How are you?'

'Good,' I tell him. I don't ask how he is.

He gets the hint and says, 'I'll leave you guys alone. Have a good night.' He turns to Jade and says, 'If you change your mind, I'll be around. See you later.'

She says, 'Bye.'

I look at this guy as he turns to leave. He's such a fucking pretty boy that I can hardly stand it. It's obvious that he spent at least an hour in front of the mirror before he came out and he's wearing expensive clothes and nice shoes and he just looks so good that I hate him for it. He's neat and clean shaven and well dressed and is just so totally pathetic. He walks off, obviously intending to try his little pick-up act on someone else.

I ask Jade, 'A friend?'

'No,' Jade says, 'just some guy.'

'Oh. Was he bothering you?'

'No, he was fine, really. Don't worry about it.'

'Are you sure?'

She smiles. 'Yes, I'm sure. Thanks for the water,' she says.

'No problem.'

We continue dancing and I try to concentrate on Jade but I'm continually distracted. I watch the guy amid the sea of bodies. Every now and then he looks my way.

One time, I see him looking at Jade, and he sees me watching. I shake my head slowly, once to the right, once to the left. He looks down guiltily. I look up at the stars in the ceiling and try to control my anger. I try counting backwards from ten, but with the pumping music and the heat of the room, it makes it seem more like a countdown and it actually increases my bloodlust.

I have to get away from him for a second to calm down so I ask Jade if she's finished her drink. She holds up the empty glass and says, 'Thank you,' and I take it and mine back to the bar.

George is still in the same place and he asks me how it's going.

'I can't fucking believe that guy. Who does he think he is?'

'I don't know,' George says.

The bartender brings me a beer that I didn't order.

George tells me he ordered it for me, and to drink it. I tell him thanks and drink from the cold bottle.

George tells me not to worry about feeling angry.

'It's just human nature,' he says. 'We're programmed to think in certain ways. It's all in the genes,' he says.

He says that a computer cannot think for itself, it can only do what it is programmed to do.

I tell him, 'Thanks. That makes me feel so much better.'

'What are you going to do?'

I think for a moment. I tell him, 'I have no idea. Nothing, I guess. If he tries anything again then I might have to have a talk with him.'

'Good idea.'

'Thank you.'

I finish most of the beer in a single drink then walk back to where our little group is standing. I stop dead in my tracks on the way. I'm shocked to see the guy standing right where I was standing, and he's talking to Jade.

My heart speeds up and my chest begins to burn and I storm over. As if sensing my approach, he turns around. I notice a small laminate on his shirt pocket with the logo of an animal charity and it becomes clear: he's pretending to collect for charity so he can talk to girls. Part of me concedes this is a great idea and I wish I'd thought of it myself, even though I see through his act straight away.

'Hey, man,' he says. 'Listen, I didn't mean to bother either of you before. I was just apologising to your friend here.'

'That's okay,' I tell him, trying to end the conversation and get him to move on. 'Forget about it.'

He holds out a brochure of some sort and says, 'Can I interest you in…?'

'No,' I cut him off. 'You can't.'

'Oh,' he says. 'Well, if you change your mind…'

'I won't,' I tell him. 'Bye.'

He looks at Jade, then at me, and tries to smile. I don't return it and he looks down, then walks away, vanishing into the crowd.

'Are you okay?' Jade asks. 'You look… flustered.'

I tell her I'm fine. 'It's just a little warm in here.'

'I know,' she says. 'I don't think we'll be staying much longer, it's getting late.' She checks her watch, then adds with a smile, 'Early, I mean. We'll have to be getting up in a few hours.'

I nod. I tell her I'm just going to the bathroom and then we can go.

I cross the room towards the toilets and open the door. The room is empty, except for one cubicle. The door is open and in the mirror I can see a guy sitting on the floor, snorting something off the seat.

The door opens behind me and George walks in.

I tell him we are leaving soon.

'Are you going to let him get away with it?'

'What?'

'That guy. Are you just going to forget about it?'

'What else can I do?'

'You know what you can do. The real question is, if you don't do it, will you be able to sleep tonight?'

I ask him what he's talking about.

'Will you be able to sleep knowing what he did?'

George tells me, 'People aren't all different. They're not unique. We all look different close up but take a step back and look again and we're all interchangeable with the next. People from the same area may have similar coloured hair, or eyes, or skin, whatever, and their accents and the way they talk may be the same. People from a similar background may share beliefs and opinions.'

George paces back and forth behind me, his voice a loud whisper.

'Take a wider look. It becomes even harder to tell them apart. Everyone living in a city will have things in common. The climate, the landscape and the society they live in will all have had an impact. Soon the commonalities begin to outweigh the differences. At a global level there is almost no difference between one person and the next. In silhouette, you can't tell us apart.'

I ask George what the hell this has to do with anything.

'It means, will anyone miss him if he's gone?'

'Don't be stupid,' I mutter.

George says, 'A nest of ants all look the same. If you stomp on one, it is quickly replaced by another, identical ant. To us, no ant is unique. They're all the same and aren't worth anything. If we stand on an ant, we don't sit up at night feeling guilty, wondering how its children are going to cope without a father. The ant's life is worthless to us. If you look at humans, as a species, it's the same. If one is killed, another two take its place almost instantly.'

I look in the mirror and my reflection shimmers briefly. George says, 'Why are farmers not punished every time they kill a pig or harvest a crop? Why is human life considered more valuable than the life of an animal? We're all made of the same chemicals and components so why are we regarded as being superior? Is it because we can't understand the way a pig communicates, therefore it's stupid and inferior, which gives us the right to kill it? Is it because we can dream? Because we're self-aware, whatever the hell that means? Because we're the only creatures that know about our own death?'

He says, 'Stronger beings kill the weaker beings to survive.'

I lean on the washbasin and look at myself. My eyes look like doll's eyes. Like they're just plastic. Windows of the soul.

'What should I do, George? You think I should kill him?'

The guy in the stall behind me looks up at this and I can see from here that he's barely even conscious. I yell at him to mind his fucking business.

Still staring at the guy, I say to George, 'Is that it? Is that what you think I should do?'

There's no answer and when I turn my attention away from the stoner, George is gone.

I splash some water on my face and walk out.

I'm crossing the dance floor again and when I get back to our spot, the group has stopped dancing and they all have their coats.

'We're ready to go,' Jade says. 'You have your own car, right?'

'Yeah, I do.'

We all walk towards the exit. The line outside is gone; it's early in the morning and the club will be closing fairly soon. There's just us and a bouncer on the door.

Down the street, I see the guy. He's standing at the side of the building, obviously waiting for us. Jade and I walk behind the others and when the group gets closer, the guy steps forward, smiling, still holding his brochures. Then he notices me and his smile fades. He steps back against the wall and doesn't say anything, letting us pass.

We walk to their car and the others climb in. One of the guys starts the engine.

'Thanks for coming,' Jade says.

'Thanks for asking me,' I tell her. 'I had a great time.'

'No problem. I'll see you.'

She gives me one last smile then gets into the car. It departs and I watch it until the tail lights fade away.

The next morning I wake up, my dream fresh in my mind, clear enough to be memory.

In the dream, I am sitting in my car in the car park, and I can't let it go.

What the guy did, it pisses me off so much that I have to do something about it.

I get out of my car and I walk down the street, back towards the club, and sure enough, the guy is still standing there. He sees me walking towards him and when I get up close he says, 'Hello again.'

'Hi.'

'Did you have a good night?' he asks and I suddenly want to see half his teeth sticking through his lips and the rest lying on the pavement.

'It was okay. But are you blind?'

He cocks his head slightly and asks, 'What?'

'Couldn't you see I was with my friends? Couldn't you tell we were trying to have a good time, and didn't want to be hassled by some asshole like you?'

He takes a slight step backwards and says, 'Listen, man, I think you got the wrong idea...'

He goes to say something else but I cut him off. I say, 'Couldn't you see I was with a girl? Couldn't you respect that and just leave us alone?'

'I'm sorry, I didn't know you'd...'

I'm tired of his explanations and before I know what I'm doing, before I even realise, I'm holding a beer bottle by its neck and I'm bringing my hand up in an arc and the thick rim around the bottom of the bottle connects with his cheekbone, just below his eye. Glass explodes out in every direction and the guy utters a quick yelp of surprise and stumbles backwards.

In my dream, blood is streaming down his cheek, which has been completely torn open, and I can see his teeth through the hole. He lifts his hand to his eye and tries to stop it from running down his face. The fluid inside looks clear in the darkness and as he brings his hand away, sticky strands cling to it like honey.

He hasn't made a sound since his initial whoop of surprise. I think he's shocked about what's happening to him and for that I am thankful.

I put one hand behind his head to hold him in place and, holding the remains of the bottle tighter, drive it into his stomach, once, twice, three times. He brings his hands down from his face and tries to stop me, but it's no use; the jagged ridge of the bottle tears the backs of his hands and cuts his fingers. I stab his belly once more and after this the bottle disintegrates, some of it falling to the pavement, most of it sticking out of his gut. Blood is streaming down from his stomach, soaking his pants. He's making little gargling noises and my hand is still grabbing a handful of hair on the back of his head, so I drag him into the alley between the two buildings.

In my dream I throw him into the alley and he stumbles and falls. Instead of trying to get up he curls into a ball and holds his stomach. I walk over and kick him, aiming for the places I stabbed.

He tries to scream again but it sounds like all the air has been knocked out of him and he can only make a feeble coughing noise.

I roll him onto his back and sit on his belly, with one leg on either side of him.

I ask him, 'Couldn't you just leave us alone?'

I punch him once in the face and his head rocks back and slams into the pavement.

'Don't you have any respect for other people's privacy?'

Punch.

'Can't you just mind your own business?'

Punch.

In my dream, my knuckles have been cut on his teeth, which have snapped off in several places. I don't know where the teeth have gone; he's probably swallowed them.

'You fucking asshole,' I say, savagely but quietly. 'Don't you have any brains?'

He mumbles something but he can't speak anymore.

'What? What did you say? Speak up, I can't hear you.'

He mumbles again and moves his head around, as if he's trying to look around the alley but he can't because the bottle punctured his eye. He's breathing heavily and blood is bubbling out his mouth.

I tell him I still can't hear him. 'What's the matter? Are you thirsty? Hungry?'

I punch him once more to ensure he won't try anything then get off him. I go back to the mouth of the alley and kneel down to pick up a fistful of broken glass.

Back into the alley and I'm sitting on him again.

I tell him I've got some food for him, if that's what he was saying. 'See?' I lift my hand to his face so he can see the glass lying in my palm. I make sure to hold it in front of his one remaining eye and I resist the urge to puncture that one too.

He mumbles something and I push the handful of glass into his mouth. He tries to block it with his tongue but it doesn't work, the pieces are too small. I put one hand under his jaw and the other on top of his head and make him chew, and the glass slices the inside of his mouth and his gums and tongue and I can hear something crunching from inside.

I'm suddenly very tired and very bored with this whole thing and I stand up. He doesn't move. The pool of blood around him is quite large and if he's not dead yet he will be very soon. The legs and seat of my jeans stick to my skin.

As I leave the alley I step on something. It's the laminate from his pocket. I kick it away into a drain.

I get back in my car and drive home.

That's when I wake up.

Eleven

Jesus calls and says he's going to pick up some album that he'd had to order in and would I like to come along? I have nothing better to do so I tell him, yeah, sure.

We go to the music store and I browse their selection while Jesus talks to the guy at the counter. They talk for a long time before Jesus signals to me that he's done.

We exit the store and walk down the sidewalk, avoiding all the yuppies doing whatever it is they do, ignoring the bums that litter the alleys and the so-called street performers playing their shitty songs or singing their tuneless melodies, begging for our change.

We decide to stop off at a café and get something to drink. It's not that I want to, it's just that I'm a million miles away, thinking random thoughts, and when Jesus asks me I've already said yes before I even know what the question is.

We sit in a booth at the side of the café. There are fans hanging from the ceiling which don't even seem to be moving the air around and I'm suddenly feeling suffocated and claustrophobic. The vinyl on the bench seat is ripped and yellow stuffing protrudes like pus through a wound. The table is scarred with cuts from a million knives and stained with the rings of a million coffee cups.

The waitress comes over and we both order coffees, no food. She walks away without smiling.

I try to remember why we chose this particular café but I can't.

Jesus opens the bag and takes out his CD. He looks at both sides and I can tell he's waiting for me to ask him about it, but I don't. Whenever I see him glance up at me, I avert my eyes to the other side of the room, as if studying the other patrons.

Eventually, he says, 'Have you heard this?'

I look back at him and shake my head. 'No, I don't think so.'

He passes the CD over to me and reluctantly I take it.

Jesus says, 'They're gonna be playing that in all the clubs pretty soon. Just wait and see.'

'So it's dance music?'

'Sure is. The best.'

I nod and pretend to read the back cover.

'So what do you think?' he asks. I can tell by the way he asks that my approval is important to him for some reason.

I decide to keep him happy and say, 'It looks pretty cool.'

He smiles, relieved, and I pass the CD back to him. He puts it back in the bag on the bench beside him.

The waitress brings our coffees over and they look like muddy water. I'm hesitant to put the cup to my mouth in fear of contracting some rare disease, but I close my eyes and decide to risk it.

It tastes almost as bad as it looks.

'Did I tell you about my cat?' Jesus asks.

'Uh, no, I don't think so.'

'He's been feeling pretty sick lately so I took him to the vet. They kept him in for a few days and did some tests, you know, and anyway they asked me to go down there one day. So I went down and they told me they thought he might have feline leukaemia.'

'I didn't know cats could get leukaemia.'

'Yeah, they can. I think it's different to human leukaemia, though. I'm not sure.'

'Oh. Does the cat's hair fall out when they give it treatment?' I ask, and laugh.

Jesus doesn't think this is funny. He just gives me a look and I clear my throat and apologise, trying not to smile.

'So anyway, they kept Mister Snuggles in for a few more tests, just to be sure. Yesterday, I got a phone call from the vet again, asking me would I go down again? So off I went. It turns out, he doesn't have feline leukaemia after all.'

'Really? That's great news.'

'Yeah, I know,' Jesus says, smiling. 'It turns out he has some problem with his white blood cell count. There's either too many or not enough, I don't remember.'

'Mister Snuggles has a white blood cell problem?'

'Yeah.'

'I'm, uh, sorry to hear that.'

'Thanks. I'll be sure to give him your best regards.'

I nod.

'Honestly, sometimes I don't know what I'd do if I ever lost him. He's been with me through the worst of it.'

'He sounds really... special.'

'Oh, he is,' Jesus says, smiling broadly. 'He's the most fantabulous cat in the world.'

I look around the café again, unsure of what I'm looking for, then back at Jesus. Trying to find something to say, I ask, 'Have you seen Nick lately?'

'No, not for a while,' Jesus says. 'You?'

'No.'

'We'll have to go out one night and catch up.'

'Yeah, we will,' I say, trying to sound enthusiastic.

'What have you been up to lately? I haven't seen you around for a while.'

'Not much,' I tell him. 'Just the usual. I went to that new club, Cosmic.'

'Oh cool, I haven't been there yet but I heard it's pretty good. When were you there?'

'Last weekend.'

'Were you there when that guy got beaten up?'

My heart stops and I start sweating. I know it was only a dream but I'm suddenly very nervous. I tell myself to calm down and I reach for my coffee but my hands are shaking so I clasp them together below the table.

'No,' I say. 'What happened?'

'I'm not sure, you can never believe anything you hear on the news,' Jesus says. 'Apparently some guy was beaten up in the bathroom. They didn't say who did it or anything.'

'He was beaten up in the bathroom?'

'Yeah.'

I lean back and let out a long sigh.

Jesus laughs lightly and says, 'You look relieved.'

I tell him, 'I'm not relieved, I'm just… tired.'

'Oh,' he says, and smiles.

I suddenly can't be bothered with this at all. For some reason I'm feeling very restless and irritable today and I just want to go home.

I say to Jesus, 'Listen, I really have to be going. Thanks for inviting me here today.'

'No problem, man,' he says, though he looks vaguely disappointed. Then: 'Is there anything wrong?'

'No, nothing,' I say, unsure if this is a lie. 'I'm just really tired and I've remembered something I have to do.'

He nods but doesn't look pleased. 'Are you sure? I haven't done anything, or said anything wrong, have I?'

I could be really mean here but instead, I say, 'No, of course not.'

I stand up and put some money on the table for my coffee.

Jesus says, 'I'll call you sometime and we'll go clubbing again. Give us all a chance to catch up.'

'Sure,' I say, nodding. 'I'll look forward to it.' I try not to grimace.

Finally he starts to smile a little, and says, 'Great. I'll speak to you again soon.'

I nod, force a smile, and say, 'Okay.'

Before he can say anything else, I turn and quickly walk away.

He calls out, 'Bye,' and I raise my hand without turning around.

I knew I wanted to kill Dawson from the first moment I saw him.

It's raining outside and I walk down the centre of an outdoor arcade, ignoring the drops splattering on my face. The weather is perfect for my mood – the sky is almost as black as my temperament. I don't know what has put me in this state of mind. I'm very frustrated but I can't figure out why.

Mister Ennui.

Thunder booms overhead and the rain picks up, and I'm forced to move to the side of the street and take cover under the awnings of another café.

This café is slightly different to the one I was just in.

Inside is well lit, with elaborate globes hanging from ornamental fixtures. There are potted plants throughout the room, which is painted in soft, soothing tones. There are no booths around the perimeter, instead there are tables made of dark, expensive wood.

The waitresses are all good-looking and they smile as they walk through the room. The clientele are all businessmen, dressed in suits that cost more than I'd see in a year, eating large servings of delicacies that I'll probably never taste.

I stand outside, soaked through, watching these people go about their lives. The wind whips down the arcade and thunder booms in the sky and a shiver runs up my body.

The people in the café, they don't even look up.

The man sitting in the window, he hasn't even noticed me.

I hate this man with all my heart. He has everything I don't, and probably never will. He's sitting there in his expensive suit, eating his gourmet feast, drinking coffee that doesn't taste like mud, while I'm standing outside in the rain.

I hate him for all these reasons. And more.

The man in the window, he still hasn't looked up.

I consider saying something to him but then I decide against it. I'm not in the right frame of mind and would most likely say something I will regret.

Instead, I walk through the downpour to the other side of the arcade. I press myself as close to the wall as I can, trying to keep out of the rain. I am drenched from head to toe and my teeth have started chattering. This barely registers though, as all my concentration is on the man in the window. I am completely numb, except for the hate I feel at this particular moment.

I stand pressed against the wall for another twenty minutes while the man finishes his meal. In this time, no one inside the café notices me. No one walks down the arcade. I stand alone in the rain, listening to the thunder, and no one sees me.

It's hard when everything you know changes.

When everything you believe is wrong.

It's hard to deal with change. All your life, you believe one thing, and it becomes your foundation. You build the rest of your life around it. It becomes the structure for your life.

Then, like any other building, when the foundation is wrong, the structure collapses.

The man walks out of the café and puts up an umbrella. I can tell from here that this umbrella wasn't bought from some department store. From the looks of it, you could feed a small family for a week with what it cost.

He holds the umbrella in one hand and his briefcase in the other and walks down the arcade, his leather shoes stepping over puddles. The suit fits him too well to have been bought off the rack; it's obviously tailored at a great expense.

I follow him as he walks along the street, keeping at a discreet distance so he won't notice me. We walk for a block or two before he turns and walks down a small flight of stairs below a large building.

I recognise the logo on the building as that of a major investment company.

I wait for a moment then quietly walk down the stairs behind him.

The parking garage is darker than the street, despite the fluorescent tubes covering the roof. It's warmer down here and the sound of the rain echoes from the street. The garage smells faintly like oil mixed with something else, something darker, something rotten.

I'm aware that there's probably security cameras hidden in the roof somewhere, so I try not to look suspicious, even though I'm soaking wet and slinking through a large company's parking lot, following someone.

The man has closed his umbrella and shakes it to clear the water. He walks over to a car, a Porsche, and puts the briefcase down, reaches into his pocket and brings out some keys. He opens the car and puts his umbrella inside.

I watch this, crouching behind a nearby car.

He closes the door and locks it before picking up his case and walking towards the elevator. He waits for a moment before the doors open and he steps inside.

As soon as the doors are closed, I'm out from behind the car and walking towards his.

I have visions of me kicking it, slashing the tyres, breaking a key off in the lock, scratching the paint, snapping the aerial or the wipers, stomping on the exhaust, putting things in the fuel tank, breaking windows or the side mirrors, numerous other things, but I know I won't.

Instead, I stand and look at the car for what feels like forever, when it's really only about ten seconds.

I take one last look before turning and walking back the way I had come, up the stairs, and back into the rain.

I walk, not seeing anyone else, my mind processing what I have just witnessed.

No matter what I do, I can't get him out of my head.

I ignore everything and my mind keeps racing back to the man in the café, the car in the car park, and the sign on the wall in front of the parked car.

My mind reads the sign, over and over.

Over and over.

'RESERVED FOR MR R. DAWSON.'

Twelve

I'm sitting on the couch when my phone rings. I check the screen and it's Jesus.

I say, 'Hello.'

'Hey,' Jesus says. 'How are you?'

'I'm good,' I tell him. 'What's up?'

'You ready to hit the town tonight?' he asks.

Mister Confused.

'Tonight?' I ask. 'What's happening tonight?'

'That's what I'm calling you for,' he says hurriedly. 'We've got to organise something.'

'Oh, okay. What do you want to do?'

'I dunno,' he whines. 'I just want to go out and have fun. We haven't all been out in a while.'

'No, we haven't,' I agree. 'Have you spoken to anyone else yet?'

'Nope, you're my first call,' Jesus says. 'So, any ideas?'

I think for a moment. 'What do you feel like? Clubbing? Or do we all just wanna go see a movie, or have a drink somewhere?'

'Hmm. Are there any good movies on?'

'Probably not.'

'I think a club is the best idea, knowing Nick and Beau. Where do you want to go?' he asks.

'I don't know. Somewhere where they play decent music.'

Jesus laughs. 'That narrows it down, doesn't it?'

I don't know if he's being sarcastic or not. I don't say anything, hoping he'll clarify, but he doesn't.

'That reminds me, you know that CD I got last week?'

'Yeah.' I try to sound enthusiastic but I'm thinking, Oh no, not this again.

'Man, you have to hear it, it's one of the best albums I've ever heard in my life.'

'No shit?'

'No shit. Every song is great. You know how on a CD there's usually a couple of tracks that suck? They just put them on there to fill up space? Not this one. This one doesn't have any bad songs, at all. It's great. And the sound, my god, it's crystal clear.'

'Dance music usually is,' I tell him. 'It's because they don't use real instruments.'

'Yeah, I suppose. But it's still great.'

'Good, I'm glad you're happy with it.'

Mister Bored.

'I am, man, I am.'

My phone beeps and I tell Jesus to hold on, I've got another call. I press the button and say, 'Hello?'

Nick McCarr says, 'Hey dude. What's up?'

I say hello.

'What're we doing tonight? Nick wants to go out and paint the town red.'

I tell him, 'I'm talking to Jesus now.'

'Oh, cool, cool. He told Nick to call you tonight and you'd tell Nick what was going on.'

'Hold on.'

I press the button.

'Jesus?'

'Yeah man, I'm here.'

'It's Nick on the other line. He wants to know what we're doing tonight.'

'Tell him we don't know yet, we're still deciding.'

'Okay.'

Click.

'We don't know yet, Nick, we're still deciding.'

'Okay, dude, that's cool. You tell Jesus not to fuck around. You tell him to make his mind up before everywhere closes.'

'Okay.'

Click.

Mister Secretary.

'Jesus, Nick says not to fuck around, and to make your mind up before everywhere closes.'

Jesus laughs. 'You tell him to go fuck himself.'

Click.

'Nick, go fuck yourself.'

Nick starts laughing uproariously and I quickly click back to Jesus.

'This is going to take all night,' he says. 'Don't you have three-way?'

'Sure. Hang on.'

I press a button on my phone and the sound of Nick laughing comes on the line.

'Nick, shut up,' Jesus says. 'We've got to decide what we want to do tonight.'

'Sorry,' Nick says, and clears his throat seriously. 'Let's get to it.'

'How about Cosmic?' Jesus asks. 'I've heard that's pretty cool.'

'I was there not long ago,' I say. 'Can't we go somewhere different?'

'Yeah, I guess,' Jesus says, although slightly grudgingly. 'Any suggestions?'

'Um… how about Hole?'

'Hole?' Jesus says, shocked. 'Why would you want to go to Hole?'

'Because the people there are sort of real. They're not fake and, you know, superficial like they are everywhere else.'

'That's because they're freaks,' Jesus says and Nick starts laughing again. 'They go to Hole because nowhere else will let them in.'

I don't know why I feel obliged to defend the patrons of Hole but I argue anyway. I say, 'The people at Hole act differently and dress differently because they think differently. They're not sheep like the rest of society. They have their own minds and…'

'Listen to him, social philosopher,' Nick says, still laughing. 'Look, we all agree that the only people who go to Hole are those who wouldn't fit in anywhere else, right? For better or worse. Right?'

'Yeah, I guess.'

'Right. So are we different or are we just like everyone else?'

Jesus says, 'We're different but not like those guys. We're different but we're still normal.'

'Speak for yourself,' I say.

Nick ignores me and says, 'So we're different but we're still the same?'

'Yes,' Jesus says, 'that's right.'

'Okay, so are we or are we not going to Hole?' Nick asks.

'No, we're not,' Jesus says before I have a chance to answer. 'I don't want to go somewhere where everyone is dressed in black and has bits of metal stuck through parts of themselves. Don't get me started,' Jesus says. 'Besides, Hole is dark and crowded and noisy and the music there is always terrible.'

I interrupt, 'Just like everywhere else?'

'And I'm not in the mood to put up with that sort of thing. I just want to go somewhere, relax, have a drink or two, do a bit of dancing. I'm not in the mood to put up with the people at Hole.'

I run my free hand through my hair in frustration.

'Okay,' Nick says, 'so Hole is out. Where else?'

'Hold on a second, guys,' Jesus says. 'My cat is… I'll call you back. Mister Snuggles! Don't!'

Click.

He's gone.

'That fucking cat,' Nick says. 'One day, Nick is going to kill it. It's more trouble than it's worth.'

'You don't like cats?'

'Nick likes cats fine, he just doesn't like Mister Snuggles.'

'Why not?'

'Have you ever met him?'

'No, I haven't.'

'That explains it then. One day, you'll meet him and you'll hate him just as much as Nick does.'

I'm not sure if I want to know any more and luckily my phone beeps. I tell Nick to hold on.

Click.

'Hello?'

'Hey sexy,' Melinda says. 'What's up?'

'Mel?' I say. 'You sound very bloated this evening.'

She says, 'What are you doing tonight?'

'Going out with the guys. How about you?'

'Nothing,' she says.

'Want to come with us?'

'Where are you going?'

'We haven't decided yet. Hang on, I'll connect you up.'

Click.

Nick is singing to himself.

'Nick,' I say, 'Mel's here.'

'Oh, hi Mel,' Nick says.

Knowing it's hopeless, I ask, 'Where are we going tonight?'

'Nick doesn't know,' Nick says.

'How about Cosmic?' Melinda offers.

'We're not going,' I tell her, 'I was there the other day.'

'And you don't want to go back?'

'No.'

'Okay. So where else?'

There's silence on the line for a moment.

I start rubbing my temple.

'How about Perspective?' Nick suggests. 'That's always fun.'

'Hmm, a possibility,' I say, considering. I don't know if I actually want to go there, or if it's just better than anywhere else I can think of, namely Cosmic.

'I'm cool with Perspective,' Fatty Mel says.

'Do you think Jesus and Beau would come to Perspective?'

'Nick doesn't see why not,' he says.

'Okay, Perspective it is. Nine o'clock?'

'Yep, that's fine,' Nick says. 'Nick will see you both then.'

'Bye.'

Click.

'That wasn't so hard,' Melinda says. 'Hey, you know that essay I had to write?'

'Yeah.'

'Well I did it, and guess what I got for it?'

'A hard slap across the face?'

'Idiot,' she says, but I can tell she's smiling. 'I got eighty-six per cent.'

'Well done,' I say. 'We'll have a drink tonight to celebrate.'

'Definitely.'

My phone beeps.

I tell Mel to hold on.

Click.

'Hey man,' Beau exclaims. 'What are we doing tonight?'

'We're going to Perspective.'

'Aw, not Perspective. I was there last weekend.'

Mister Not Surprised.

'Oh. Hang on.'

Click.

'Mel, Beau is here.'

'Hey Mel,' Beau says. 'What's up?'

'Hi Beau,' Mel says.

I tell Mel how Beau doesn't want to go to Perspective, he was there last week.

'Oh really? Where do you want to go then, Beau?'

I start pacing.

Beau says, 'Let me think,' and goes completely silent. After about ten seconds, he says, 'How about Cosmic?'

I tell him, 'We're not going to fucking Cosmic.'

'Okay, man, calm down,' Beau says. 'We'll go someplace else.'

'Where?' I demand.

I go to the fridge and take out some water. I drink it in a couple of large gulps, hoping it'll settle my stomach.

'Umm... Hole?'

Melinda says, 'Yeah, Hole is fine with me. I haven't been there in a while.'

'No, no, we can't go to Hole. I already suggested that and Jesus doesn't want to go.' I tell them this with my eyes squeezed closed, my hand rubbing my temple again.

'Where does he want to go?' Beau asks.

'He said he wanted to go to Cosmic but I told him no.'

'Okay,' Beau says. 'So Cosmic is out, Hole is out, Perspective is out. What does that leave?'

I say, 'Utopia, Emetic, Grind, Babylon, Paramount, Jezebel's, Existence...'

'Surely we must all be able to agree on one of those?' Mel says.

'How about Babylon?' Beau suggests. 'I haven't been there in at least three weeks.'

'Babylon is good,' Mel says, 'but I'd rather go to Paramount.'

'Paramount?' Beau says. 'Why do you want to go there?'

'I dunno,' she replies, 'I just like it there.'

'But you like Babylon too, right?' Beau asks.

'Yeah.'

'So let's go there instead?'

'That's fine with me,' I add quickly.

'Me too, then, I guess,' says Fatty Mel, without enthusiasm.

'Great. Babylon it is.'

I tell them, 'I'll call Nick and Jesus and let them know what's up.'

Beau says, 'Okay. Nine o'clock?'

'Sure.'

Beau says, 'Bye,' then hangs up.

Click.

'I never thought it'd be this difficult,' Mel says.

'Tell me about it.'

'I still think Paramount is better. The music there is cooler, the colours are nicer...'

'The drinks are more expensive.'

'... yeah, I guess. But the music and the colours more than compensate.'

'No, they don't. Cheap drinks win, every time.'

'God, don't be Mister Cheap. You get what you pay for, you know.'

'I know. But if I'm buying you a drink for your essay result then I don't want it to cost an arm and a leg. I like being able to get a beer for less than ten bucks.'

She laughs. 'Okay, fine. If that's how much I'm worth to you...'

'You're worth every cent.'

'Great, thanks, I'll remember that.' She laughs and says, 'I'll see you there at nine.'

'Sure. Bye.'

Click.

Reluctantly I dial Nick's number.

He picks up on the third ring.

I tell him we're not going to Perspective anymore, we're going to Paramount instead.

'Why is that?'

'Because Beau was there last week and he doesn't want to go again.'

Nick says, 'Jesus called a minute ago and told Nick that he couldn't get through to you.'

'I was talking to Mel and Beau.'

'Nick told him we were going to Perspective.'

'We're not going to Perspective, we're going to Paramount.'

'Yeah, Nick knows that now, but he didn't know when Jesus called.'

'So call him back. Tell him we're going to Paramount.'

'Okay, hang on.'

Click.

I'm waiting.

Beep.

Click.

'Hello?'

Beau says, 'Guess what?'

'You're pregnant?'

'Jesus just called me and asked if he could have a lift with me tonight to Perspective.'

'Oh.'

'What is going on? Did we not come to the conclusion that we were no longer going to Perspective?'

'Yes, we did, but Jesus doesn't know that yet.'

'He does now,' Beau says. 'I corrected him and told him we were going to Babylon.'

'Babylon? What happened to Paramount?'

'Paramount? Mel wanted to go there, but we never agreed we would. We agreed to go to Babylon. We never agreed to Paramount.'

'Shit. I was talking to Mel about Paramount after you left, it must have, you know, confused me.'

'You get confused pretty easily.'

'I just told Nick to go to Paramount.'

'You'd better tell him we're going to Babylon or else he'll end up at the wrong place.'

'He's on the other line. I'll tell him as soon as he comes back.'

'Okay. I'll see you at Babylon at nine o'clock. Okay?'

'Okay.'

'Bye.'

Click.

I'm waiting again.

Click.

Nick says, 'Okay, Nick called Jesus and told him we're going to Paramount, but he told Nick that he had just called Beau, and Beau had told him we were going to Babylon. He wasn't too impressed, either. But Nick managed to convince him we weren't going to Babylon, we were going to Paramount.'

'Nick, we're going to Babylon.'

'What?'

'I'm sorry, I fucked up, I didn't know what I was talking about.'

'So are we going to Babylon or Paramount?'

'Babylon.'

'You're sure?'

'Yes.'

'Positive?'

'Yes.'

'Okay,' Nick says. 'That's cool with Nick, but Nick doesn't know if Jesus will go to Babylon.'

'Then he can go somewhere else. I'm sick of wasting time trying to decide where to go. Babylon is fine with everyone else, so if he doesn't like it, he can stay at home.'

Nick laughs and says, 'It's good to see you taking charge.'

'Thanks,' I say. 'Can you call Jesus back and tell him we're going to Babylon?'

'Yeah, okay,' Nick says. 'Hold on.'

Click.

I wait around, not wanting to talk to Jesus, but knowing I can't avoid it.

After a minute Nick comes back with Jesus.

'What's going on?' Jesus asks. 'We're going to Babylon now?'

'Yes.'

'What about Paramount?'

'I'm sorry, I told Nick the wrong thing, I was–'

'What happened to Perspective? Wasn't that where we were going all along?'

'Beau was there… look, it doesn't matter, okay? We're going to Babylon.'

'Come on, dude.' Nick says. 'It'll be heaps of fun.'

'Why can't we go to Cosmic?' Jesus asks. 'I really want to go there.'

'Cosmic is not an option,' I say, barely keeping my temper in check. 'Perspective is not an option. Paramount is not an option. We're going to Babylon. Now, are you coming or not?'

Jesus says, 'Umm,' and stretches it out for a few seconds, then says, 'yeah, I guess so.'

I tell him not to sound too enthusiastic.

He laughs and says, 'I've only been there once before and I didn't have a very good time.'

'Tonight will be better,' Nick says, 'Nick is sure of it.'

'Okay, okay,' Jesus says, 'you've talked me into it.'

'Great,' I say, with only a slight hint of sarcasm. I tell them I'll see them both at Babylon at nine o'clock.

Click.

George and I arrive at Babylon at eight forty-five. We wait in line and it's five past before we get inside. We split up and I head straight for the bar.

I had tried to call Jade to invite her but my calls went straight to her voicemail. I left a message asking if she'd like to meet up later but had so far heard nothing.

The walls inside the club seem to be made out of sand, or mud bricks, but of course they aren't. The floor has the look and feel of compressed dirt, but it's really something else. There are lights on the walls that resemble flaming torches. There are statues of gods and heroes from Babylonian mythology, and they tower over everyone, watching silently.

At the bar I order a B&C then begin the slow task of searching the club for the rest of the group.

I push my way through the crowd and head towards the garden area. Outside there is a small paved area with a waterfall and a pond at the far end. The pond has large koi fish swimming in it and the bottom is covered with coins, tossed in by those still hopeful or drunk enough to believe in wishes. There are torches on the walls and standing in various parts of the garden and these torches are real fire, unlike the ones inside. There's an ant crawling on my wrist so I brush it away.

I turn a corner and see them sitting around a table. This area is not as crowded as inside or in the main garden area, and in the firelight it looks ghostly.

Nick sits on the chair backwards with his arms folded along the backrest. He has a glass of something in his hand and is laughing in his usual loud way.

Jesus sits to his left, his right leg resting on the left, the ankle on the knee. He sits back in the chair, also holding a drink, smiling at whatever it is Nick is laughing at.

Beau sits across from the others with his feet up on a vacant chair. He's rocking back on his seat, balancing on the rear legs. He's laughing along with Nick and nursing a beer.

Fatty Mel sits with her back to me, her arms folded, not holding a drink, and from here I can't tell if she's smiling.

I walk over to the table and say hi to everyone and they all say hi back. Beau holds up his hand and I slap him high-five, then push his legs off the chair and sit down between him and Mel.

We all exchange greetings and Jesus says, 'I'm glad you remembered to come here and not to Paramount.'

I smile, groan and cover my eyes with my hand.

Beau says, 'He gets confused easily,' as if he's explaining to the rest of them. I don't know whether he's defending me or not.

'It was just…' I stop, not bothering to finish.

I sit back and take a drink. Nick is already half drunk, his voice gradually getting louder. He's talking about some girl he met and what they did and it's obvious no one is interested. I don't even pretend to listen.

Jesus is looking at me and he goes to say something but Nick speaks over him and I'm quietly relieved.

Mel leans in to me and says, 'At least you got here in the end. Better late than never.'

Nick continues talking and, although I've only been here a matter of minutes, I'm already finding him irritating.

I tell Mel, 'I'm glad you're here.'

She says, 'Me, too. I don't mind this place, really.'

'We'll go to Paramount next time,' I tell her. 'I promise.'

She smiles at me and says, 'I'll hold you to that.'

'That reminds me, I owe you a drink.'

She smiles and says thanks, and when I ask her what she wants, she asks for a Stoli, please. I tell her sure and head off towards the bar.

*　*　*

I'm walking through the garden towards the doorway when a hand lands on my shoulder. I turn, expecting Mel or George, but it's Beau.

I ask him what's up.

'I've got something for you,' he says.

I ask him, 'What?'

He puts his arm around my shoulder and steers me towards a back corner of the garden area, away from our table.

'I didn't want to give it to you around the others, because there's not enough for everyone.'

'What are you talking about?'

He reaches into his pocket and takes out a small baggie. He holds it in the palm of his hand so no one else can see it and brings it up into the light.

The baggie is filled with small, green leaves.

Beau Branson presses the baggie into my hand and I put it in my pocket.

I ask him, 'What was that for?'

'I dunno,' he says. 'From the look of you recently, man, you look like you could use some chilling out.'

'What is that supposed to mean?'

'Nothing, man, nothing,' Beau says, 'it's just that you haven't been looking so good lately. I mean, you've been looking good. Your hair is great. But you've been looking kinda stressed. I thought you could use a little something to calm you down.'

I tell him, 'Great, thanks. I'm sure it'll come in… handy.' I tell him I hope I don't turn into a stoner like him.

Beau Branson, the master of the witty comeback, says, 'Fuck off.'

I laugh and he smiles and says, 'I'm gonna head back before they come looking for us. Enjoy it, man.'

'I will.'

'Use it, don't abuse it.'

'I will and I won't.'

'I'll see you later.'

'Sure. Thanks again.'

He walks away and I turn and go inside. I'm instantly aware of all the security guards along the walls and each of them seems to be eyeing me suspiciously. I coolly walk over to the bar, as if I'm doing nothing wrong, and casually lean against it. After a moment, the bartender comes over and I order a B&C for myself and a Stoli for Fatty Mel. On the counter there is a bowl full of matchbooks and a dish of papers for rolling cigarettes and I reach over and grab some. The bartender brings the drinks for me and I give him the money.

When I turn around, George is standing in front of me.

I ask him where he went.

'Just looking around,' he tells me.

'Oh.' I look around, and upon seeing no one paying us much attention, I motion for him to follow me back outside. He does, and when we get out to a relatively empty part of the garden, we sit at a small table and I tell him about Beau's gift.

George nods and asks me if I'm going to smoke it.

I tell him I think so.

He nods again and says, 'Cool.'

'You're okay with it?'

'Sure, go ahead,' George says. 'Why would I mind?'

'I dunno, for some reason I thought you'd be against it. I was worried you were gonna be pissed off and give me the whole lecture.'

George laughs and says, 'The world is going to hell and it's not drugs that are doing it. It's not any one single thing that's doing it. It's a group effort.'

I put the drinks down on the table and take the baggie out of my pocket.

George tells me, 'Don't believe any of that stuff you hear on television, it's all bullshit. Most of what everyone tells you all your life is bullshit.'

'What are you talking about?' I open the baggie and inhale. It smells thick and herbal, slightly spicy. I take a small pinch of the weed and place it on a cigarette paper. I'm only half listening to George. I'm concentrating on not spilling any of the pot, and I'm keeping an eye out for bouncers.

'We have no freedom in life at all,' George says. 'Even before we're born, everything is decided for us. Contraception can murder us before we're conceived. We're born and our parents make our choices for us. We go to school and they tell us everything they think we need to know. We all learn the same things, we watch the same movies, we listen to the same music. We chat together on the internet.'

I begin to roll the paper around the pot.

'A smaller group evolves faster,' George says. 'Birds on an island will evolve faster than a group on the mainland because the gene pool is smaller. Now you've got a huge percentage of the world's population all having access to the same information. We all get access to the same news and entertainment. We're all thinking the same thing at the same time.'

George says, 'That can't be good for the species, as a whole.'

I lick the paper and stick it closed.

'Our society is a man-made institution. There's nothing natural about how we live. Nothing free. Society tells us how we are supposed to act and live. We are free to do whatever we like as long as we do not transgress its rules.'

I pull out the book of matches.

'So what do we do?' George asks rhetorically. 'We rebel. But even our rebellion is within the confines of society. We're expected to rebel, so when we do, it's still acceptable. People get tattoos, piercings, wear black, whatever. We have businesses that cater especially for people who don't want to be part of mainstream society. They're all socially-accepted outcasts.'

George says, 'We grow up with our global corporations and our mass media, our fast food and bulk education. Everything you do in life will be spoon-fed to you by someone else. Everything you ever experience will have already been experienced by someone else. All your ideas have been given to you by someone else. Your life is a repeat of someone else's, a recycled plotline, a cliché.'

He says, 'If you believe what some people say, even your soul is second-hand.'

George says, 'You have to find a way to do something unexpected. Step outside the square. See things differently. You have to live a little.'

I ask him, 'How am I meant to do that?'

George tells me, 'If you want to see things differently, you have to change your perspective. You have to think differently.'

He says, 'If you want to think differently, you have to not be yourself. You have to be out of your mind. And the quickest way to do that…'

I look down at the joint in my hand.

'It's a matter of binary opposition,' George says. 'You have to know what something is before you can compare it to something else. So how do you know what normal is if you've never experienced anything else?'

I tell him that's a good question.

'They say, once you reach the top, there's only one way you can go.' He looks at me and says, 'That works both ways.'

'So... I have to get sick before I can get better?'

'Crash and burn, man.'

I take a match from the matchbook and George says, 'With the world the way it is today, you're never going to experience anything new.'

I put the joint in my mouth and the paper is instantly soggy. I strike the match, then again, then it lights. I bring the flame to the end of the joint and inhale softly.

The pot begins to burn and smoke.

'Go ahead and destroy yourself,' George tells me. 'Then you can put yourself back together, better than before.'

I inhale slowly and the tip of the joint glows brightly. White smoke, thick and hot, courses down my throat and into my lungs. My initial reaction is to cough but I fight it and hold the smoke down. I inhale as much as I can until I can't hold any more and my eyes are watering.

George says, 'This is one of the only ways you're ever going to experience anything for yourself. No one else can tell you how to think or feel. This isn't filtered by technology. This is real.'

I hold the smoke inside me and it feels like my lungs are sweating and torn and full of liquid. The smoke is heavy and hot and thick and burning and it fills my chest completely. I exhale in a white cloud. My chest and mouth are burning and I have to take a swallow of my B&C to try and cool them.

I take another drag, long and deep, but this time I can't fight off the coughing. My chest explodes and I cough for almost a full minute before I get myself under control again. I wipe the tears from my eyes and offer the joint to George.

He smiles and shakes his head. 'No, thanks.'

'No? But what about all that stuff you just said?'

'It's a metaphor,' he says. 'Live and learn, man, you gotta grow up sometime. Do what you like.'

With that, he stands up and walks away.

I watch him leave, wanting to say something, but I don't.

I sit and alternate between smoking, watching out for security, and drinking my B&C. Eventually the joint is finished and I drop it to the ground. My throat and chest are burning and my drink is almost finished. The smell is strong in the area so I get up and walk away, back towards where my group is sitting.

I approach the table with my empty glass in one hand and Mel's Stoli in the other. There are more people sitting at the table now; obviously Beau and Nick have made new friends. They're all laughing loudly, except Jesus, who is back a little way, obviously not enthralled by the conversation, and Mel, who is missing.

My head is spinning. Beau is standing beside me yelling something, his hand on my shoulder. He says something to the group and they all cheer loudly and raise their glasses. I start to laugh and raise the Stoli.

Beau steps in front of me and asks, 'Where have you been, man?'

I tell him I was off using his gift.

Beau's smile widens. 'Oh man,' he says excitedly and claps me on the shoulder again. 'That's great news. How are you feeling?'

Laughing, I tell him I'm feeling pretty good.

'Great. Come join the party, I'll introduce you to everyone.'

'Sure.'

I sit down on a vacant chair and Beau points to everyone and tells me their names but I don't remember any of them. I'm still smiling and there's nothing I can do to stop it. Colours seem more vivid, the sounds clearer. It's like I'm seeing everything for the first time and nothing is boring any more, everything is new and exciting.

I'm listening to the people talk and the rhythm of their voices is soothing. Someone is telling someone else that someone OD'd last week, and how it's so terrible that there's so much bad coke around, but the second someone doesn't know who the person who OD'd is.

I tune out and listen to the music playing, the dull thumping coming from inside the club. I don't like it so I listen to another conversation, one I can barely begin to decipher.

Jesus appears out of nowhere and stands in front of me.

'Where did you go?' he asks.

'When?' I ask, peering up at him.

'Before. When you were gone.'

'Oh. I was… just walking around.'

'Uh huh,' Jesus says, and I'm not sure if he believes me and am surprised at the amount of energy it takes for me to care.

I ask him where Mel is.

'She went to look for you,' he tells me.

'Why?'

'I dunno, I guess she was worried. And I don't think she likes our new friends much,' he says, and motions with his thumb to the new group sitting around our table. 'To tell the truth, neither do I.'

I nod.

Jesus looks up quickly and it startles me. I try to follow his gaze so look up too and Mel is standing beside me, which startles me even more.

'Where have you been?' she asks.

'Nowhere,' I tell her. 'I was here all along.'

'You were gone for ages.'

I hold up her Stoli and tell her I was getting her drink.

She smiles and says, 'Thank you.'

I tell her it's not a problem.

I look at Fatty Mel and I realise that she isn't fat at all, she's actually quite slim. I think of all the times I've made jokes about her being fat and I start to laugh.

She looks down at me quizzically. 'What's so funny?'

'Nothing,' I tell her. I clear my throat and try to stop smiling. I bring my glass to my mouth to take another drink before I realise that the glass is empty, and this sets me off again.

Mister Wasted.

'What?' Mel asks again, smiling. 'Are you okay?'

I tell her I'm fine.

She nods, not quite believing me, but still smiling. 'Would you like to come and dance?'

'Sure.'

I stand up and it feels like I'm in someone else's body. My feet are a thousand miles away and it's as if I have no control over them; they move on their own volition. I follow Mel through the garden, back into the club, everything happening in slow motion.

Inside, the flashing lights and loud music combined with the pot and alcohol make it hard for me to see. I squint in the darkness and the music seems incredibly loud but I can hear every note with crystal clarity.

We find a place on the dance floor where there's a bit of room and Mel starts dancing. I try to join in but I can't get my body to do what I want it to do. I just move around, amazed at how my arms and legs move, how the muscles and bones all work together without me having to consciously think about it. I hold my hand in front of my eyes, watching in awe as the coloured lights flash across it.

Mel leans in to me and yells over the music, 'Are you sure you're okay?'

'Yeah,' I tell her, and ask, 'Why wouldn't I be?'

'I dunno,' she yells back. 'You're acting really weird, like you're, I dunno, stoned or something.'

I laugh and tell her, 'I'm fine, really, I'm just…'

She nods and continues dancing.

We keep this up for a while longer; her dancing and me throwing myself around, trying to look like I'm not completely out of it.

'Hang on, I'll be right back,' Mel says.

I ask where she's going.

'Just stay here,' she instructs. 'I'll be back in a second.'

She walks away, fighting her way through the crowd towards the DJ platform.

I watch people dancing, watch the lights flashing, listen to the thump of the music.

A few moments later, Mel comes back.

I ask where she went.

'Nowhere. Don't worry about it, I'm back now.'

'Okay.'

We keep dancing, then, at the end of the song, the lights dim and a slower song starts. At first I don't know what is going on and I'm panicked by the sudden change in sound and light, but then I look around and realise that everyone is still there and nothing has gone wrong.

Mel steps towards me and puts her arms around my neck. I look at her, surprised, wanting to ask what's going on, but not caring enough to actually do so.

'Dance with me,' she says.

I tell her I am.

She laughs lightly and rests her head on my shoulder. I put my hands on her back and we sway slowly back and forth.

I ask if she's okay. 'Are you tired?'

'No, I'm great.'

'Good.'

There's a silence.

'What time are you leaving?'

'I don't know,' she says, 'whenever. What time are you leaving?'

'Whenever.'

She nods against my shoulder. 'So I've been meaning to ask, how was your date the other night?'

'It wasn't a date,' I tell her. 'There were other people there.'

'But you like her, don't you?'

'Yes.' The thought makes me weak at the knees.

'There's something I've been meaning to ask you,' Mel says.

'Yes,' I tell her, 'that outfit does make you look fat.'

She hits me on the back and says, 'Shut up. It's not about that.' She says, 'I just wanted to say…' She stops, considers. 'I want you to know that…' She stops again, takes her head off my shoulder, looks at me. 'I wanted to ask you…'

Beau appears beside me out of nowhere. 'There you are,' he yells. 'I've been looking for you.'

I tell him we were right here.

Mel removes her arms from my neck and steps away from me. 'Hi, Beau,' she says quietly.

The slow song ends.

I ask Beau, 'What's up?'

'We're leaving, man,' he tells me.

'Already?'

He gives me a look and says, 'What do you mean, "already"? We've been here all night, they're closing soon.'

'Really?'

I look at my watch.

Somehow, I lost a few hours somewhere.

I start to laugh, again.

Beau laughs too and asks, 'Are you alright?'

I tell him, 'I'm great. Fantastic.'

'I think you'd better come home with me,' he tells me. 'I don't know if you're in any condition to drive.'

I tell him I'm fine.

'Okay, suit yourself,' he says.

'Don't drive home,' Mel says, stepping forward.

I'm sick of telling everyone how fine I am, so I ask her, 'Would it make you feel better if I spent the night at Beau's?'

She forces a smile and says, 'I guess.'

I smile at her reassuringly and the three of us walk outside. Jesus and Nick are standing by our table, and for some reason, I am relieved that I didn't get to talk to them any more than I did; I feel as if my patience is at an all-time low.

We all say our goodbyes, people arrange lifts, and we assure each other that we'll go out again soon. Jesus tells me that he's sorry he didn't get to talk to me more tonight and I assure him it's alright.

We go back through the club and I don't see George anywhere; he must have left already. Out in the parking lot, I look up and the stars seem bright and wondrous and they make me think of Jade.

Everyone leaves in a bunch and Beau tells me I shouldn't leave my car there by itself and that I should follow him back to his house.

I tell him okay.

After what seems like hours we finally make it to Beau's. His place is dark and his dog, Phydeaux, is barking outside. Beau yells at it to shut up.

He takes me through the house and shows me to the spare room. I tell him thanks and five minutes later I'm in bed.

The house is silent.

A little while later the dog starts barking again. I wait, thinking it'll stop, but it doesn't. I wait for Beau to get up and yell at it again, but he doesn't.

I hear a noise outside. It's a scraping, scratching sound.

Coming from the neighbours' house, I can hear a baby crying.

There is a bang from the backyard and the dog's barking intensifies.

I get out of bed and it feels like a dream. I can't feel my body and I have no control over what I'm doing.

I walk back through the house into the main room and it's lighter than before; there seems to be a dull blue glow and a low bass drone radiating from the walls. Slowly I walk toward the sliding glass door that leads into the back garden. I slide it open and step outside.

The dog is standing in the far corner of the yard and is barking at something I can't see.

I kneel down and whisper, 'Hey boy,' to the dog, trying to calm it.

I can still hear the baby crying from somewhere.

I hear the scraping sound again and I turn and slowly start to walk in its general direction, unable to stop myself.

It's too dark for me to see anything; the garden is shadows. I think I see something move but I'm not sure.

I turn around and start to walk back towards the door. The dog stops barking and starts whimpering and I hear the scraping again, behind me.

I don't turn around.

I walk calmly back towards the house. The dog's whining has become more persistent and the baby's cries are now more like urgent screams.

The sound from inside the house, the bass drone, is louder and pulses rhythmically.

The dog screams and there is a thud behind me and then panic hits and I run inside. The dog's whimpering, the low pulse sound and the baby's screams cut off as I slam the door closed.

I lean my back against the cold glass for a moment, in total silence. The only sound is that of my long, deep breaths.

Inhale.

Exhale.

Silence.

Inhale.

Exhale.

Something slams against the glass behind me and I jump in surprise.

I turn around, my heart thudding, and see the dog standing on its hind legs with its front paws resting on the glass. It's whimpering softly and it taps the glass with its paw.

The scraping comes again, from closer this time, and the dog turns its head in the direction of the noise. It looks back at me through the glass and taps the window again, more urgently this time. The whimpering is louder and its eyes plead with me to open the door.

I close my eyes and turn around and start to walk back towards the spare room. The dog yelps and I hear it run away to another part of the garden.

There is a thud at the door and I stop dead in my tracks. I can hear a low breathing, deep and harsh, coming from something large. I straighten up and a shiver runs along my spine.

Mister Terrified.

I force myself to keep walking without looking around.

There is another scratch then a louder thump on the glass as I close the door to the spare room. Again there's silence.

I get back into bed and pull the covers over my face, thinking of those times when I was younger that I would get scared and lie between my parents until morning. Thinking how things have changed.

It's silent for a while longer, but then, faintly, I can hear a baby crying.

The cries get louder and louder and I pull the pillow over my face and clasp it across my ears but it doesn't block the sound out.

I finally drift off to sleep with the screams still clearly audible, as if they were coming from inside my head, and I'm wondering what the hell is going on.

THIRTEEN

My family used to go to the fair every year. We'd spend the whole day together, eating ice cream and going on the rides. We'd stay all day and at night we'd sit and watch the fireworks and laugh and my dad would sit in between my mother and me and he'd put his arm around us both. I would lean against him and he'd be warm and comforting and I would look up at them both and they'd be watching the sky and smiling, thinking their own thoughts, and I would be consumed with love for them and I would know that nothing could ever go wrong and life would always be perfect.

One little thing can change everything. It all hangs on the smallest thread.

All you do is pull the trigger and everything's different.

When I wake up it's still dark so I close my eyes and try to get back to sleep but I can't so I open my eyes again and bring my hand up to rub my face and discover I'm wearing sunglasses that I don't remember putting on, so I take them off and it's still dark without them but I can't sleep so I sigh and get up.

The social worker is coming in a few hours so I decide to spend my time writing before she comes.

Sometime during the week, Beau had told me that girls like poetry. I had always thought this to be a cliché and I doubted Beau had ever written a poem for a girl; I figured he'd just use his blessed doll. But he assured me that poems did actually work so I thought I'd give it a try. The first one was okay, it was about a puppy that played in a field of flowers. George read it and said he liked it; that it was very good in a nihilistic, post-modern sort of way.

The biggest problem I had was finding a word to rhyme with Jade. So far, the best I had come up with was:

On the beach, she changed my life,
I met a girl named Jade.
And I will love her, all my life,
Every night and day–d.

I didn't think it quite worked; it didn't say what I wanted it to say.

After that, however, things had gone downhill.

I had gone shopping and bought a pair of shoes but they didn't fit so I returned them and exchanged them for a pair that did. I had been clubbing the night before with Nick and Beau and had quite a hangover so I kept my sunglasses on at all times, a shield against the sunlight making my head pound. I decided to shortcut through a large and expensive suit retailer; I knew no one would bother me because I didn't look like a potential customer in my blue jeans, sneakers, V-neck T-shirt, post-clubbing stubble and sunglasses.

I'm walking through the store, cutting between the rows of suits and racks of shoes, approaching the exit door. I'm walking through the tie section when I see him, browsing their selection. I stop dead, my heart racing. I no longer hear the soft music playing throughout the store or the soft murmur of the other shoppers. Nothing else registers with me.

He hasn't seen me so I hide behind a rack of shoes where I can see him between the shelves.

Dawson is looking at ties on a rack and I am instantly furious. I don't even own a single tie and here he is, wearing an expensive suit, looking to buy another one to add to his collection, which, no doubt, is already huge.

I brush away an ant that's crawling around my ear.

I consider going over and saying something to him but I decide against it.

I consider telling one of the clerks that I've seen him putting something into his briefcase so the security staff will go over and hassle him and, although I like this idea, I simply don't have the energy to go to all the trouble.

I throw Dawson one last hateful glance from between the shoes then walk swiftly towards the exit.

In the family room I find Gran chewing on the leftovers I had put out last night. She's sitting on the couch, pushing handfuls of cold spaghetti into her mouth.

I take the bowl from her lap. She follows it with her eyes and holds her hands out for it, like a baby. I shake my head and tell her, 'No, it's not for eating.'

The social worker arrives twenty minutes later. It's Christmas Eve so she's wearing a Santa hat. She reminds Gran who she is, tells her Merry Christmas, asks her a few questions (to which Gran replies, 'I don't know' to almost every one), makes a cup of coffee and then sits in the front room with me.

She rubs her eyes and tells me, 'That was as productive as ever.'

I ask her if she ever wishes she'd chosen a different line of work.

'All the time.' She sighs. 'Helping people is so unrewarding. Especially when you see them twice a month for, like, nine years and they still don't know who you are. I might as well have become a maid; it's much the same thing, only the messes are easier to clean up.'

She asks me how I'm doing and I tell her I'm doing okay.

I don't want to tell her about Dawson. For now, I'm keeping that between him and me.

Mister Scheming.

Instead, I tell her to wait a minute.

I go through to my bedroom, returning with the poem. She reads it, looks down at it, confused, then reads it again. She turns the paper over to see if there's anything on the back, then looks up at me.

'What do you think?'

She reads it again, then asks, 'You've been writing poetry?'

'I've been trying to. That one is the best.'

'Yeah? What else have you written?'

'A couple more poems. One was about a puppy.'

'Oh. That's… sweet.' She smiles and asks, 'You're doing this for a girl?'

I tell her, 'Not just any girl.'

'The one you met on the beach?'

'Jade.'

She smiles. 'She sounds like she's really something.'

I decide to tell her the truth.

I say, 'She makes me think there's hope.'

'Wow,' the social worker says. 'That's quite a statement, coming from you.'

My eyes drift up to the pictures on the wall. There's one of me sitting on my dad's knee when I was little. It looks as though he's bouncing me up and down and there's a huge smile across my face and my dad is looking happy, too.

I try feverishly to remember what this is like, but I can't.

The wounds left behind from when we were happy.

She follows my gaze and says, 'It must be hard, this time of year. Harder than usual, I mean.'

I shrug. 'I don't think about it that much.'

'Do you miss them?'

I tell her I don't know. 'Sometimes. Sometimes I wish things were back how they were. Everything was so much easier then. I don't miss them, exactly, but I miss the way life was. They'd look after me and I didn't have to worry about anything. Does that sound selfish?'

She considers for a moment then shakes her head. 'I don't think so. The only thing that concerns me is, over the past nine years, you've hardly mentioned them. In fact, I don't remember you ever really saying anything about them at all. Not recently, anyway.'

I shrug. 'It's not that important to me.'

'It must be,' she says. 'You lost both your parents in a relatively short period of time. That can't be an easy thing to go through. It leaves scars.'

I tell her it had nothing to do with me. It wasn't my fault.

'I know that,' she says. 'But do you? Maybe a part of you blames yourself? Especially for your mother's suicide. You think that you could have saved her. You knew she was sick and depressed but you didn't do anything. The truth is there was nothing you could do. It wasn't your fault. It's only natural for a small child to blame himself for things he has no control over. The problem was entirely your mother's.'

I tell her, 'Suicide can sometimes be prevented.'

You don't need to die to destroy yourself.

She says levelly, 'You sound like you're speaking from experience.'

I shrug. 'I think you need the right reason to come along. That's what's lacking in people. A reason. A purpose.'

'But you have to know that, at your age, you were too young to do anything. Don't blame yourself.'

I tell her I don't.

She closes her eyes and sighs. Softly, she asks, 'Did you ever think that maybe you feel the way you do because of some unresolved feelings about your parents? This sense of worthlessness you have about yourself. The idea that you're no good, the idea that no one will love you. This fear of rejection.'

'I do not have a fear of rejection.'

'No? Then why haven't you told this girl Jade how you feel?'

I don't say anything.

'Could it be because you think that, if your own mother didn't love you, then why would anyone else?'

Again, there's silence on my part.

The social worker continues, 'Could it be that you believe your mother would rather kill herself than be with you? That you were worthless to her? And if she didn't want you then no one else will either, right?'

Silence because of the lump in my throat.

'Let me tell you, that's wrong. You deserve the same happiness that everyone else does. And if you dealt with your past you'd be able to move on with your life and realise that not only are you capable of loving someone but that other people are also capable of loving you.'

Part of me wants to believe this, desperately, but the overwhelming voice of negativity crushes it and smothers the hope like a shoe stubbing out a cigarette. The voice I have grown so used to over the years, that black voice without a face, assures me that everything she's saying is wrong. I don't even bother to fight this voice anymore, I know it's too strong, so no matter what the social worker says, or anyone else for that matter, I know it's useless.

I brush off an ant that's crawling on my arm.

I look up again at the pictures on the wall. I look at my dad, me on his lap, the ghosts of Christmas past. I'm perilously close to tears so I close my eyes and bring my hand up, pretending to rub them, thinking.

There's a long silence before she says, 'I'm sorry.'

'No,' I tell her, 'it's alright.' I move my hand from my eyes and offer her a reassuring smile which I'm sure looks more like a grimace.

'I just hate to see you like this, that's all,' she says. 'Especially on Christmas. Listen, the next time I see you, it'll be next year. A new year is a new chance. You can start again. Leave all this stuff behind. Will you do that? At least try to?'

I nod. I tell her I'll try. And maybe I will.

She smiles, more naturally. 'Good. And on that note, I better be going.' She stands up and we walk over to the door. 'I'm just making short visits today. Everyone is really busy so I have to get home and get out of everyone's way.'

'What are you doing tomorrow?'

She shrugs. 'Nothing much. A quiet day at home.'

I'm suddenly very sad for her. She is also spending Christmas alone and I know this is just a small snapshot of her life. What else does she do alone? Movies? Holidays? I get an image of her, spending weekends alone with a stack of DVDs, every now and then throwing a casually eager glance at the telephone.

It occurs to me briefly how selfish I can be; seeing only my own problems and not recognising everyone else's. But then it's gone, as quickly as it came, and my vision is once again crowded with anxiety.

She walks out the door, stops, turns. 'Merry Christmas,' she says. 'I'll see you next year.'

I nod and smile, then watch her climb into her car before closing the door.

Fourteen

A while ago George and I went to a Fun Run. The streets were packed with joggers and George and I sat on a pedestrian overpass that stretched across their main route.

I tell him, 'I don't know why I can't just talk to Jade.'

He says, 'You're terrified of being let down again.'

From my backpack I produce a small hand-reel of fishing line with a silver hook. George takes out a box of donuts.

He says, 'Everyone has to play the hand they're dealt. The trick is to keep a poker face, no matter what, and play out the cards as best you can. Bluff your way through and never show anyone your weaknesses.'

From somewhere, a gun goes off and the noise of a thousand runners resounds along the city streets. I take a donut from the box and thread it onto the hook.

'You don't have a good poker face,' he explains. 'People know what your story is before you open your mouth. That's why you lose all your bets. It's why you won't say anything to Jade.'

A few minutes later the first runners emerge from around the corner in the distance. I lower the fishing line off the side of the overpass, the donut hanging about seven feet off the ground.

George says, 'You've lost every bet you've ever made. You're afraid because, in your mind, this bet is so huge that you can't bear the thought of losing.'

The runners begin to pass below us. George has to raise his voice to be heard over the constant thunder of their footfalls.

George says, 'There's only so many bets you can lose before you have to call it quits.'

He says, 'They say that if you fall off the horse, you have to get right back on it. But you can only fall off so many times before you have to wonder whether equestrianism really is your sport.'

Someone reaches for the donut and I yank the reel up, jerking it out of his reach.

George says, 'You're afraid because, in your mind, this is your last bet and if you lose it, you lose everything.'

'And that's a risk I'm not willing to take.'

George shrugs. 'Maybe one day you'll realise it's not such a big bet, after all. Maybe you'll find some change in your pockets that'll give you another chance. Or maybe you'll realise you had your cards facing backwards all along.'

Every time someone reaches for the donut, I pull the line. I can imagine someone jumping for it when I'm not ready and getting the hook snagged in the webbing between their fingers.

George looks out over the mass of bodies running below us. 'What are you running from?' he yells. 'Stand and face your fears.'

I tell him, 'Thank you for those words of wisdom.'

* * *

There's a safe sex poster in the bathroom that tells me to remember to use a water-based lubricant.

Beau is standing at the next urinal and he asks, 'Are you coming with us on New Year's, man?'

We're at another club somewhere in the city. It's night and it's the weekend sometime. I don't much bother remembering the days anymore. Everything is just happening and I'm watching it all sail by.

I ask Beau what's happening on New Year's.

'We're going to some beach party,' he says. 'They're having this big party and it's, like, on a beach.'

I don't ask him who 'they' are.

On the poster, someone has scribbled, *Like Olive Oil.*

'Sure, I'll come.'

'Cool,' Beau says. 'It's on the thirty-first of December. Jesus told me about it, I think the whole group is going.'

I tell him, 'Cool.'

Someone else has written, *Or Peanut Butter.*

I walk over to the washbasins and wash my hands.

From the urinal, Beau says, 'You can bring Jade, if you want.'

On the poster, someone has written, *Lighter Fluid.*

I think of kissing her at midnight. I tell Beau, 'Okay, I'll ask her.'

'Cool,' Beau says. 'The more the merrier.'

Someone has written, *Battery Acid.*

Beau is drying his hands with a paper towel, leaning against the bench. He says, 'When I was a kid my dad used to drive me to church every Sunday morning for Sunday school. My mum would still be at home, usually in bed, sometimes making breakfast or cleaning something. My dad would leave me at the door and then drive home again. Neither of them ever came in with me, or went to church at all, as far as I know.'

On the poster, someone has written, *Motor Oil*.

Beau says, 'One day I asked my dad why they sent me every week and he said it was to make me into a better person. He told me it was so I wouldn't turn out like them. Eventually I got sick of going, I didn't believe half the stuff they were telling me, it all seemed like stuff from a comic book or a movie and, for something that was supposed to be real, it required a lot of suspended disbelief.'

Beau throws the scrunched up paper towel into the trash and says, 'My friends would go to the video game arcade down the street, so it got to be that, after my dad dropped me off, I'd wait for him to drive away, then walk down to the arcade and play with my friends until it was time to go. Then I'd walk back to the church and he'd arrive and take me home. That was the story of every Sunday morning for about a year. After that, my dad said I was too old for fairy tales and I didn't need to go anymore.'

I nod, taking this in. I ask him, 'What's the moral of the story?'

He shrugs. 'Does every story need a moral?' He smiles at me cryptically and says, 'I'm sure you can figure it out.'

On the condom machine, someone has written, *For Refund, Insert Baby*.

The beach is lit by huge floodlights and it's almost like daytime until you look up and see the stars. Dance music is pounding from large stacks of speakers. I've never seen this many people at the beach at night before.

Absently I wonder if Beau will bring his doll. I decide it's most likely.

I spot Jade standing next to a small kiosk, our arranged meeting place. She looks beautiful, amazing. I start towards her when I spot Mel coming through the crowd. She smiles when she sees me then looks down at the kiosk. Her smile fades.

Even before she walks closer, I can see how pale she is.

I think of Mel coming up to me at the beginning of the year in the university cafeteria. Do you mind if I sit with you? I don't much feel like sitting by myself.

It seems like a lifetime ago and I'm suddenly very sad.

'Is that her? I didn't know she was coming,' is all Mel says.

I tell her, 'Sorry, I didn't think you'd care?'

'What does that mean?' she asks.

'It means, why is it important? Why does it bother you?'

'It doesn't bother me,' she says. She laughs humourlessly and says, 'Why would it?'

'I… don't know.'

'Whatever. Let's just have a good night, okay?'

I'm confused by Mel's reaction but decide not to upset her further with questions. We both start towards the kiosk, towards Jade. I do the introductions. Mel smiles falsely and says, 'Nice to meet you.'

We stand around, no one talking, Jade looking at the stars, me looking at Jade, Mel looking at me looking at Jade. I look at Mel and shrug questioningly, and I mouth, What? She stares back at me, hard, and I'm forced to look away, wondering why she's mad at me. I look at Jade, who is looking at me. I look away, embarrassed, and Mel looks at Jade. Jade looks at Mel then they both look at me. I look at the stars, then back at Jade. I see Jade look at Mel once more, then she looks around the crowd. Mel looks at Jade, then at me, then down at the sand. I also look down at the sand.

Nick appears next to Jade, breaking the silence by yelling, 'Happy New Year.'

'Hey, Nick,' I say, wishing he were Beau instead. At this point, I'd even settle for Jesus.

'You must be Jade,' he says, kissing the back of her hand. Mel rolls her eyes and looks away. 'It's a pleasure to meet you.' He leans in to me and says, 'She's way too good for you, dude.' Then, louder, 'So what's everyone's resolutions? Nick just wants to go out and meet new people.'

I don't see anything wrong with Nick finding new friends and leaving us alone, but I keep this opinion to myself.

'Your turn, Mel,' Nick says. 'What do you want to achieve next year? Maybe you should try and get some taste?'

'I have taste,' she says.

'No, you don't, sorry,' Nick says. 'Your favourite movie is *Pretty Woman*. And need Nick mention…' He rubs under his nose with a finger pointing at me.

'What the fuck does that mean?' I ask.

He smiles at me for a moment, like I'm some poor idiot who's missing the whole point, and says, 'You don't get it, do you?'

Quietly, Mel says, 'Drop it, Nick.'

'Maybe that can be your New Year's resolution?' Nick says. 'Get a clue.'

The tension is broken by a voice calling out, 'Evening, ladies,' and I turn around to see Beau walking toward us. Jesus is with him and his eyes look red, teary. He quietly says, 'Happy New Year, everyone.'

I introduce Jade for what I hope is the final time. Beau says, 'Well, now that we're all here, let the fun begin. So, who wants a drink?'

We set up camp with blankets and an icebox further down the beach.

'Thanks for coming,' I tell Jade. 'I'm glad you're here.'

'My pleasure,' she says. 'Your friends seem really nice.'

I don't bother to correct her.

Later, Beau and I are walking up the beach, both of us carrying cold bottles of beer. I hadn't wanted to leave Jade, especially after Nick's comments, but Beau talked me into coming for a walk with him.

'Come on,' he says. 'Help me pick one.' He lifts up his shirt and I see the doll's head sticking out of his hip pocket. Its hair is blonde.

I ask him why Jesus looks like he's been crying.

'I don't know, man. He didn't want to talk about it.' A moment later he asks, 'Do you like him?'

I shrug. 'He's just one of the bunch, you know? I guess he can be a bit annoying sometimes,' I say, and Beau laughs.

I watch him scanning the girls and I ask him if he ever gets sick of using the doll.

'What do you mean?'

'I mean, don't you ever get tired of using it? Cheating your way through? Don't you want something more?'

He shakes his head. 'All this is just for fun. It's not cheating, it's more of a safety net. I'll settle down when I get older and find someone worth settling down with. That's the hard part.' He looks at me and asks, 'Do you believe in soul mates?'

I shake my head. 'I don't think so. I don't believe in souls.'

He nods. 'I can understand that. I'm not sure if I believe it or not. It's a pretty big thing to buy; the idea that there's one person in the entire world who is perfect for you. The chances of finding that person aren't very high at all. It's discouraging, ain't it?'

I nod.

'But we have our whole lives ahead of us. We're young,

healthy, good looking and intelligent young men. The world is ours for the taking. All we have to do is stand up and take what is ours.' He pauses, letting that statement ring out.

'If only it were that easy.'

He claps me on the shoulder. 'Whether or not you succeed is not important.'

I snort a laugh without any humour in it and say, 'What is?'

He looks at me and says, 'The fact that we tried.'

We walk back towards the others. I finish my beer and drop the bottle onto the sand. Beau holds his empty bottle by its neck and throws it into the ocean, into the crowd.

When we get back to the group only Nick and Mel remain. Nick is looking through the icebox for another beer and Beau calls out to him to get an extra two. Nick throws my bottle more at me than to me.

I ask where Jade is and Nick says, 'Nick doesn't know. Maybe she's gone? Maybe she finally came to her senses about you. What a shame that would be.'

I ignore his remark. 'And Jesus?'

Mel doesn't say anything. She simply points up the beach and stares out into the sea.

I walk away along the beach, looking for Jade.

Instead, I find Jesus sitting on a bench, wiping his eyes with the back of his sleeve. I sit beside him.

'Hey,' I say, 'have you seen Jade?'

He shakes his head but doesn't speak.

'Are you alright?' I ask, not caring but asking anyway. 'What's wrong?'

He shakes his head again. 'It's nothing. Don't worry about it.'

'Don't be that way. Tell me. What happened?' I should be looking for Jade, not wasting time here.

'Well, if you really want to know…' he starts. He pauses, looks as if he's fighting back tears. He continues, 'Uh, well, it's about Mister Snuggles.'

'Yeah? How is the little guy?'

'Umm, not so good, I'm afraid.'

'Oh?'

'Yeah, he, uh…' Now the tears start to flow. 'He died earlier today.'

'Oh, man, I'm sorry to hear that.' I put a hand on his shoulder. 'What happened?'

'Well,' Jesus says, 'I was running a bath this afternoon and I walked out of the room to get something. I was gone only a few seconds…' He stops, choked up, unable to continue.

After a moment I gently urge him to go on.

He nods and takes a deep breath. 'I had the radio on the bench-top beside the bath. I don't even remember what I was listening to now… maybe that CD I got that day we went into town. Anyway, I leave the room for a minute and all of a sudden the power goes off. I go back into the bathroom, and there…'

He leans forward, face in his hands, his body racked with sobs. He wipes his face, his breath hitching, and says, 'I went into the bathroom and the radio was in the bath and so was Mister Snuggles. The power had cut out automatically but not before it was too late. It was only a little shock but it was enough.'

His eyes are red from crying and he looks up at me. 'Why?' he asks. 'Why would Mister Snuggles kill himself?'

'You think it was suicide?'

'Of course it was suicide,' Jesus says. 'What else could it be? I knew he was depressed but I had no idea it had gone this far.'

I tell him, 'I'm sorry, I had no idea…'

He waves me away with his hand. 'Don't be sorry, there's nothing you could have done.'

I nod. What can you say at a time like this?

'Anyway,' he sniffs, then snuffs, 'thanks for asking. It felt good to tell someone.'

He puts his arm around me and I pat him on the back.

He doesn't let go.

I ask, 'Are you okay?'

He nods, looking down. He laughs at himself, embarrassed, and says, 'Excuse me. I'm just gonna go splash some water on my face. I'll see you later.'

I watch him disappear into the crowd then resume the search for Jade.

I head back to camp when I run out of beer.

Some time passes and the countdown starts. It begins quietly then builds in strength as more people join in. I suddenly feel very sad. I think about trying to kiss Jade at midnight and am sad that this won't happen; that her face won't be the first thing I see this new year.

When the countdown reaches two, I close my eyes. When it reaches one, I squeeze them together so tightly that I see colours dancing in the blackness. Then, everyone screams, 'Happy New Year', but I still don't open my eyes.

A split second later there is a loud bang. I open my eyes and the black sky is lit up by a huge golden flower. More flowers open around it, some red, some blue, some green, and I watch as they are fired into the air from a barge anchored offshore.

Then Mel is beside me and she says, 'Happy New Year.' She leans in and kisses me on the side of the mouth. I return the kiss, more in surprise than anything, but all the while I'm wishing she were someone else. I say it back to her and she smiles.

Beau's hand grabs mine and he shakes it vigorously, then pulls me forward into a clumsy drunken hug. He pats me on the back a few times, then pushes me back and keeps one hand on my shoulder, like a proud father. He tells me happy new year and I think if I hear that any more tonight I will go crazy.

Jesus shakes my hand quickly and doesn't look at me when he wishes me a happy new year.

Nick doesn't offer me his hand and I don't care.

The sky continues to explode above my head as I walk along the beach. The layers of people soon begin to thin out and before I know it, I'm standing above the cliffs.

This is the calmest it's ever been. For the first time, there is no wind and the sea is sleepy. It laps gently against the cliff face and everything is very peaceful. Aside from that, it's the same as always. This is when it hits me. It's a new year, but really there's nothing new about it. It's just another number added to the date. The cycle begins again. Everything I did last year I will have to do again this year: university, my birthday, then before you know it, it's New Year's again. The year is punctuated by holidays where people celebrate all the things I don't have.

But, fuck it, I don't care. I am beyond the point of caring. The novelty of life has well and truly worn off. I simply do not care.

I tell myself this all the time, but this time I mean it. Really.

A voice says, 'Hey.'

I turn around and it's Jesus.

'What are you doing up here?' he asks. 'Didn't you want to watch the fireworks?'

I tell him I can see them from here.

'Yeah,' he says, 'but…,' and his voice trails away.

He takes a couple of slow steps towards me, maybe worried I'll throw myself off the cliffs.

'Thanks again about before,' he says, and I shrug.

This time he walks closer, maybe thinking he'll catch me if I fall. He looks at me as if he's going to say something, but doesn't. I look back out at the sea, the sky, the fireworks.

'Do you come here a lot?' he asks, then laughs. 'Man, that sounds like a bad pick-up line,' he says. I try to smile.

He looks at the ground for a long time, then out to sea, then back at the ground. He sighs. 'I just want… I wanted…' He pauses, then says, 'Happy New Year.'

He steps forward and, before I know what's going on, he's kissing me firmly on the mouth. He has one hand on each side of my head, holding me in place. I pull my head back and push him away. He stumbles backwards.

'I'm sorry,' he says, looking down. 'I didn't… I… I'm sorry.'

'What did you do that for?'

'I don't know, I'm sorry. I just thought, maybe, I didn't know how you felt…' He looks away, at the sea, at the sky, anywhere but at me. I think I am thankful for this.

'Jesus,' I mutter.

'Yeah?' he asks hopefully.

'Not you,' I say. 'I meant the other one.'

He looks puzzled for a moment.

'I'm really sorry,' he says. 'I've been drinking, and it's New Year's, you know. And everything with Mister Snuggles… I'm sorry. I shouldn't have… I… I don't know, I just…'

'It's okay,' I tell him. 'Just forget it, okay?'

'I'm sorry,' he says. 'I'm so sorry…'

I yell, 'Just fucking forget it, alright?'

He nods quickly. 'Okay. I'm sorry. Let's just, you know, forget it.'

'Okay,' I say. 'Come on, let's go back to the others.'

He nods, looking down. 'Okay.'

I start to walk but he doesn't follow. I ask, 'Are you coming?'

'Yeah,' he says. 'I just…' He stops talking and waves an arm towards the sea, then drops it to his side. He sighs quietly and mumbles something to himself.

I tell him I'll see him down there and I walk away.

The final explosion of colour blasts through the night.

Back at the camp, Beau hands me a beer and points to a guy who is sitting on a blanket with a group of friends. 'You see that guy?' Beau asks.

I nod. His group is just like ours, except there are a couple more people and they seem to be getting along well. They're sitting a few feet away from our blanket and they all appear to be drunk or stoned.

Beau says, 'He ate a plant.'

'What?'

'A plant. Like, from a pot.'

'He ate a whole plant?'

'Yep. The whole thing. From the leaves down to the… what do you call the other bit?'

'The trunk?'

'The trunk? Maybe. I was thinking stalk, but trunk might be right. I dunno. But he ate all of it.'

'Why?'

'Why not? Shit,' Beau says, frowning. 'Now I'm hungry.'

I shake my head in confused wonder. I ask myself aloud, 'What the fuck is going on?'

Beau looks at me and smiles.

*   *   *

There is still no sign of Jade. I get another beer from the icebox and lie on my back, watching for shooting stars.

Jesus hasn't come down from the cliffs.

Beau is talking to the guy who ate the plant.

Mel is sitting on the blanket, pulling at loose threads.

Nick is taking ice-cubes from the icebox, throwing them up and catching them in his mouth.

There are no shooting stars and there is no Jade.

The beer runs out at about two-thirty in the morning.

Jesus comes back from the cliffs and sits at the other end of the blanket from me. I have moved off the blanket onto the sand, watching people dance and drink. He looks over at me and tries to smile but doesn't say anything. Mel sits beside him and says something and he looks away, down the beach.

Nick is lying on the sand with his head resting on the side of the icebox, passed out. I absently hope he gets alcohol poisoning.

I decide it's time to go home.

We pack everything away and head for the cars.

Mel puts on a cheery smile and claps her hands together. 'Well,' she says, 'I hope we all had a good night.' Nobody says anything and her smile fades.

'Happy New Year,' Jesus says and walks away. Mel follows him, looking down.

Beau looks at me. He claps me once on the shoulder, leaves his hand there for a moment, then drops it to his side. I get in my car and he watches me drive off.

Fifteen

I start plotting to kill Dawson not long after that.

It's a sunny day and I find myself in the city. I don't know how I got here, or why, but I'm sitting on a bench outside the building I saw Dawson go into that first time I saw him. I idly look up and try to count the number of floors but I can't get past twenty-seven; after that my mind reaches some sort of block. I wonder which floor he works on and what he does all day, what his secretary looks like and what he has for lunch.

I think of walking inside and asking the receptionist where he is. I'd get into the elevator and ride up to the appropriate floor. I'd knock on his office door and when he opened it…

Visions of me pushing him out an open window flood my mind.

Sticking a letter opener into his face.

Using a stapler.

A box cutter.

My fists.

Then security would arrive and my worries would be over.

I see myself following him home, waiting in his bedroom or behind a door. I smother him with a pillow in his sleep, or raid his bathroom for pills, needles, razor blades.

I stare at the tall, concrete walls of the building. It stands high above me, blocking out the sun.

I try calling Jade to see where she went on New Year's. Her phone goes straight to voicemail and I end up leaving a rambling message saying how I hoped she'd had a good time and that everything was okay and how I hoped to see her soon. I end the message with a very awkward, 'I'll catch you round, then,' before hanging up.

George asks if I gave her my poem and when I say no, he puts his hand on my shoulder and says, 'Good move.'

I spend a lot of time with Beau for reasons I am not really sure of. I go to his house and we watch television, usually music videos or old movies, and eat pizza. The fridge is always stocked with beer and one time there is even some kind of melon but I don't know where it came from and I don't ask.

We sit around on the couch watching television and drinking beer and eating pizza and not really talking about anything. The dog barks sometimes and Beau tells it to shut up but I hardly hear him and after a while I stop hearing him at all. The same movies and music clips play and soon I know exactly what is going to happen and when. Each time I watch carefully to see if anything changes but it never does. It's always the same recorded people doing the same recorded things, over and over, but we watch them anyway.

On some nights we go out to clubs and Beau leaves me at the bar while he dances with girls and I drink more beer and have lots of Cokes with double shots of bourbon. The clubs all look and sound the same and after a while the people in them start to look the same too and sometimes I forget where I am and I think I am in one of the music videos we watch and I look around for a camera and a director. I never see one and that is when I realise I'm not in a music video at all and I am actually at a club somewhere and then I go to the bathroom and close the stall door and start to cry.

After the clubs we go back to Beau's house and sit on his couch and drink beer and eat pizza and watch television.

One night I tell Beau I think I should probably go home.

'Where?' he asks.

'Home.'

'Oh,' he says, and looks back at the television. During the next commercial break, he asks, 'Why?'

'I don't know. I just think I should.'

He says, 'Do you want another beer?'

I tell him I do and he gets him and me another drink and we sit on the couch and watch television.

We go to clubs and I drink while Beau is dancing. We go to a different place every night and Beau always knows lots of people and they buy us drinks. Sometimes the club closes and we have to go to a different one but they all look the same. We leave when the sun is coming up and go back to Beau's house where I fall asleep and dream of cactus plants and small birds that fly towards the sky, and I wake up sweating and shivering and I get up and Beau is sitting on the couch watching television.

Beau goes to work during the day and all I do is sit around, but at night we go out to clubs and drink and meet new people and meet old people and dance and try to have a good time. I never know what day it is or where I am or even really who I am, but I go out and drink and meet people and have fun and don't worry about tomorrow because I don't care if it comes or not, and all we do is go out and get drunk and it should be more fun than it is and some people find it boring but most people don't.

Beau called me at home during the day and asked if I wanted to go to a party and I said yes, unsure of who I was speaking to. Four hours later I checked my phone and saw that it had been Beau, so I drove to his house later that night. Nick was there, as was Jesus and Fatty Mel.

I walk in and they all say hi, and I half-heartedly offer the room a peace sign with my right hand.

'You ready?' Beau asks.

'For what?'

'The party. We're leaving pretty soon.'

I nod. 'Yeah, I'm ready.'

I open the beer bottle Beau has pushed into my hand.

'Cool,' he says. 'It's at some guy's place. You've met him but I doubt you'd remember.'

'Probably not,' I agree.

'Are you sure he's not going to mind us coming?' Mel asks from the couch.

Beau shakes his head. 'Nah, it's cool,' he says. 'I told him you'd all be coming.'

I'm staring out the back window but it's so dark outside I can't see anything. I take a drink of beer and I can see Jesus from the corner of my eye. He looks at me occasionally, then away.

Beau asks, 'Is Jade coming?'

I snap out of my trance at the mention of her name. I say, 'No, she's not.' I see Nick look down in disappointment.

'Okay then,' Beau says. 'Seeing as we're all here, let's go.'

We all get up and walk outside, Jesus and Mel in the lead, then Nick and Beau, with me at the back. Beau stops and locks the door, then claps his arm around my shoulders.

'You and I are getting drunk,' he tells me. 'Deal?'

I nod. 'Deal.'

'Cool,' he says, then louder, to the group, 'Who's driving? Not me, that's for sure.'

We arrive at the house in Mel's car twenty minutes later. There is a long driveway up to the building, which is double storey with balconies and windows lining the front of the house. It's white and looks like one of those Hollywood mansions you see in the movies. I'm wondering if we've got the right address because it seems unlikely that any friend of Beau's could afford something like this.

My concerns are alleviated once we get out of the car and I can hear the music coming from inside. It's so loud from where we're standing that I'm amazed anyone could possibly be in the house for even a second without going totally deaf.

'This is gonna be good,' Beau says, rubbing his hands together.

We walk up the steps with Beau in the lead and he opens the front door without knocking. The music seems to be coming from within the walls and all the rooms are full of people. Some of the faces in the crowd look familiar but I can't place any of them; I figure I must have seen them when I've been out with Beau. They all look about our age, a lot are wearing sunglasses and a disturbingly high number of people are wearing bathrobes. I wonder if this is some kind of dress-up party that we weren't told about, but I realise I don't care, seeing as how the people with bathrobes look far more stupid than those without.

Eventually we find a door and I follow the others through it and I find myself in a room with grass instead of carpet and it takes me a moment to realise that we have gone outside. I determine the reason for this confusion is the large marquee that is stretched above our heads; it gives the impression we are still inside, but the grass below my shoes and the ants crawling down my back convince me otherwise. There are lights hanging under the marquee that flash different colours, painting the crowd in reds, blues, greens.

The party is huge. There are hundreds of people crammed in the house and under the marquee. The air is thick with smoke from cigarettes and pot and the atmosphere of the place is more like that of a club than a party. I keep following the others, not knowing where we're going and not caring. We push through the people until we arrive at a bar at the end of the garden. One of the girls serving drinks is quite attractive but the very idea of talking to her makes me want to cry.

Beau has reached the bar first and already has a beer in each hand. He gives one to me and we clink our bottles together. I up-end mine and drink most of it in a single mouthful. My mood drops even further and there is a heavy feeling in my chest and a lump in my throat. Beau puts his arm around my shoulders and leads me away from the bar.

'What's up?' he asks.

'What do you mean?'

'You don't seem like yourself. In fact, you haven't for quite a while. I'm not even sure what yourself is anymore.'

I sigh. 'I don't know. I think I'm depressed.'

Beau laughs. 'Don't worry about that. We're all depressed. That's the single main defining characteristic of our generation. But what can you do? Just roll with it, man. And try not to let it run you over.'

I nod. 'Good advice,' I tell him. 'Though it doesn't make me feel any better. There's this little niggle in the back of my mind, like there's something wrong. It takes me a moment to identify what the problem is, but then I remember it's just my life. For some reason, knowing that everyone feels this way does not help. Why can't we fix it? If we're all so depressed, why can't we do something to change?'

Beau shrugs. 'Because we're all so fucking lazy? I mean, where do you start? Changing the world isn't easy. It's a scary thought. Most people would much rather bury their head in the sand and wait for it to fix itself. Of course, we all know this isn't going to happen, but it's a nice thought.'

He sighs and says, 'The world isn't going to change itself but we're not going to change it either. This is our chance to fix the place, make it better for everyone, but instead we're choosing to get drunk and go dancing.'

Beau says, 'It's going to get harder and harder for every generation. We're just throwing the world away, wishing it was a better place instead of getting up and actually doing something to fix it.'

He says, 'You want another beer?'

I tell him, 'Definitely,' and we walk back towards the bar.

The five of us are standing around in a small circle but I'm not really listening to anything that's being said. I'm on my third beer and we've only been here fifteen minutes. I really want a double B&C but I don't have the energy to ask for one. Beau is telling Nick about some girl named Becky who has a sister named Sarah but the two of them look almost identical. Some guy named either Paul or Jamie was seeing them both at the same time, somehow without either of them finding out, but then Becky got her hair cut real short and looked like a guy so Paul or Jamie stopped seeing them.

A woman walks up to us holding a tray of food and asks if we'd like any. Everyone takes a handful and I tentatively put some in my mouth and it's not bad so I eat the rest. Beau and Nick keep talking but Mel doesn't look like she's having a good time.

'Don't you like it?' I ask.

She looks up and around before realising it's me who's talking.

She smiles, embarrassed, and says, 'Sorry, you caught me off guard. You haven't said a word all evening.'

'I'm just quiet,' I tell her, as if this explains everything. 'Don't you like the food?' I ask again.

'Um, yeah, I think so,' she says, 'but I'm not sure what it is.'

'Me neither, but it tastes alright.'

'Okay,' she says, and nods as if steeling herself. She takes a mouthful and looks at me. 'Yummy,' she says.

I nod, strangely satisfied.

The lady comes back with the tray and I take another handful. I look down but I can't make out what it is I am holding. I don't think it's because of the beer; the food seems to be made up of unnatural angles and substances I have never seen before. The dynamics seem to be completely impossible and just looking at it makes my eyes hurt so I close them and put the food in my mouth.

Mel takes another one and eats it with what appears to be great effort. She forces a smile and tries to swallow.

'Don't you like it?' I ask for the third time.

'It's nice, really, I'm just… full.'

I nod and try to suppress a shrug. She really doesn't look full. In fact, it looks like she hasn't eaten in months.

Summoning up all my courage, I say, 'Excuse me,' and head towards the bar.

When I get there I ask the girl for a double B&C, hold the Coke. She pours two shots into a glass and hands it over then moves onto the next person. I realise I don't have to pay for any of this and my first idea is to get as drunk as I can as fast as I can, but then I decide not to; not for any real reason, just because getting drunk seems like a lot of work. A final thought fills my mind: I'll probably end up getting drunk anyway, so I stop worrying about it and an enormous sense of relief washes over me.

I ask for another, and she brings it over to me.

I walk back towards Mel, but when I get there, she's gone.

A voice says, 'Hi.'

It's Jesus.

'Hey,' I say dutifully. 'What's up?'

'What are you drinking?' he asks.

'Bourbon,' I tell him. 'Double. Straight up.'

He raises his eyebrows and says, 'That'll get you pretty drunk.'

'That's the idea,' I say and try to move past him.

'Hey, listen, wait a sec,' he says, and steps in front of me. I stop walking and force myself to meet his eyes. He gives a small smile when he realises I am going to stop, then recoils when he looks in my eyes. He stutters, then continues, 'I, uh, just wanted to apologise again, you know, for New Year's…'

'Oh, you've got to be fucking kidding,' I mutter. 'Why did you have to bring this up again?'

'I'm sorry,' he says, 'but I had to. I can't let this go.'

'Yes, you can,' I assure him. 'It's really not that big a deal. Let it go.'

'Don't you understand, I can't?' he asks. 'I have… feelings for you and they won't go away.'

'Jesus…,' I start, but stop to take a drink. I start again, as gently as I can. 'What you're experiencing is a delusion. Whether you're thinking this because you're drunk, or whatever, I don't know. But the fact is, it's not a rational way of thinking.'

'I think it is,' he says. 'I think it's very rational.'

'Well, you're, like, wrong. So just, you know, deal with it, okay?'

'Wait, please, can we please talk about this?'

'There's nothing to talk about. Nothing.'

'Yes, there is…'

'I have nothing to say to you.'

'Please don't say that…'

'Jesus, I'm leaving. I don't want you to bring this up again, okay? Now, I'm leaving.'

I start to walk off and he puts his arm up and says, 'Wait,' but I push past him and walk away. I can feel him looking after me, deciding whether or not to follow me. He doesn't.

The crowd is so thick that visibility is almost zero, making navigation very difficult. I end up inside the house before I know where I'm going. I go into the kitchen and open the fridge and spot a block of cheese and suddenly it's hard to breathe and a lump rises in my throat. On the verge of tears I slam the fridge door closed and take another drink and the feeling passes as suddenly as it arrived.

I stumble towards the stairs that lead to the upper floor of the house, looking at the pictures hanging on the walls, each one portraying a different bleak, dark image. The second storey is dark and the music is a lot quieter up here than downstairs; for the first time since I arrived I can hear things other than the deafening thump of the bass. I walk down the corridor, the darkness becoming more complete as I go deeper into the hallway, and the pictures on the walls become more threatening and disturbing. I round a corner and there's a light coming from below one of the doors.

I walk up to it and rest my ear against the wood. It's silent for a moment but then I hear what might be someone vomiting. It must be someone who's had too much to drink. The sound comes again and this time it's followed by a sob.

I reach down and gently try the doorknob. It's unlocked. I push it open and peer inside.

It's a bathroom. A mirror lines the wall over the vanity and the room is incredibly white.

Fatty Mel is on her knees, leaning forward over the toilet bowl. At first I think she is trying to get something out of her mouth but then she removes her fingers and vomits into the bowl.

'Mel?' I ask. 'Are you okay?'

She sits back suddenly, startled by my appearance. 'What the hell are you doing in here?' she yells.

'Sorry, I…'

'Get out!'

'Mel…'

'Get out!'

I back out the door, closing it behind me. I lean against the wall on the other side of the hall and wait. I finish my drink and after a little while I hear water running. The door opens and Mel stands there, silhouetted against the white porcelain.

'You're still here.'

I nod. 'Are you okay?'

'Peachy,' she says, and smiles falsely.

'Was it the food? I know it was weird, but…'

She snorts and shakes her head. 'Jesus Christ, you are so fucking stupid.'

'Whoa, hey, Mel, what's wrong? Everyone gets sick, it's nothing to worry about.'

She stares at me for a moment before turning and walking quickly down the hall.

'Where are you going?' I call after her.

'Away,' she replies.

I chase after her, repeating her name, asking her to stop, to wait, to slow down. Before I know it we're out the front of the house heading towards her car.

'You can't go home,' I tell her.

She stops and turns to face me, furious. 'Really? Why the hell not?'

'Because... you drove us here.'

She grits her teeth in frustration and starts off towards the car again. She takes her keys from her pocket and opens the door. I lean in and push it closed. She looks up at me, absolutely fuming.

'Hey, don't be Miss Pissed,' I say, trying to smile.

She doesn't laugh. 'You have two minutes,' she says, staring at me. 'What do you want? What could we possibly have to talk about? It's a little too late, I'm afraid.'

I ask, 'Too late for what? Mel, what's going on?'

'Have you ever known? Really? Have you ever known what's going on?'

'I... don't think so.'

'Most people pretend,' she tells me. 'They pretend they know what's going on, and I know you try, but you're not very good at it.'

'I don't know what to say, Mel. I don't know what's happening anymore.'

'Do you even care? You have Jade now.'

'She's a good friend.'

'But you want something more.' She makes this sound like a statement rather than a question.

I ask, 'Does that bother you?'

'Does it matter?'

Pause.

'No,' I say. 'I don't think it does.'

She nods. 'Well, I'm glad we understand each other. I'm glad we got that sorted out.' She closes her eyes and brings her hand over her face. I don't know what to say, whether to put a hand on her shoulder or not, so I just stand there. She turns and walks towards the back of the car, and she lifts herself up, with what seems like great difficulty, and sits on the boot.

'I don't have the energy to cry anymore,' she says after a while. 'It feels like I want to, but I can't, you know? Do you ever get that? Where there's all this bad stuff inside, you can feel it building in your chest and your throat, but it won't come out. It's like there's a sob that you can't quite get out and it grows and grows inside you until it feels like you're about to burst. Do you ever get that?'

'Sometimes.'

'Things start slowly, they just come out of nowhere. You don't expect them, or even really want them, but soon you get used to it. Soon you just stop thinking about it and it becomes part of your life. Soon you need it; you start looking forward to it. At first you think you can't live with it, then you can't live without it.'

'What exactly are you talking about?'

She shrugs. 'Just things. You should know what I mean.'

'Maybe I do.'

She laughs sourly. 'No, you don't.'

There's a pause before I say, 'Mel, I know I can be a little... strange... sometimes, but sometimes I lose track of what's going on, I forget things and my mind seems all jumbled up. I wake up and I wonder why I bothered. But even when I'm acting strangely, I never stopped being me. I'm still your friend.'

'Are you?'

'Yes. Well, I hope so.'

She nods. 'I haven't been feeling so well lately.'

'Have you seen a doctor?'

She shakes her head, no. 'I don't think it's that sort of sick,' she says, and starts to cry. She laughs at herself sadly and says, 'I guess it could come out, after all.'

'It's okay to cry,' I tell her.

'I know. I've been doing it a lot lately.'

I nod, unsure of what to say.

'I've started having dreams,' she says. 'I have these nightmares where I see all these terrible things; people I care about doing these things, and it upsets me. I wake up shivering, feeling totally depressed. Or worse: sometimes I dream that everything is okay. I wake up and I'm happy for about three seconds before I remember. I think that I'm not trying hard enough to be a good person, that I can always try that little bit harder, then the dreams will stop, all of this will stop, but it never does. No matter how hard I try, it never stops. The dreams just get worse and worse. It gets to the point where I dread going to sleep. Then the only thing worse than being asleep is being awake.'

She wipes her eyes with her sleeve and looks up at the stars. 'You think that you're being punished in some way, but the only person who is punishing you is yourself. You're not living up to what you want to be. So you try harder, but it makes no difference. Things get worse and worse and you keep telling yourself, I deserve this.'

I wait for her to continue, but she doesn't. I look over at her and realise she's crying too hard to speak.

'It's so hard,' she sobs after a minute. She sniffles, 'I thought I could...,' she stops, her voice trailing away.

'Thought you could what?'

'I don't know. Just that, I guess. I thought I could. But I can't.'

'You can, you just need to keep fighting.'

'It shouldn't have to be a fight,' she says. 'I thought it was meant to be beautiful...' She sighs, her breath hitching. 'But it's so hard.'

'Yeah, it is. And it hurts. Most of the time it hurts bad. But sometimes that's all you can hope for.'

She slides down off the car boot and looks at me. 'I'm sorry if I've been at all... harsh with you. I didn't mean to be.'

'That's alright. We all get a little messed up sometimes.'

'Yeah. Well, I'll see you around, okay?'

I nod. 'Okay. We'll catch a cab home.'

She tries to smile, fails, walks around to the driver's door and gets inside. I stand back and watch as she drives off.

Sixteen

'Where are you going?' George asks as he follows me around the house.

'To the hospital,' I tell him.

'The hospital? What's wrong?'

'It's Mel,' I tell him, pulling on my shoes. 'That was Jesus on the phone, apparently Mel was admitted earlier this morning.'

'Why?'

'I don't know, he wouldn't say.'

'Is she okay?'

'I don't know. I'll tell you everything when I get back, alright?'

I push past him and get into the car, heading towards the hospital.

Jesus is sitting in the waiting room and he stands up to greet me as I walk through the sliding glass doors. His eyes are red.

'What's going on?' I ask. 'What happened?'

'She collapsed at work,' he tells me. 'She was serving a customer and just passed out.'

We walk quickly along the corridor, then up the elevator, towards her room.

'Do the doctors know what's wrong?' I ask.

'They think it's weakness, malnutrition, suspected bulimia.'

'Bulimia? Wouldn't we have noticed that?'

Jesus shrugs. 'I don't know. The doctor says it's not always obvious.'

'Is she going to be okay? I mean, this isn't going to kill her, is it? It hasn't gone that far, has it?'

Jesus stops walking and I turn to look at him. He looks down and when he looks back up at me I can see fresh tears in his eyes. 'It's not looking good, I'm afraid. Her... her stomach has ruptured.'

'Oh, Christ.'

'Yeah. Don't mention anything to her though, okay? She doesn't need to know.'

'Alright.'

He nods. 'The doctors say she doesn't have long. A week at the most.'

It's suddenly hard to breathe and I have to turn away from him and continue walking.

Mel's room smells of antiseptic. The window lets in yellow light and I can see the sun shining between the buildings.

Beau sits on a chair next to the head of the bed. His hair is messy and he hasn't shaved. He smiles at me when I walk in but there is more fear behind the smile than he wants me to know about.

A doctor stands at the foot of the bed, reading pages attached to a clipboard. He looks up at us as we walk in.

Mel is lying in the centre of the bed and she looks much the same as she always does, except very pale. The sheet lifts with the regular rhythm of her breathing.

Absently I wonder how many people have died in this bed, on these sheets.

'Doctor, what's going on?' I ask.

He smiles professionally. 'I'm sorry, I can only discuss her health with immediate family…'

I look at Beau. 'Where's her parents?' I ask, cutting the doctor off.

'On their way,' he says. 'They were out of town, her dad was on a business trip of some sort.' He shrugs. 'They should be here soon.'

The doctor continues, 'If you'd like to wait for her family to arrive…'

I cut him off again. 'We are her family,' I yell. 'Don't you see that? We are her fucking family.'

Jesus' hand lands on my shoulder. 'Calm down,' he says. Then, to the doctor, 'Please, he's a very close friend. Tell him what you can. Please.'

The doctor rubs his eyes. 'Okay,' he says, sighs, like he's doing me a huge favour but really doesn't want to. 'Your friend here passed out at work this morning. We examined her and she is very, very weak. It's as though she hasn't eaten in months. Further examination led us to believe your friend was suffering from bulimia nervosa.'

'How do you know that? How can you tell?'

'She has severe dental decay, namely the erosion of tooth enamel, caused by the upbringing of stomach acids.' He ticks them off on his fingers. 'Swollen parotid glands, slight hair loss, small holes in her oesophagus, unusual levels of certain gastrointestinal chemicals… Do you want me to go on?'

I shake my head. 'No, it's alright. It's just a bit of a shock, that's all.'

He smiles reassuringly at me, a smile that has obviously been used thousands of times. 'I know. It's alright to be shocked.' He addresses the three of us, 'Do you mind if I ask you all some questions?'

The three of us nod our consent.

'Alright,' the doctor says. 'First off, has Melinda been moody lately? Any sudden changes in her behaviour?'

'A little,' Jesus says. 'She was a little depressed lately.'

'And what did you do about that?' the doctor asks.

'Well, nothing…,' Jesus starts. 'I mean, everyone is depressed these days, right?'

The doctor looks at him for a moment before writing something on his pad. 'Did she mention anything about menstrual irregularities?'

The three of us shake our heads, answering quickly, telling him no, never, nothing like that.

'Did Melinda have any steady boyfriends? Anyone she used to see? Was there anyone she was pursuing?'

There's a silence in the room that's surprisingly uncomfortable. I wait for Beau or Jesus to answer, but they don't, so I say, 'No, not that I was aware of. Doctor, what does this have to do with anything? Why would this cause her to… do what she did?'

'No one really knows exactly what causes this disease. Some people say it's cultural, some say it's genetic. I'm just trying to get an idea, here. Listen, I have to get going. I'll be back when Melinda's parents arrive. I'll see you guys then, I'm sure. Try not to wake her, she needs her rest.'

He walks past us and out into the corridor. I sit on one of the chairs beside the bed and Jesus leans against the wall near the doorway. It feels like my legs are crawling with ants.

I ask Beau how long he's been here.

'I came as soon as Jesus called, which was right before he called you, I guess.'

I try to laugh. 'You look like shit.'

He smiles tiredly. 'So do you.'

'Is Nick coming?'

'I couldn't get hold of him,' Jesus says. 'Let me try again.' He walks out of the room.

There's a pause. Quietly, Beau says, 'Did Jesus tell you? About her stomach?'

I nod. 'Can't they fix it?'

'I don't know. I don't think so.' He leans forward, head in hands. 'God, man, we're going to lose her.'

I look at her lying silently in the bed. It's almost like there's nothing wrong with her.

'Is she in any pain?' I ask.

'I hope not,' Beau says through his hands.

A week. The person lying in the bed will be gone in a week. She'll be Melinda, then she'll be nothing. How long does dying take? Is it instant or can you feel it coming? A week. She'll lie here for a week then she'll die and they'll wash the sheets and move someone else in to take this bed. We'll plant her in the ground and begin the process of forgetting.

'She's too young,' Beau says, interrupting my thoughts. 'She shouldn't have to go through this. Not yet.' He stands up and runs his hands through his hair. 'I've been trying to imagine what life will be like without her. There'll only be the four of us.'

'Don't talk like that. She's not gone yet. What if she can hear you?'

He walks over to me and kneels down in front of my chair. 'How did we not see this coming?' he asks. 'Are we really that blind? Are we that selfish and preoccupied? We didn't even notice one of our best friends killing herself under our noses?'

'How could we? She was doing it in private, she looked the same as always.'

'Oh, come on, no she didn't. She looks like a rag doll.'

'But with make-up, and bulky clothes you couldn't tell.'

'Yes, you could tell; we just didn't pay enough attention.'

'So what do we do now?'

'I don't know. I just don't know.'

When I leave the hospital she still hasn't woken up. Her parents are due any time, but Jesus still can't find Nick. Sitting in her room won't help any and I can't stand the sterile smell of disinfectant any longer.

I take one last look at Mel, lying on her back peacefully. She looks like she's sleeping calmly and I hope her dreams are of happier times and happier places. I hope she doesn't feel any pain and if it has to end that it ends quickly and quietly with no fuss, just the way Mel liked things to be. I hope that when this ends, one way or another, she finds peace. She rolls her head and in her sleep she seems to smile.

I feel a lump rising in my throat. I tell Beau I will be back tomorrow and I leave.

The phone rings the next morning.

It's Jesus.

I listen to him speak, then hang up.

The first time I met Fatty Mel was at the university cafeteria. It was back at the beginning of the year, when things were still new and exciting and the novelty hadn't worn off yet. I was sitting at a table by myself when she walked over and smiled. *Do you mind if I sit with you? I don't much feel like sitting by myself.*

It's a beautiful sunny day and I realise this is the first time I've ever been to a cemetery. I didn't attend either of my parents' funerals.

There are chairs set up in two sections, divided by an aisle. At the front of the chairs there is a lectern and beside that there is a large, dark hole.

There are lots of people standing around, all wearing black and most of them are crying. I look around for Beau but I can't see him. I keep away from the main group, watching the sun streaming through the trees and listening to the birds chirping and it amazes me that a place of death is so alive.

I walk slowly through the trees, adjusting the tie Beau has lent me, trying to catch one of the thoughts that are buzzing around in my head. My hands are shaking uncontrollably and I stuff them deep in my pockets in the hope they'll stop. Instead, the shaking spreads up my arms and into my shoulders and I have to sit on the warm grass with my eyes closed until it passes.

Beau walks up to me from the group. He says, 'Come on, it's starting soon.'

'I don't think I can.'

'Yeah, you can. You just need to sit there. It'll be okay.' He holds out his hand. Reluctantly I take it and he pulls me up on my feet.

'It'll all be over soon,' he says and puts his arm around my shoulders as we walk towards the gathering. We sit at the back and Beau spots Jesus and Nick sitting in the next row up on the opposite side of the aisle. I ask him if we should go over and join them but he shakes his head, no.

We watch as the coffin moves down the aisle supported by men who must be Mel's uncles, cousins, her father. They lower it down onto bars over the hole then slowly move to their seats. Straps are threaded through the coffin's handles, ready to lower her into the dirt. The preacher or priest or whoever he is moves to the podium and addresses the crowd through the microphone, delicately concealed behind a small bunch of flowers.

'Ladies and gentlemen, we are here to celebrate the life of Melinda Jane Evans. A life that was taken from us much too soon.'

Jane, I think. Her middle name was Jane.

'Melinda was a joy to everyone who knew her. Everyone she met, she would fill their lives with warmth and happiness. Daughter of Michael and Janice, sister of Katie, friend of many, Mel touched the lives of so many people and she will be sorely missed.'

I think of us at Babylon, dancing, her head on my shoulder, my arms around her.

'Mel was studying to be a teacher,' the minister continues, 'because of her love of children. She never knew it but she was teaching all of us, every day. We all learned something from Melinda and through her, we all learned something more about ourselves.'

The minister says, 'She loved going out and having fun. She had a laugh that would make anyone around her smile because of its sheer innocence and the joy it contained. Mel had a gift: she could make anyone smile and was always smiling herself.'

I think of her vomiting into the toilet bowl.

'Most of all, she loved her friends and family,' the minister says. 'She had a very tight-knit group of friends she would do everything with, and she would do anything for them and they would do anything for her.'

Beau asking me how we didn't notice she was sick.

'Mel was a strong, committed member of her family. She always put her parents first and always exceeded their expectations. Her whole family was incredibly proud of Mel and the wonderful person she had become.'

When I left the hospital, her parents still hadn't arrived.

The minister continues to talk but I stop hearing him. Mel's father stands up and says a few words but I don't hear him, either. I keep staring at Mel's mother, who has her head bowed forward and a handkerchief pressed to her face. Her body shakes with sobs and Mel's sister puts her arm around her mother's shoulders.

I notice an ant on the back of my hand and absently brush it away.

Everything seems to have had the volume turned down; everything is muffled and unclear. It all seems as sterile as the hospital. I look up and can see the sun streaming through the branches of the tree, then everyone is standing, people are talking, people are walking away.

Beau leans in and says, 'We're all coming back to my house for a while. We all need a drink. Come on.'

I'm pulling up at Beau's house before I realise that 'we all' is now only Nick, Jesus, Beau and myself.

Nick and Jesus are in the kitchen and Beau is sitting on the couch with his hand over his eyes, tie loosened and top button undone. Phydeaux paces back and forth at the glass door then sits down and scratches behind its ear. I sit down on the armchair mimicking Beau with the button and tie and let out a long, deep sigh.

Jesus exits the kitchen, jacket off, carrying a bottle of whisky and four glasses. Nick follows, also with his jacket off, eating from a packet of corn chips.

'Hope you don't mind,' he says to Beau, and Beau raises his shoulders and shakes his head – that look that says, whatever.

Jesus sits down and pours the drinks, topping up the glasses just a little more. He gives one to everyone and we all look down into the thick liquid. After a moment, Beau raises his glass and we join him. We hold them there for a moment, then, without a word, we drink.

The drinks keep coming.

The level in the bottle drops dramatically over what feels like a very short period of time and my head starts to buzz pleasantly, almost enough to drown out everything else that's going on in there. For a moment I forget why it is we're here, dressed in black suits, but it only lasts for a second and then I remember and it hits me hard in the stomach. I find myself on the verge of tears and no one is talking and the silence is overwhelming so I have to say something, anything, just to distract myself.

I ask, 'What time is it?'

Beau shrugs and sighs tiredly. 'That depends.'

'On what?'

'On what,' he repeats. 'I dunno, on a lot of things, I guess.'

'Well, what time is it now? Here?'

He shrugs again and sighs. I look over at Jesus but he's staring into his drink. Beside him Nick is glaring at me, his jaw clenched.

I stare back for a moment before asking, 'What?'

He snorts, shakes his head, smiles, looks down.

'What?' I ask again.

There's silence before he says, 'Nick doesn't know how you can sit there like that. Asking for the time.'

'What do you mean? You don't think it's a valid question?'

'How can you sit there and ask for the time, knowing what you've done?'

'Done? What have I done, Nick?'

'Nick,' Jesus says softly.

He laughs. 'You dumb fuck,' he says to me. 'You really don't get it.'

'Nick,' Beau warns. 'This is not the time.'

'No, this *is* the time,' he says. 'This is the perfect time.'

I stand up. I say, 'Look, I really don't know what you're talking about. But I'm not in the mood for your shit right now so you can fuck off.'

I start walking towards the bathroom and Nick stands up, cutting me off.

'It's your fault,' he says.

'What's my fault? That you're talking shit?'

'It's your fault she's dead, you dumb fuck.'

This stops me.

Mister Shocked.

'What did you say?'

'You heard Nick.'

'Say it again,' I say loudly, looking straight into his eyes, daring him.

Beau is standing behind me. 'Nick,' he says, 'be cool, man. Be cool.'

'You could have saved her any time you liked,' Nick says.

'That's bullshit, Nick,' Beau says from behind me. 'It's bullshit and you know it.'

'Come on, Beau,' he says. 'You knew it, Nick knew it, even Jesus knew it.'

Jesus is sitting on the couch, leaning forward, head in his hands. I hear him sob quietly.

'You don't know what you're talking about,' Beau says. 'You're drunk. Now sit down.'

'Sit down, Nick,' I mimic, teeth gritted.

Nick steps towards me. 'Or what?'

Now it's my turn to snort. 'Fuck you,' I mutter and push past him.

He grabs me and yanks me backwards. I stumble a few steps and Beau catches me and I regain my footing. I look up just in time to see Nick's fist speeding towards my face.

Seventeen

'What happened then?' she asks.

'I dunno. It's all blurred. We hit each other a few times then Beau got between us. That's about it.'

The social worker sits on the couch in her usual spot, her files discarded beside her. When I opened the door to her and she saw my eye, black and swollen, she pushed past me to dump her books on the couch. She then turned around and examined my face.

'Does it hurt?' she had asked, pushing and prodding the flesh.

'Only when you do that.'

She sat me down and insisted I tell her the whole story. I told her about Mel. The hospital. The funeral. I told her about the drinks at Beau's, the argument, the accusations, the punches. She listened attentively and nodded in all the right places.

When I'm finished relaying the story there's a silence before she says, 'I'm sorry. It's so sad,' she continues. 'She was so young.' She looks at me and asks, 'How are you handling it?'

I shrug. 'As well as can be expected.'

'Have you talked to anyone about it?'

'Just you.'

'Not Beau? Or Jesus?'

'No. Why would I talk to them? They were there, they know what happened.'

'It doesn't matter if they were there or not. They don't know how you're feeling. That's what you should be talking about.'

'They know how I'm feeling. They're probably feeling exactly the same way.'

'And what are you feeling?'

I shrug again. 'I dunno. Sad, I guess.'

'That's all?' she asks.

'What do you want me to say? That I feel guilty? Yeah, okay, fine, I admit it – I feel guilty. Happy now?'

'No, I'm not happy. Why do you feel guilty? You have no reason at all to feel that way.'

'Maybe I do. Maybe what Nick said is true.'

'No, it's not. He didn't know what he was talking about,' she says sternly.

'But what if he did? What if I could have saved her?'

'How would you have done that?' she asks.

'I don't know. But maybe I could have.'

There's a pause before she says, 'I think we've had this conversation before. Remember?'

'Vaguely,' I say, and scratch at an ant on the back of my neck.

'You blamed yourself for your mum's death. Now you're blaming yourself for this. Why do you do that?'

'I don't know. I just keep thinking there must have been something I could have done.'

'I know you do and that's only natural. In bad times, we always wonder what went wrong and what we could have done to fix it. But you have to realise that this was her problem, not yours. You didn't force her to do any of this.'

'I know that but I could have noticed earlier. I could have gotten her help.'

'Beau could have noticed. Jesus could have noticed. Her parents could have. Don't take the whole weight of this situation on your own shoulders. The fact is, there's no one to blame here. It was just one of those things, that's all. So go ahead, feel sad. In fact, I encourage you to feel sad. But don't feel guilty. Guilt can be very, very destructive, especially when it's over something you couldn't control.'

I let out a long, deep sigh. 'So what do you want me to do?'

'I want you to mourn,' she says. 'I want you to go to your friends and share your grief. The healing process is much faster and more thorough that way.'

I nod. 'Sure. I can do that.'

After she leaves, I call Beau and tell him she told us to get drunk tonight. He says that sounds like a good idea and he'll see me around seven.

On the phone I can hear George making himself a cup of coffee.

'Fuck Nick,' he says. 'What the hell was he thinking?'

'He was mad.' I shrug.

'Don't do that,' George says. 'Don't make excuses for him.'

'I'm not making excuses, I'm just saying it's understandable to want to hit someone under these circumstances.'

'No, it's not. He blames you for Mel's death when you had nothing to do with it. He hit you for something you had no control over. He overstepped the line.'

'I don't like Nick any more than you do.'

'Then why are you standing up for him?'

I sigh. 'I don't know. I shouldn't.'

'Damn right you shouldn't. You should be pissed off at him. Big time.'

'I am pissed off, I just…'

'Good. Stay that way. Don't let him off the hook for this. He's put you through too much shit to let it slide. Remember what you told me about New Year's? That he said Jade was too good for you? That he kissed her hand? God knows what he said to her while you were gone. Not only does he try to steal your girl in front of you but then he blames you for your friend's death. What sort of a friend does that?'

I'm pleased to hear George refer to Jade as my girl but I have to correct him anyway and tell him that she's not.

'I know that, but she might be if Nick would keep out of it.'

'Yeah. Maybe.'

'Something to think about,' George says. I'm about to ask him what he means but he's already hung up.

When I get to Beau's it's not the usual drunken Beau that answers the door; instead, it's a quiet, subdued Beau. He says hi as he opens the door then stands aside and lets me pass. I put my beer in the fridge and take one into the main room. The dog scratches at the glass but I ignore it.

Beau is sitting on the couch and I crash down into the armchair and open my beer. I would prefer a B&C but it's much easier to open a beer than to mix a drink.

Neither of us says anything for a while.

'This is all very…,' Beau says, then trails off.

'Very what?'

He shrugs. 'I don't know.' His usual charisma is gone; the easy-spoken Beau has been replaced by a sedate, inexpressive Beau.

'Are you okay?'

He stares into space for a while before shaking his head softly. 'No. Not really.'

I nod. 'Do you want another beer?'

He looks at me and says, 'Not just now.'

There's another silent period before he leans forward on the couch and runs his hands through his hair. 'Don't you ever feel, you know, bad?'

'Sort of. I miss Mel, if that's what you mean.'

'I just... I wish there was more we could have done. I still can't get over the fact we didn't notice this was going on.'

'How could we have noticed? It was her problem. She kept it to herself. She didn't want us to know.'

'We should have known something was wrong. We were supposed to be her friends, yet we didn't realise she was killing herself right in front of us.'

'You can't force people to tell you things if they don't want to.'

'I'm not saying she should have told us, I'm saying we should have seen it. You didn't notice she looked sick?'

'Yeah, but I thought that was just... Mel.'

'God, we are so fucking stupid.'

I nod, unable to disagree.

'I've never known anyone who died before,' he says.

'I have.'

He nods slowly. 'How did you get through it?'

'I don't know. I don't think I did.'

He sighs tiredly. 'Where do we go from here?' he asks.

'We can only go forward. It keeps coming at us and we have to keep moving.'

Beau looks at me and says, 'Something tells me it's not going to be that easy.'

* * *

The rest of the evening is fairly quiet. Neither of us talks much and the more beers I have the worse I feel. There's a short period when my head spins pleasantly but it doesn't last very long and I'm quickly thrown back into the depression that has been creeping out of my chest for the last week or however long it has been since Mel died.

I know I should be using this time to share my feelings with my friends like the social worker said, but it seems like a lot of work and somewhat inappropriate. My grief is something that seems more comfortable inside where it belongs, where I can nurse it and sweat it out. It is something that needs to be kept inside because Beau is feeling the same thing and he does not need to hear about my troubles. I know I should be offering support and comfort but I cannot. I am so lost within myself and my own sense of loss that bringing it out into the open is too much.

At one point Beau has tears in his eyes and this strikes something in me; the fact that Beau is always strong, always in control, always cool and collected and yet he shows this sign of weakness, this chink in his armour. It makes me think that it is perhaps alright to comfort him, to show support and tell him we are all going through the same thing but the words will not come out. I can do nothing but sit in the armchair and drink the beer, staring at the wall, fighting off the tears that cloud my vision.

The despair settles over me like a blanket. There is a feeling of uselessness, of hopelessness and I know that I have nothing to offer Beau, or myself, in these circumstances. I know that he will have to get through this by himself, as will we all, and this once more reinforces the fact that we truly are all alone.

Eighteen

A few days later the group gets together and we go out to a club, Paramount, and it reminds me of Mel's attempts to get us to go there the night we went to Babylon. This is something that happened only between the two of us and I keep this memory to myself in an almost sacred fashion, holding on to something Mel left behind that I can say is truly mine. Something we shared and no one else knows about or can take away.

We're sitting around a smoky table, away from the dance floor so we can hear ourselves talk. Tonight there is myself, Beau, Jesus, Nick, and somehow, Jade. I'm holding a double B&C and my calves are crawling with ants.

Nick and Jade are sitting on the other side of the table. Nick keeps talking to Jade then looking at me, making sure I've noticed and smiling with satisfaction. This makes my chest hurt, my breath come in short, deep gasps and pushes me to the verge of tears. I have never been so close to standing up and punching Nick as I am now.

Jesus sits on one side of me, Beau on the other. Neither say very much.

'I'm sorry I didn't make it to... the funeral,' Jade says. 'I didn't think it was appropriate. I hardly knew her.' She looks at Nick and says, 'Thanks for inviting me tonight.'

Nick says, 'That's okay.'

I keep staring at Nick, my teeth clenched.

'How are her parents?' Jade asks.

'They're pretty much... destroyed,' Jesus answers.

'Oh,' Jade says, and takes a sip from her drink.

'They're strong,' Nick says, as if he's trying to cheer everyone up. 'They'll get through it.'

'I just feel so bad about it all,' Jade says, almost crying.

'Shh,' Nick says quietly and turns towards her, shutting us out. 'There was nothing you could have done.'

He puts his arm around her.

'I'm empty,' Beau says, holding up his glass. To me, he says, 'Come on.' He stands up and it takes me a moment to find the strength to get to my feet. I have the urge to pounce on Nick but Beau pulls me away.

At the bar, Beau says, 'Maybe we've been looking at this all wrong.'

'What do you mean?'

'We're sitting around crying over things that we can't change.'

'Yeah.'

'That's what everyone does. And that's why nothing ever changes. We should accept the things we can't change as a learning experience and use them to make our lives better.'

'It sounds good in theory.'

'Yeah, it does,' he continues. 'I've been thinking about this over the last few days. Instead of crying over what has happened we should be learning from it.'

'Death doesn't teach us anything.'

Beau says, 'What have we come to realise because of Mel's death?'

'You'd better not get all preachy on me, because I really don't want to hear it.'

'No, I'm not,' he says. 'I'm not going to preach. I'm just telling you what I've discovered. Listen, we screwed up. We screwed up one of the most important things. We had a friend who needed us, who was dying in front of us, and we didn't notice. We were too busy stressing over insignificant matters like which club to go to, where to get drunk, shit like that. We didn't notice that something big was happening, something that actually mattered, and we screwed up. Mel died. So let's not let her death go to waste. Let's learn from it. Let's try and become better people.'

'This all sounds very nice but it's not that easy.'

'Yeah, it is.'

'No, it's not. How do you plan on becoming a better person? How are you going to concentrate on bigger things? How are you going to become less self-obsessed?'

Beau smiles. He reaches into his pocket and brings out the doll.

The blessed doll that can win any girl, sweep her off her feet then sweep her under the rug.

'This,' he says, and holds it up.

'What about it?'

'This is where the trouble lies. This has made me false. You were right before: it is cheating. This doll symbolises one thing:

self-gratification. That's all. It benefits me, and no one else. And what is the point of that?'

'What're you going to do?' I ask. I don't like the way Beau is talking, it's all very New Age-y and totally unlike him.

'I'm going to stop being so selfish and think of others for a change. Become a better person, become a real person.'

He looks at the doll clenched in his hand, its blonde hair resting on his fingers. 'From now on, everything I do, I do for real.'

He tosses the doll into a bin.

'Wait,' I yell, diving after it. 'What are you doing? You can't throw the blessed doll away. Don't you know how great it is?'

He laughs. 'Let it go. It didn't matter. Nothing it did matters. Nothing it did was real. It was a cheat and I'm through with that. If I died tomorrow, how would I feel about having cheated my way through life?'

'You probably wouldn't be feeling anything if you were dead. Enjoy life. Keep the doll. Or at least give it to me.'

He shakes his head. 'No. It's gone. I'm through cheating, I'm through faking.' He sighs. 'It's a shame Mel had to die to make me realise all this.'

I'm peering into the bin, searching for a glimpse of blonde hair.

'What about you?' Beau asks.

'What about me?'

'Are you going to do the same?'

'Um. Yeah, sure. Sounds good to me.'

Beau smiles. 'Glad to hear it. Don't cheat your way through life. Come on, let's get a drink.'

He starts to walk away and I hesitate for a moment, searching through the rubbish, but the doll is gone.

*   *   *

Throughout the rest of the evening I hardly see Jade at all. She spends the night talking with Nick and I'm sure he's doing a good job faking that he cares about what she's saying.

I'm both Mister Furious and Mister Drunken Resignation.

I'm sitting watching them and Jade looks over at me. She smiles sadly and I try to return the gesture. My breath catches in my throat and I have to stand up and walk around the club until the feeling passes.

The funny thing about grief is, just when you think you have it under control, it comes back with a vengeance.

I'm standing at the bar, trying to get the image of Nick and Jade out of my head, and the girl next to me orders a Stoli.

This is the drink I bought for Mel at Babylon. The drink I bought her for getting a good result on her university paper. The drink I bought her after I promised that, next time, we'd go to Paramount.

It strikes me that Mel will never drink another Stoli. I will never buy her another drink. She will never call me to tell me the results of her assessments. I will never again dance with her at a club or hear the sound of her voice. I will never again tell her she looks fat in that outfit.

Then I'm leaving the bar, pushing through the crowds and into an empty cubicle in the men's bathroom. I'm sitting on the closed lit of a toilet, sobbing into my hands. I would give anything to get her back though I realise this is a pointless way of thinking because there is no way she is coming back, ever, so I really should follow Beau's example and learn from this experience. Take control of the situation and use it to make things better.

This thought is overwhelming and I know I cannot do it. I feel a profound sense of loss and it makes me want to curl into a ball and go to sleep. Above anything else, it all seems so unfair.

Later, at the table, I notice how everyone looks worn out. They all look exhausted and sad and I think maybe I should talk to them about things, about how we're feeling and how we're coping. I see Jade sitting with Nick and the thought of me talking about my feelings, making myself even more exposed and vulnerable, is totally unwelcome. If I'm losing Jade to Nick, of all people, then this is not the time to be weak.

I take a beer off the table and up-end it, finishing it in one gulp.

I wonder when Jade and Nick got so friendly. George's question floats back to me: what did Nick say to her while I was gone at New Year's?

The next time I see the social worker, I tell her about what is going on.

'Have you told Jade how you feel?'

'No.'

'What about Nick?'

'Not exactly.'

'So maybe, as far as either of them knows, they don't think they're doing anything wrong. Maybe they don't know they're hurting you.'

'Nick knows,' I tell her.

'Are you sure?'

'Yes. He's just doing it to piss me off.'

'Maybe he really is interested in her. Maybe it has nothing to do with you.'

'It has everything to do with me. He knows I'm in love with her so this is his way of getting back at me for Mel.'

The social worker sighs. 'It sounds like Nick wouldn't listen even if you did talk to him. His mind is made up. The only thing you can do now is talk to Jade. Maybe she thinks you're not interested. Or you were, and have moved on. She does have her own mind, you know. She doesn't have to do what Nick wants her to do.'

I nod. 'Alright, I'll talk to her.'

She smiles. 'Good idea.'

The next time we all meet, Beau is not there, much to my disappointment. This leaves Jesus and Nick, who has once again brought Jade.

'Are you okay?' Jesus asks. 'You seem pissed off.'

'I am,' I tell him.

'Oh,' he says, but doesn't pursue this any further.

Nick stands and walks towards the bar. I get up and follow him.

'Hey,' I say, sliding up to the bar beside him.

He looks over at me, then back to the bottles lined up behind the bar. He doesn't say anything.

I ask, 'So what's going on with you and Jade?'

'Does it have anything to do with you?' he asks.

'Well, yeah, kinda.'

'Oh, were you guys together? Sorry, Nick didn't know.'

'No, we weren't, but...'

'You weren't? Then Nick guesses it really doesn't have anything to do with you, after all.'

'You could have at least asked me first.'

'Why? She can do whatever she likes, or whomever she likes.'

My temper flashes and I feel my fist tense, ready to strike. 'Have I ever told you you're a fucking asshole?'

He smiles sweetly. 'No, Nick doesn't believe you have.'

'Stay away from her,' I say.

He looks at me. 'Are you threatening Nick?'

'I hope so.'

He laughs. 'She doesn't love you. Nick doesn't think anyone does.'

Infuriated, I am on the verge of tears. There are ants crawling under my shirt and I want to strike Nick as hard as I can. More than that, I want to see him bleeding, sobbing.

'And she loves you?' I demand. 'A guy who can't even speak in the first person? What do you have to offer her? What could she possibly see in you?'

'Why don't you ask her?'

He starts to walk away with his drinks.

'You don't deserve her,' I say. 'You'll never be good enough for her. You're the one who should've died, you piece of shit.'

He turns to face me. 'You're the one who deserves to die. You killed Mel and for that, you'll die alone. Nick will make sure of that. You'll die alone because who else is there? These guys just hang around with you because you're part of the group, as unfortunate as that is. We don't want you here. We never have. Why don't you do us all a favour and go kill yourself? Go stick your head in the oven like your fucked-up cunt of a mother.'

I am shaking violently. There is so much adrenaline pumping through my body that I cannot stand still. I have never been so furious in my entire life and I try to stalk after Nick but I can only make it halfway across the room before I have to turn and bolt for the bathrooms, barely making it before I vomit into a bowl. I kneel down, trying to get a grip, but I can see only red.

Nick has gone too far this time and I know, for him, there is no chance of redemption.

* * *

I get home and I cannot sleep. I think over the events of the evening and my anger does not subside. I know talking to Nick is pointless from now on; there is no way we will ever be able to speak civilly again. I decide to follow the social worker's advice and go straight to Jade. After all, Nick didn't say they were actually together and she does have a mind of her own. I make up my mind to call Jade tomorrow.

I think of George telling me to face my fears. To stop running. To fight back.

I finally fall asleep and I dream of Jade saying yes, she does love me, and the only thing better is seeing Nick's face when he hears the news.

Nineteen

Oh, Nick. You don't know it but I'm watching you.

Throughout the day I tried to call her but there was no answer so I drove to the beach in the hope she'll be there.

She is, but so are you.

I get to the beach and see you sitting with her in the moonlight, staring up at the stars. The sand is pale in the darkness and you are just two shapes sitting beside each other. The night is completely still; the air is calm and quiet and the only sound is that of the waves breaking against the shore.

My knees give way when I see you and I sit down heavily on the sand. I'm behind you, high up in the dunes, and you don't know I'm here.

I think about going up to you and saying, hi, and calmly asking what is going on. I think about going up to you, kicking and screaming, but my legs refuse to move.

The sound of the waves drowns out your voices and all I can hear is an occasional muffled laugh.

It hurts. Deep inside, it hurts. It is a feeling I'm accustomed to but it begins to subside into something new, something much more pleasant. A kind of dull fury builds in my chest and swells into my skull where it aches and throbs and burns. The need to break down and sob is very strong but it begins to take second place to this new guest, this wild rage that builds with every beat of my heart.

Is she telling you about the stars? About how the sun is so far away we will only ever see its echo? How things are only clear in retrospect? Is she telling you all the things she had told me? Or is she telling you something new? Something unique and special and something I will never be a part of?

The stars look down, watching us like a million eyes. There's you and her sitting on the sand, watching the waves, and there's me, sitting behind you on the dunes, watching your every move.

How long have you been here? Had you just arrived when I stumbled upon you? Or have you been here for hours? Have you been sitting together through the night, sharing each other's company without sparing a single thought for me?

You're sitting next to her but not touching. I can almost see you put your arm casually around her, pulling her close. Part of me thinks I would die if it happens. It would surely be the end for me; my breath will catch in my chest and my heart will give one final strained pump and then, welcome blackness.

But part of me wants you to touch her, to put your arm around her. I don't know why I want this to happen but part of me sits here on the sand thinking, I dare you. I dare you.

She laughs again and it's too much, all of it is too much.

I try to stand but stumble before I make it to my feet. I walk back to the car. My hands are trembling and I drop the keys and it takes me several attempts to unlock the door.

I start the engine and begin to drive, the car heaving itself drunkenly forward. I drive around for hours, not paying much attention to anything. The streets bleed into one another and I seem to look through things as much as at them. I watch the moon sail across the sky as I drive around, losing all sense of time, and before I know it, I'm parked outside your house. There is a light on inside and your car is in the driveway, so I know you're home. The question I refuse to ask myself is whether or not she is with you.

I stare at your front door, my hands strangling the steering wheel so the knuckles are white. I don't know for how long; I just look at your door, waiting.

I see your shadow pass across the window. At first I think it is just your silhouette, but the curtains are open and I can see your every move. You are holding a bottle, probably tequila, and are wearing jeans but no shirt. You always were a fucking poser.

The urge to vomit comes and passes. Then I need air, some fresh air to breathe, so I open the door and get out.

Then I'm walking towards your door, approaching enemy lines, then knocking and listening to your approaching footsteps, eager to see the look on your face when you see who has come calling.

'Oh, great,' you say, throwing the door open. 'What the hell are you doing here? What's going on?'

'We need to talk,' I say, pushing past you.

You start to say something but I don't bother to listen and you close the door and follow me deeper into the house.

'Are you alone?' I ask.

'What? Of course Nick is alone, what do...,' but then you stop, your voice trailing off into silence. The confused look has faded from your eyes, leaving something like aggression and possibly a trace of... what was that? Guilt?

'I came by earlier,' I lie, 'but you weren't in.'

'No. Nick was out. He wasn't home.'

'Where were you?' I ask, staring straight into your eyes that try to meet mine but don't quite make it.

'What's it to you?' you ask and take another swig from the tequila bottle.

I tell you I need a drink and walk into the kitchen while you say sourly, 'Help yourself.'

On the counter there is a cutting board with slices of lemon lying next to a knife and a salt shaker, the usual production line. I look in the fridge for a beer but there's none, then search the cupboards for bourbon but again come up empty. I have to settle for Coke, which tastes bad without any bourbon in it.

I lean over the counter, breathing heavily, my head throbbing. I turn around and see you standing in the doorway, watching me.

I laugh shakily. 'What a night.'

'What are you doing here?' you ask. 'Nick thinks you should go,' you say, and start to walk away. 'Nick doesn't want to see you again. You're not welcome here.'

'What were you doing with her?' I ask.

You stop and straighten up. 'What did you say?' you ask without turning around.

I roar, 'What the fuck were you doing with her?'

Then you turn to face me, trying to look angry but the alcohol is working and your eyes are hazy and far away.

'That's none of your goddamn business,' you say. 'Hasn't Nick made that clear to you yet? She doesn't have to answer to you and neither does Nick.'

How can I put it into words? The fact that you knew how I feel about her, the fact that you went behind my back and betrayed me, how can I make you understand how that feels? I can't so instead I spit, 'If I see you with her again, I'll kill you.'

You raise your eyebrows. 'You'll what?'

'You heard me, Nick,' I say through gritted teeth. 'If I see you with her again, I'll fucking kill you.'

'What?' you yell. 'You come into Nick's house in the middle of the night and you stand in Nick's kitchen and you threaten to kill Nick?' You close your eyes and smile like you can't believe how stupid I am. 'Dude,' you say, 'you are fucking with the wrong guy. Now get out.'

I don't move. You stand there and repeat, louder, 'Get out.'

'Fuck you,' I snarl, pulling away from the counter and standing tall.

The fury hits me in a wave, bursting its banks and flooding my vision red.

You advance towards me and take a swing, a drunken wide roundhouse that I easily avoid. The momentum pulls you around and I give you a hard push. You stumble away, falling drunkenly, landing heavily on the tequila bottle that is still clenched in your left hand. The bottle shatters, sending glass shards across the floor, and I hear your surprised, pained yelp while the smell of tequila stings my nose. You roll over and sit up, then look down at your hands and the fragments of glass embedded deep in the flesh, dribbling blood down your arms and dripping from your elbows onto the kitchen linoleum.

You look up at me in a drunken fury. You get to your feet slowly, never taking your eyes from mine. The blood from your split palms drips off the ends of your fingers and in the fluorescent light I can see the slivers of glass ground deep into the meat of your hands.

You take a deep breath and say something like, 'You are dead,' through clenched teeth and then you charge me, head down and forward like a bull. You catch me around my waist and drive me backwards into the kitchen counter which crashes painfully into the small of my back.

I try to push you away but you remain locked around me, no matter how hard I beat at your back, your neck, your head. Blood from your hands is on my shirt and I can feel it wet against my skin. I hammer on your back while you pin me to the counter, smashing me against it, sending shocks up my spine. You have a hand pressed into my face, pushing my head backwards, and I feel around blindly on the counter for something, anything, and my hand closes around a handle. I pick it up and bring it around, hard, into your side.

The knife plunges into you in that meaty part just below your ribs. I feel a warm splash on my hand as you cry out and pull away. I hold onto the handle and the blade twists as it tears out of you, ripping your side. You clench your hands over the hole, blood running between your fingers, collecting in your belt and running down your leg, turning your jeans red.

Your face is white and shocked and scared and as you stumble backwards you almost trip.

You pull your eyes away from the hole in your side, your life pumping out red between your fingers, and look at me. You are panting roughly through your teeth, your breath coming in jagged snarls, and you are having a hard time standing up.

'Bastard,' you growl and turn away, limping as fast as you can. I follow as you bounce off the walls, leaving dripping red smears as you stumble through the house. You take one hand off your side and pick up the telephone.

Oh Nick. I can let you call the police, or the ambulance, and it will save you. But what will become of me? I think of her, sitting on the beach. I will never see her face again, or hear her laugh or the music of her voice. Knowing she will hate me for what I have done is a thought too terrible to live with.

Only one of us will come out of this situation and the fact is, Nick, I love her more than you ever could.

'Nick, don't do that,' I warn.

'Fuck you,' you yell. The phone slips out of your hand, dripping, and crashes to the floor. You shake your hand back and forth as if to dry it and blood splatters onto the wall.

You kneel down to pick up the handset and yelp as the gash in your side splits further open. The skin around the edges is peeling back white and jagged and the flesh inside is dark red with flecks of yellow. The wound is wide and open like a pair of bloody lips and you try to hold it closed with your fingers.

'Nick,' I say, 'put the phone down.'

'Get out of here,' you scream at me. 'The police will be here soon. Get out.'

'I won't let you call the police,' I say softly.

Then the first tears begin to spill down your cheeks. 'Get out,' you say again, your voice breaking. 'Please, just leave.' You hold the phone to your chest like a source of comfort.

'Put the phone down.'

Oh, Nick, if only you'd listened. We could have avoided all of this if only you'd listened.

You start to dial and then I'm stepping forward and pushing the knife into your exposed belly. You cry out, double over and drop the phone. I put my arm around your neck to hold you steady then pull the knife out and slam it in again as hard as I can, then again and again, until I lose count of how many times, until your stomach is hanging open, until the carpet around us is sopping wet with blood. I release my grip and you stumble away from me, your hands holding your belly together, tears dripping from your chin.

Your sobs become more intense; there is no anger now, only pain and fear. You take a step backwards and then you slip. You fall onto your back, hard, your head banging against the floor and I hear your teeth slam closed, shattering, biting your tongue. Somehow staying conscious, you try to back away from me, using your feet to push yourself along while I stand above you, watching.

Oh, Nick. The way you wriggle along the ground, leaving a bloody snail trail. It would be funny if it weren't for your sobs, your hitching breath, your tears.

You make it as far as the wall but then your legs lose strength and will push you no further. Your shallow screams become retches that bring black blood, thick and sticky, out onto the floor. The alcohol is preventing your blood from clotting so it runs thinly from your wounds.

On the wall where you have come to rest is a picture, a family photo, you and your parents and some other kids, your brothers and sisters. It's a studio shot, with professional lights and everyone wearing their best clothes. Your mother sits on a chair and your dad stands behind her, the rest of you scattered around. You're all smiling into the lens and, on the ground below, you've backed into the wall and are sobbing, violently retching blood, crying out.

You try to talk as I kneel on the floor beside you, running my fingers through your hair that is matted with sweat. You try to push away, gargling, but your hands fall limply to your side. You say, 'Wait.'

Your legs begin to twitch when you see me bring the knife up again, trying to escape, but it's no good.

I say, 'Let me do this. Be still.'

I stab the knife towards your neck but you move your head down and the blade catches your face, just in front of your ear, and slices all the way down to your mouth, leaving your cheek a ragged flap.

You curl up into a ball, sobbing, trying to speak, maybe to plead, and when you see me bring the knife up once more, your eyes grow wide and you begin to shudder violently.

I bring the knife down into your throat, slamming it into something that pulses just below the skin. The end of the blade jars against something hard and blood erupts in a geyser, spraying my hands and face. I spit blood and wipe it from my eyes, watching as you begin to spasm, your eyes rolling wildly. I put my other hand on your chest and hold you down and as I push the blade deeper, slowly forcing it in, I say, 'I'm sorry, Nick,' even though I don't mean it.

Then the knife will go no further. Blood is running out of your throat and side, and your mouth is opening, closing, opening, closing. It looks like you're saying something, over and over, and it takes me a moment to realise it is mamma. Your eyes stare straight ahead, your chest sinks and you exhale one last time.

Then you are gone. The person that had been Nick McCarr is gone and all that is left is this, this remains of a person, this piece of meat that is sliced and torn and hacked open and bleeding. Your eyes are starting to glaze and when I push you you don't move, you just rock a little as blood spills from your wounds.

You die on the floor with tears drying on your face.

The house is silent. I can hear my own breathing and the tiny drip, drip of blood trickling into the puddle around you.

I look at you and feel nothing.

* * *

It's sometime later and I'm trying to hold back the vomit that creeps up my throat. The stench of blood is overwhelming and I can hardly think straight; it hovers over my thoughts like a toxic cloud.

The kitchen floor is covered in tequila and glass. Blood trails from a puddle on the linoleum through to the phone, where the carpet is soaked and its original colour is indiscernible, all the way to where I am now, where even the walls have not escaped.

I sit on the carpet and stare at the body. It's creeping me out and whenever I avert my eyes it looks like it moves. I look away, then swing my eyes back quickly, trying to catch it out, but it's always lying completely still.

I go through to the bathroom and get a huge white towel and lay it over the body. Red patches instantly appear and I have a vision of it sitting up like a creature from an old horror movie.

I start to pace back and forth.

Panic swells with the vomit and I'm feverishly trying to figure out what to do. I'm trying to string thoughts together in a coherent fashion. Ideas are flashing randomly through my head at a million miles an hour and it is impossible for me to snare even one. I'm desperately trying to formulate something that resembles a plan but everything that comes to mind is full of holes.

I run into the front room and draw the curtains. The last thing I need is a nosy neighbour taking a peak into the slaughterhouse that was the living room.

I pull my phone from my pocket.

Who do I call?

My first thought is Beau. I dial his number but it goes to his voicemail.

I call George but his phone is off.

I call Jesus but there is no answer.

The thought of implicating them in a murder barely crosses my mind.

I stare at the white towel, waiting for it to move, but it stays still. I almost scream when my phone starts to vibrate in my hand. I answer and it's Jesus.

'Hey man,' he says groggily. 'Did you just call me? What's happening?'

'I called but there was, like, no answer.'

'I know, I was asleep. What do you want?'

I don't know how reliable Jesus is. I know that, of everyone, he is the weakest and the most likely to squeal but at this point I have no choice but to trust him. Desperate times call for desperate measures so I tell him I am in some serious trouble.

'What's happened now?' he asks, tired. 'Can't afford beer? The video store already rented out your movie? What? What could possibly be so important that you have to disturb me at...,' I hear him stretch to look at the clock '... three a.m.' he yells. 'Shit man, it's three a.m. in the morning. What the hell are you doing calling me at three a.m.?'

I tell him he needs to get up and get dressed.

'Why?' he asks. 'Where am I going?'

'You're coming to Nick's house.'

'Must be a pretty good party. I dunno.'

'Please, just come here, please. Oh, and park a little way down the street, okay?'

He sighs and yawns. 'Okay,' he says, 'but unless somebody died, you're in so much trouble.'

I stand over Nick's body, pointing at it. Jesus looks up at me and I drop my hand dumbly.

'What the fuck happened?' he asks, then, 'No, wait, don't tell me. I don't want to know.'

I peel the white towel off Nick. Livor mortis is setting in, where all the blood seeps to the lowest point of the body, leaving the top pale and the underside bruised and spongy. Jesus looks down at what is left of Nick and wrinkles his nose. I replace the towel and step away.

'He must have pissed you off pretty bad.'

I tell him it was all an accident.

'Man, this isn't an accident. One stab wound is an accident. Maybe two. But not fifty. You don't accidentally stab someone fifty times. You don't accidentally hack them open and slice up their face.'

I shake my head, warding off panic. 'What are we going to do?'

Jesus looks at me, eyebrow raised. 'We? What's all this we talk?'

'You've gotta help me. You can't leave me here to do this alone.'

'Do what alone?'

'Get rid of it.'

He smiles unbelievingly. 'You want to dispose of the body? It's not like it is on the movies, you know. The police have DNA and fingerprints and all sorts of shit.'

'No, I've figured it all out. I'll tell them we were friends, I visited him all the time, like friends do. There'd be nothing unusual about my fingerprints being here. As for DNA, what is there? He only hit me a couple of times and I'm not bleeding anywhere.'

Jesus is looking at me through narrowed eyes.

'Look,' I tell him, 'all we need to do is get rid of the body and the knife.'

'What about all this blood?' Jesus asks, waving his arm.

'Fuck the blood,' I yell, the first notes of panic creeping into my voice. 'They'll know he's missing in a day or two anyway. As long as we clean this up and get rid of as many traces of me as possible, then who cares? Let them know he's dead. If there's nothing to lead them to me then who gives a shit.'

'And I'm involved in this because…?'

'Because you're my friend. You're my friend and I need your help and this is what friends do.'

'Oh, man,' he says. 'I really don't know about this. I mean, this isn't like changing a tyre or something, this is big. This is really big. We could go to prison for this, you know? Forever. Did you think of that?'

'Jesus, please,' I say, hating myself for doing this, for needing his help. Of all the people who could have answered the phone, it had to be Jesus. I say, 'He's dead. There's no changing that now. He's gone and he's not coming back. The only thing that can be changed now is whether I make it out of this or not. You don't want to see me get arrested, do you? Locked away in prison for the rest of my life? Because that's what's going to happen if you don't help me. I don't want that to happen, especially over Nick. Come on, you know Nick was an asshole. Please. I've never asked you for anything before. Just do this one thing for me. Please.'

I can see him starting to waver. 'We could end this,' he says hesitantly. 'Just call the police and explain…'

'I can't do that, don't you see? There's too much at stake. Now, I'm going to get rid of this body, with or without your help. I'd really appreciate it if you'd give me a hand, but if not, fine. Leave. But let it be on your conscience when I'm arrested. And maybe I might let your name slip when they ask if anyone else was involved. Who knows.'

He looks conflicted. He looks around the room desperately.

'Come on,' I say. 'Be my partner in crime.'

Jesus sighs and rubs his eyes. 'What the fuck am I doing?' he asks himself. 'Okay, fine. Seeing as how I'm already involved. Seeing as how you didn't actually tell me what I'd be doing when I got here, I guess I don't have much of a choice, do I?'

I sigh with relief. 'Thank you. I owe you, big time.'

'Fuck you,' he growls. 'Let's just do this.'

Jesus and I start in the kitchen.

We're carrying tissues and wiping all the surfaces I may have touched. I run the tissues across the handles of the cupboards I opened when I was looking for a drink. I wipe the Coke bottle, then the fridge door. He wipes the bench top where I was pinned, from where I grabbed the knife.

From here we move into the other room, being careful not to step in any of the blood. Jesus asks me if I touched anywhere in here and I tell him no, I don't think so.

After we have scrubbed every surface, including the phone, Jesus looks down at the towel covering Nick's remains and says, 'Now we have to deal with this.' He goes into the kitchen and comes back with a roll of garbage bags.

'What are we going to do?'

'Wrap him up,' Jesus says, taking the towel away. He hands me the bags and says, 'Put one of these around each end, then one in the middle, then tie them down. Easy.'

I nod. 'Okay.'

'Okay. So pick him up and I'll pull the bag down over him.'

'Wait, wait,' I say. 'You pick him up and I'll pull the bag down.' I look down at Nick, sliced and diced and starting to smell.

'No way am I touching that,' Jesus says.

'Why do I have to do it?'

'Because you're the one who cut him open. You're the one who called me here, you're the one who needs my help, which means I am in charge.'

'So what?'

'So I'm in charge, so I'm telling you to pick him up. It'll only take a second. You hacked him up so you have to do all the gross stuff. And this is gross. That means you're picking him up. So, like, pick him up.'

'Oh man,' I say and take a step towards Nick. 'Fine, I'll pick him up. But cover him quick.'

Jesus opens up one of the bags, bringing it down so it catches the air like a parachute.

'Do this end first,' I say, pointing at Nick's feet. I kneel down and grab his legs, just above the ankles. I hold them up and Jesus slides the bag over the feet. I raise Nick's knees by the fabric of the jeans and Jesus manages to pull the bag up so it reaches Nick's stomach. I lift the body using the belt loops and Jesus fits the bag all the way around Nick's waist.

'There's one,' Jesus says. 'Now for the fun part.'

We stand looking down at Nick's glazed eyes, his torn face and the knife embedded in his neck.

'We should probably take that out,' he says.

'Let me guess. That's my job too, right?'

I step around and place one hand on the handle of the knife and pull but it doesn't budge. I put my other hand on the knife and pull again but still nothing. I look up at Jesus. 'It's stuck.'

Jesus purses his lips and kneels down. He puts one hand on the top of Nick's head, keeping his fingers away from the slashed cheek, and the other hand under Nick's jaw. 'Try now,' he says.

I pull again as Jesus holds Nick's head and there's a wet meaty rip as the knife tears out of Nick's throat. Thick yellow fluid runs out of the hole and Jesus and I step back, groaning in disgust.

'Man,' Jesus says, 'this is so gross.'

'What do I do with this?' I ask, holding out the knife.

'Put it in the kitchen. We'll get rid of it later. Let's take care of this.'

When I get back from the kitchen, Jesus is standing above Nick's head, opening a bag. I place one foot on each side of Nick's waist and Jesus says, 'Do it.'

I lean down and grab Nick's shoulders. His stiffening body lifts like a zombie and there's a huge sense of relief as Jesus pulls the bag down over Nick's head, covering his eyes.

Jesus pulls the bag further down and my hand slips in something cold and the body falls out of my grip, crashing to the ground with a meaty thud, stretching the bag.

'Shit man,' Jesus says. 'Be careful.'

'I'm sorry,' I say. 'He's slippery.'

'Just do it again. Carefully.'

I nod and take a deep breath. I get a firmer grip and lift the body again. Jesus pulls the bag down and I lift Nick by his waist and my hand slips into the wounds in his guts and inside is still warm and wet and rubbery and I pull my hand away as though it were burned and there are yellow and purple bits stuck to my palm and my fingers are dripping with a brownish syrup. My gorge rises in my throat and I have to clench my jaw to keep it down.

'Hold on,' Jesus says. 'Almost done.'

I nod and pick up the body by the first bag around the waist. The second bag is stretched all the way down and the two meet in the middle. Nick is finally covered and I realise I'm never going to see him again. The only emotion this brings is relief, enormous tides of relief that hit me in waves.

'I'll wrap a third bag around the middle,' Jesus says. 'You go and find some string or something to tie them down.'

I nod and leave the room, thankful to be away from the corpse. I wash my hands in the kitchen, scrubbing as much of the blood off as I can. Most of it is caked on and deep under my fingernails, so I have to scrub hard to get it off. I wipe my face where Nick's blood is smeared and afterwards it feels cold and clean. While I'm standing facing the sink I regularly check over my shoulder for an approaching figure draped in a white towel. I pick up the knife and run it under the faucet and the blood whirlpools down the drain. With a handful of tissues I begin to open cupboards, looking for something to tie the bags down. I can't find anything except a box of freezer bags so I take it back to the front room where Jesus has completely sealed the body in black plastic.

'What is this?' Jesus asks.

'Sorry, I couldn't find any rope.'

'What about electrical tape? That always works in the movies.'

I shake my head. 'We'll have to use these.'

'Man,' Jesus moans. 'And things were going so well.'

I place the knife on the table and we take all the small, clear bags out of the box and tie them together, end to end. This takes longer than I expect. When we have several lengths we tie them around Nick's neck and knees, then a lot around the middle where the bags join. Jesus hands the empty box back to me and I wipe it with the tissues before placing it next to the knife.

'Now what?' I ask.

'Go out and back your car into the driveway. Get as close to the house as you can. Pop the boot and do it all quickly and quietly, okay?'

I leave the house and walk quickly to my car, shocked and slightly scared at how well Jesus is handling all this, how easily he is doing all the tasks that need to be done, how he is never hesitant and seems to know exactly what to do. There is a pang of excitement as I think, we may just pull this off. We might actually get away with this.

I open the car door and get in, closing it quietly behind me. I turn the key and the car gasps once, heaves, then dies.

I sit in the silence for a moment, taking a second to appreciate the irony, then try again. Again, it coughs but does not start.

There's a burning sensation in my chest and I feel my ears grow hot as a rough realisation of what this might mean seeps into my head.

I knew this was going to happen. Doesn't this shit always happen when you least want it to?

I run my hands through my hair, which is soaked with sweat. Each time I twist the key in the ignition the car sends a burst of noise through the silent street before once more taking a final gasp and staying as it was, dead and useless. I know that if we waste much more time, we'll risk running into early morning joggers and commuters.

I look around in the darkness, expecting to see a white towel with red stains walking towards me. This freaks me out and I try to set my mind back on the task at hand.

I exhale deeply and turn the key once more, stomping the accelerator quickly then releasing, and the engine roars to life. I unexpectedly laugh with relief as I put the car into reverse and back it down the driveway into the shadow of the garage. I get out of the car and ease the door closed, then pop the boot and head back inside.

Jesus has dragged the body over to the front door. There is a slight trail on the carpet but it's not too bad.

Jesus says, 'What the fuck was wrong with the car? I could hear it from in here. It probably woke up half the damn neighbourhood.'

'It's alright now. It was just, I dunno, flooded or something.'

'It doesn't matter. Did anyone see you?' he asks.

'No. We don't have much time.'

'I know. Here, help me with this.'

I bend and grab one end of the bundle and Jesus grabs the other. He says, 'One, two, three, lift,' and we both stand up, holding the body between us.

I walk backwards out the door and the dead weight between us is so heavy it feels like I'm dragging it by myself. We carry it down the front step and towards the car, my hands slipping on the smooth plastic as the body seems to get heavier and heavier with each step. Finally we reach the car and sling the bundle into the boot. My back groans with relief and I stand up straight, stretching.

'He didn't look that heavy when he was alive,' I mutter.

Jesus nods, panting lightly. 'Come on,' he says. 'Final clean up. On the home stretch.'

We go inside and Jesus closes the front door. Again, we grab handfuls of tissues and wipe doorhandles and walls, whatever we can think of. Jesus says, 'Okay, that's as good as it's going to get.' I look around and there's still blood everywhere, but this does not matter as long as there is nothing to tie it to me.

'Finish up,' Jesus says, carrying the towel. He goes over to the table and picks up the knife and the empty box. 'Come to the car when you're done. Don't take too long, we're not out of the woods yet.' He walks out the front door, shutting it gently behind him.

The first signs of fatigue begin to hit me as I wipe the last surfaces in the kitchen. My eyes are stinging and my movements are slower than they should be. I'm working in a kind of trance and suddenly there's a knock at the front door.

I freeze on the spot, simultaneously icy cold and burning up. I keep completely still, afraid to move or breathe.

The knock comes again and a drunken voice yells, 'Nick, open up.'

I don't recognise this voice; it must be one of Nick's other friends. I realise the lights are on so this is why the drunk thinks Nick is awake.

'Come on, dude,' the drunk yells. 'I just need a place to sleep for a few hours. I won't be no bother, I promise.'

I remember to exhale and I stand there listening to what the drunk is doing. He seems to be standing outside the door, waiting for someone to let him in. The thought of impersonating Nick's voice and telling him to go away crosses my mind but it seems too problematic.

I hear footsteps across the porch and I wait to see what they're going to do. They pause for a moment, then start to walk away. I close my eyes and sigh with relief.

The house is pretty much clean of prints. I'm in the kitchen taking one last look around to make sure I haven't missed anything when I hear a noise at the front door. I'm wondering what it is and then my mind reels in horror as I remember the spare key in the fake rock in the garden, and then I recognise the sound as that of a key in a lock and I hear the door swing open and it feels like I have been punched in the stomach.

I peek around the corner and see the drunk standing just inside the doorway. He's looking at all the blood splattered on the walls and carpet with a confused look on his face.

'Nick?' he calls. 'You here, dude?'

He reaches out and runs a finger across the wall, smeared in brown from when Nick's carotid artery sprayed out, then rubs his fingers together under his nose.

'Nick?' he calls again. 'Is this blood, like, yours?'

He begins to walk through the house and I'm trapped in the kitchen and I know it's only a matter of time before he stumbles across me. I wonder if Jesus would be pissed off at having to get rid of two bodies and I decide he probably wouldn't appreciate it.

I can hear the drunk shuffling through the house, opening doors and closing them. Sometimes he calls out, 'Hello?' but mostly it's silent. I try to think of a way to distract him while I escape but my head refuses to function. I peek around the corner again and I see the drunk has left the front door open. I duck my head back as he re-enters the front room and stands with his hands on his hips, looking around.

If I can somehow lure him into the other end of the house I can make a break for the front door and get to the car. But how to distract him?

I think of all those movies I've seen where the hero throws a rock and the baddies go to investigate the noise, so I look around the kitchen for a rock but there isn't one. I see myself resorting to throwing a saucepan and scaring the drunk to death and I almost laugh. Then my eyes fall upon one of Nick's shot glasses. I pick it up with the tissues I'm still holding and look around the corner. As soon as the drunk turns his back I throw the glass as hard as I can down the hallway where it smashes against the wall.

The drunk spins around and yelps in surprise. 'Hello?' he calls again and cautiously walks towards the corridor. As soon as he is a short way down I start towards the front door, moving as quickly and quietly as I can. Then the cool night air washes over my face and I'm taking my keys from my pocket, climbing into the car and it starts first time. I slam it into gear and then I'm pulling out of the driveway and down the road.

I'm driving through the empty suburban streets when the scratching starts.

It's now almost four-thirty. It seems like a lifetime ago since it all started, but it has only been a matter of hours. Jesus is... I don't know where.

I see visions of a white towel, stained with blood, standing in the street ahead of me. I periodically turn my head to check the back seat for any dead bodies that may be stalking me.

The streets are deserted and silent and I'm driving in a daze and it takes me a minute to focus on the scratching. At first I think I'm imagining it, that my mind is playing tricks, but it comes again, louder, then the scratching becomes knocking and it is, in fact, coming from the boot.

I find a dark side street and pull over. My heart is beating at a million miles an hour as I climb out of the car and stand looking at the boot. Something inside is definitely knocking on the hatch, trying to get out.

I see myself opening the boot and a white towel lunging at me from the interior.

I tell myself it can't be Nick. It can't be.

I brace myself and take a step forward, opening the boot in one smooth movement. I scream and take a step back in a horror as a white towel with red stains sits up from the darkness, crying out.

I continue to scream as I'm running down the street, putting as much distance between myself and the car as possible. My mind is yelling, I knew this would happen, I knew this would happen, with each stride. From the car I hear Nick's voice call out, 'Stop, wait,' and I am giddy with terror.

I risk a look back over my shoulder at the figure standing beside the car and it takes off the towel and then I realise it's Jesus.

I stop running and stand doubled over, panting. After a moment of collecting my thoughts, I begin to walk back to the car. Jesus is leaning against the boot and I come very close to punching him in the mouth.

'What the hell are you doing?' I demand. 'You almost gave me a fucking heart attack.'

'That guy arrived,' he says, 'and this was the only hiding space.' He looks into the boot at the black bundle and says, 'That was a really creepy ride.'

'Why the towel?' I ask. 'Why were you under that?'

'In case he opened the boot.'

'Why the fuck would he open the boot?'

'I don't know,' he yells. 'He was drunk. Drunks do weird things.'

I begin to get my breath back and my fear under control. I tell him, 'Don't you ever do anything like that again, alright? Scared the living shit out of me.'

'I'm sorry,' he says. 'Did you think I was Nick?' He starts to laugh.

'What's so funny? I don't find it funny at all,' I tell him.

Jesus says, 'Once someone is dead, they stay dead. They don't come back.' After a moment, he asks, 'Did that guy see you?'

'I don't think so. Even if he did, he was too drunk to remember what I looked like.'

'It's a good thing he was there,' Jesus said.

'What? Why?'

'Think about it. He's leaving fingerprints all over the place.'

It dawns on me.

'Come on,' Jesus says. 'Let's go.'

'What are we going to do?' I ask. 'Where are we going?'

'To the rubbish dump,' he says. 'Quickly.'

We arrive at the dump and the sky is turning orange in the east. The noise of daily life is starting to pick up and there are more cars on the roads.

'We have to do this fast,' Jesus says. 'Garbage collectors are most active in the mornings. This is their natural habitat.'

I park the car at the back of the dump and Jesus and I haul the body from the boot. We drag it over the sand and into the vast dunes of rubbish. The black bags around the body blend in perfectly.

'We need to bury it,' Jesus says.

'Okay,' I murmur, and begin to collect smaller bags from around the dump.

Bye, Nick, I think. Rest in peace. I can't help but laugh. He's where he belongs now.

We cover him with garbage.

Jesus drags an old washing machine over and pushes it down onto the body. Together we lift an old television set and hold it over the corpse, looking for the best place to put it in order to conceal more of the garbage bags.

'Put it there,' Jesus says.

'No, here,' I say.

'Up there,' he says.

We walk separate ways and the television slips from our grasp, landing on a corner of the washing machine. The set shatters, breaking the vacuum tube and a noise like a gunshot rings out deafeningly over the silent dump. A flock of seagulls takes flight and they squawk noisily, fleeing from the explosion.

Jesus and I stand there, heads lowered, afraid to move. We look around for any signs of movement, for anyone that may have heard the blast, but the dump is deserted. After a moment it becomes clear no one is responding to the noise and we both let out a sigh of relief.

'Here,' Jesus says, taking another black bag from his back pocket. 'I brought this for you.'

'Why?'

He points down and I follow his finger. For the first time I realise my clothes are dark red. They are drenched in gore and I am instantly revolted.

Jesus holds the bag while I strip off my shirt, shoes and jeans. I stand shivering in my underwear while Jesus walks away from the grave and throws the bag as far as he can.

We walk back to the car and Jesus says, 'One last thing.' He reaches into the boot and pulls out the knife and the box. He throws the box one way, the knife the other. He dusts his hands off and says, 'Let's get out of here.'

I get into the car and as soon as I sit down I am overcome with exhaustion.

'Not here,' Jesus says. 'You can't sleep here. Drive. Quickly.' He shows no signs of tiring.

I drive away, heading for Nick's so Jesus can pick up his car.

'At least that's the hard part done,' I mutter.

'That's the easy part,' Jesus says. 'Wait till you realise. Let's see how well you sleep tonight.'

TWENTY

Jesus is wrong: I sleep like a baby.

I get home and go straight to the bathroom. I get in the shower, not caring if it wakes my gran, and wash the blood off my face and out of my hair. Afterwards I dry off and stumble to bed, where I collapse from exhaustion. I'm asleep ten seconds after my head touches down.

I wake up mid-afternoon. I wonder for a moment why the muscles in my arms are sore, then I remember. If I move my arm in a stabbing motion the muscles burn all the way to my shoulder. I get up and get something to eat, feeling surprisingly well rested. I think back over the night's events and there is still no guilt. Instead there is a massive sense of relief, like a weight has been lifted from my shoulders.

I walk around the house cheerfully, thinking of Jade and how the last obstacle between us is now gone. I think I may actually give my gran something to eat instead of just leaving out leftovers. I'm feeling like there is a clear path ahead of me and nothing else can go wrong.

There's a knock at the front door.

When I open it there are two men in black suits standing there.

'Good afternoon,' the first one says. 'I'm Detective Jacobs, this is Detective Abrahams. We'd like to have a word with you. Can we come in?'

'Sure,' I mutter, and I know the surprise on my face is genuine.

We're sitting in the front room, me in my usual chair, the pair of them sitting on the social worker's couch. I'm trying not to look as panicked as I feel. Jacobs leans forward, his elbows on his knees as he speaks. Abrahams leans back with a notebook on his lap.

'We can understand you're very upset,' Jacobs says, 'but we'd like to ask you a few questions, if you feel up to it.'

'Sure,' I say. 'Sorry, this is all just a bit of a shock.'

'I know,' he says. 'We're sorry you had to find out like this.'

I nod. 'Are you sure he's dead? I mean, he hasn't just run away or anything?'

Jacobs shakes his head. 'No, he's dead. We got a call this morning from a person at the scene. Our enquiries determined that Mr. McCarr was deceased.'

'Who called you? And how do you know?'

'I'm afraid we can't disclose that at this point.'

'Was it a burglary? Someone broke in and killed him?'

'There's nothing to suggest this was a burglary. We didn't locate any signs of forced entry and at this point we have been unable to determine if anything is missing. This means that Mr. McCarr probably let the killer into the house, so it may be someone he is familiar with.'

Jacobs smiles. 'How well did you know Nick?'

I laugh nervously. 'We were part of the same group. We'd go out on weekends and stuff.'

'Would you say you were close?'

'We were, once,' I tell them, 'but lately we'd grown apart a little.' I figure by mixing truth and lies I'll have more chance of sounding convincing than if I made the whole thing up.

I look over at the other detective, Abrahams, who is scribbling something in his notebook.

'You'd grown apart?' Jacobs asks. 'For any reason in particular?'

I shrug. 'Not really. Just a few differences of opinion. Am I the only person you've talked to so far?'

'No, we've talked to a couple of others, Jesus and Beau,' Jacobs says, looking at Abrahams for confirmation. Abrahams nods but remains silent. 'I believe they're part of your group, too. Who else is there?'

Abrahams stops writing to look up at me.

'There's Mel. Melinda Evans. She died recently.'

'I'm sorry to hear that,' Jacobs says as Abrahams begins writing again. I can hear the tip of his pen scratching the paper and it sounds like ants crawling everywhere. 'How did she die, if I may ask?'

'Bulimia. Her stomach ruptured.' I tell him this straight, looking at his eyes.

He nods. 'Not a nice way to go.'

'No, it wasn't. Can I ask how Nick died?'

'We can't release that information.'

'Please,' I butt in, trying to sound upset. 'Nick was a friend. I'd just... It'd make it easier if I knew, that's all. I know I shouldn't be asking, but I'm kinda freaked out right now and it'd just ease my mind a little.'

Jacobs sighs. He looks over at Abrahams, but he is looking at his notebook. Jacobs turns back to me. 'We don't know.'

'You don't know?'

'No. I really can't say too much, you understand?'

'Couldn't you just look at the body?'

'No, because it wasn't there.'

I try to look shocked.

Abrahams starts writing again, his pen scratching on the paper.

'That's how we know it's a murder,' Jacobs continues. 'Basically, there's blood all over the house, broken glass, everything that normally suggests a struggle, foul play. Forensics are putting together an idea of what they think happened. It has all the characteristics of a knife attack, and a savage one at that. All we need now is a body and a knife.'

'And a suspect.'

He smiles cryptically before continuing. 'You told us about Melinda Evans. Is there anyone else?'

'It doesn't matter, does it? She's only on the outskirts of the group, you know? She only sees us occasionally, she'd have nothing to do with this.'

'What's her name?'

'Do you really need to bring her into this?'

Detective Jacobs says, 'We'd just like to have all of the available information, so we don't miss anything. You know how it is.'

'Please, can we keep her out of it as long as possible? I can guarantee she had nothing to do with it.'

'How do you know?'

'I just do. I know her and I know she wouldn't do this.'

He sighs. 'We'll come back to it if we need to.'

'Thanks,' I say, and sigh.

'Can you think of anyone who might want to kill Nick McCarr?'

I shrug. 'I dunno. He was getting on a lot of people's nerves lately, but I don't know if it was enough for anyone to want to kill him.'

'How was he getting on people's nerves?'

'Just the usual stuff, you know.' It feels like I'm about to start sweating and I can almost feel my face turn red.

'What usual stuff?' Jacobs asks.

'Drunken stupidity. He'd get drunk and insult people. Start fights. Hit on people's girlfriends. Just a general lack of respect for people. That sort of thing.'

'Ah,' Jacobs says as Abrahams keeps writing. 'Did anyone in particular have a special dislike for Nick?'

'Not that I can think of.'

He nods and pauses for a moment, then says, quickly, 'I heard you and Nick had a fist fight recently.'

This catches me off guard. I try to laugh and say, 'Well, I wouldn't call it recently...'

'I heard it was after Melinda's funeral?'

'Yeah, but that was...' Something's not right. 'Hang on, I thought you didn't know about Mel? I just told you a moment ago?'

'We heard about her from your friend Jesus,' Jacobs says. 'We were just confirming it with you.'

'So what else have you already heard? What else are you confirming with me? Is this a test? Are you asking us all the same stuff to see if our stories match?'

Abrahams is still writing: scratch scratch.

'Was there a fist fight after the funeral?' he asks directly.

'Yes, there was.'

'Why?'

'Personal reasons.'

'Personal enough to maybe grow into a murder?'

'Do you think I killed Nick?'

'Was the reason you had a fight big enough to warrant you killing him over it?'

'I didn't kill Nick.'

'What was the fist fight over?'

'Nothing, we were drunk, it was just a fight, it was nothing.'

Scratch scratch.

'Did it have anything to do with Melinda's death?'

'Where did you get that idea?'

'We heard Nick blamed you for what happened.'

'Like I said, he was drunk. He wasn't all that bright when he was sober, let alone when he was pissed.'

'Being blamed for something you didn't do, especially something as big as that, can be a good reason to be mad at someone.'

'Yeah it is, but that doesn't mean I killed him.'

'Do you know who did?'

'No. I don't. I didn't know Nick was dead until you told me.'

'No one comes to mind?'

'No. Why don't you ask the guy who called you from the scene?'

'The guy who called from Nick's house?'

'If that's where it happened, yeah.'

Scratch scratch.

'I thought you knew that's where it happened?' Jacobs asks, feigning confusion.

'No. How would I know that?'

'You asked me before if anything had been stolen. If it was a burglary. So you must have known it was at his house. So let me ask you this: how did you know?'

'I didn't. A lucky guess, I just assumed…'

Jacobs nods and leans back on the couch. He looks over at Abrahams, who is tapping his pen against the page. He sighs. 'We know about Jade.'

My heart speeds up and I resist the urge to lick my lips.

'She's also in your group, right?'

I nod.

'Are you involved in a relationship with her?'

'We are friends.'

'But nothing more? Jacobs asks.

'No.'

'Do you want anything more?'

'Sorry, what does that have to do with anything?'

He shrugs. 'Just curious.'

Scratch scratch.

'Was Nick in a relationship with Jade?'

'Not that I knew of.'

'We heard they were getting pretty close.'

Jacobs looks down at my clenched fists and I have to cross my arms, hiding them from view.

'If they were,' I tell him, 'I didn't know about it.'

'Would you have minded if they were in a relationship?'

I shrug, trying to look noncommittal. 'If they wanted to that's their business, not mine.'

'True love,' Jacobs says, smiling. 'When we give up our dreams to make someone else happy.'

I've decided I don't like Detective Jacobs much.

'I guess so,' I say.

'Let me get this straight,' he says. 'You weren't in a relationship with Jade and neither was Nick, although you wouldn't have minded if he had been. Right?'

'Right.'

'So there was no tension between you at all. Right?'

'Maybe a little. Nothing too bad.'

'So it would have bothered you a little if they were together?'

'A little, but nothing I couldn't handle.'

'But it would have bothered you.' This time it's not a question.

'Are you trying to, like, get a motive out of me or something? Am I going to need to get a lawyer or something soon?'

He smiles and opens his mouth to say something but then my gran walks in from the other room. The two detectives stand up. Jacobs introduces himself and Abrahams, who still does not speak.

'Would you like some coffee?' Gran asks.

'No thank you, ma'am,' Jacobs says, smiling, as they sit down.

'Are you policemen?' she asks.

'We're detectives, yes,' he replies.

'That's nice. Are you here to arrest us?'

He laughs. 'Not yet, no.' He looks at me. 'That reminds me,' he says. 'Where were you last night?' He's still smiling but watching me closely. Abrahams has stopped writing.

'What?'

'Last night. Where were you?'

'Why? Do you think I'm a suspect?'

'We're just trying to get all the available information,' he says, still smiling at me.

'I didn't kill Nick.'

'I'm not saying you did, I'm just asking where you were.'

'I was at home.'

He raises his eyebrows again. 'Home? Here?'

'Yes, here.'

'All night?'

'All night.'

'Hmm,' he says.

'What's "hmm"?' I ask. 'What are you hmm'ing about?'

'We've just got a conflict of information, that's all,' he says calmly.

Abrahams is writing, then he stops, then resumes. Scratch scratch.

My head begins to throb and it feels like my shoes are full of ants.

'Why?' I ask hollowly. 'What did you hear?'

'Are you sure you were at home last night?'

'Yes, I'm sure.' I look up at my gran. 'I was at home all night, wasn't I?' I ask her.

'I don't know,' she says. 'I don't remember.'

'I was, Gran,' I say, staring hard at her. 'Think about it. Last night. I was at home. Remember?'

She squints her eyes, thinking. 'Last night...'

'I was home.'

'You were home.'

'He was?' Jacobs asks.

'Yes,' Gran replies. 'He was home all night. I'm sure of it.'

'You're positive?'

'Yes. Positive. I'm sure he was home.'

'See?' I say, finally happy I seem to have won one.

'Hmm,' Jacobs says again. 'This is strange.'

'Where do you think I was?'

'Not here,' he says, and looks at me.

'So where was I?'

'You were out.'

'Out where?'

'According to my information, you were out with Jesus. At his house. All night.'

I pause for a moment. 'Oh,' I say, trying to laugh it off. 'That's right. I was out with Jesus last night, after all. Sorry, I just woke up before you got here, I've forgotten what day it is. With all these questions I've got mixed up… Sorry. Yes, I was out with Jesus last night.'

Abrahams is writing, writing.

'I thought you were here?' he asks.

'No, that must have been the night before.'

'You're sure?'

'Yes. Very sure.'

Jacobs looks up at Gran. 'He was at home last night?' he asks.

'All night,' Gran says.

To me, 'Which is it? Were you here or with Jesus?'

'I was with Jesus.' I look at Gran. 'I was out last night, Gran. Remember?'

'No, you were here, all night,' she says.

'No, that was the night before. Think about it. I was out last night. I was home the night before. Remember?'

She's thinking. 'Maybe,' she says. 'I'm sorry,' she says to Jacobs. 'My memory isn't what it used to be.' She laughs at herself, embarrassed.

'So you can't definitely vouch for his whereabouts over the last two nights?' Jacobs asks her.

'Not really,' she says sadly. 'But he's a good boy. And if he says he was at home, then he was at home.'

He looks at me, clearly angry but trying not to let it show.

'So you were out with Jesus last night?'

'Yes.'

'All night.'

'Yes.'

Scratch scratch.

'Okay.' He looks at Abrahams. 'I think that's about it for now. Do you mind if we come back later if we think of anything else?'

'Do I have a choice?'

He smiles again. 'That's it, then. We'll see you later. Have a good day, folks.' He says to Abrahams, 'Ready?'

Abrahams leans forward. 'One last thing,' he says.

He pauses for what seems like ages and there is an electricity in the air as I wait for him to speak for the first time. He looks down at his notebook, then up at me, then back at the book. Finally he looks back up and he asks, 'Do you know who won the silver medal for the women's speed skating in the 1986 Winter Olympic Games?'

I consider this very carefully before answering. 'No. I don't.'

He raises his eyebrows. 'Really?' he says accusingly, and turns back to his notebook.

'What the hell does that have to do with anything?' I demand.

He turns the notebook over and I can see there's a crossword puzzle sitting on his lap. Most of the squares have been filled in.

'Thanks for your time,' Jacobs says.

When George arrives an hour later I'm sweating and shaking uncontrollably. He gets me a glass of water and sits me down.

'I did it,' I tell him in rush. 'I killed him.'

'Nick?' he asks bluntly.

'Yeah. Nick. He's dead.'

'When? Last night?'

'Yeah.' I tell him the whole story, leaving nothing out. When I am finished he sits there calmly, nodding.

'So you got away with it?' he asks.

'For now, anyway. Those two detectives though, they seemed to think I had something to do with it.'

'Nah, they were just sweating you,' George says. 'Testing you to see how you'd react.'

'My reactions weren't that great. I may as well have signed a confession then and there.'

'Not yet. Don't give anything away until they come at you with evidence. And from what you've told me, that won't be the easiest thing to find.'

'What the hell was I thinking? It was a mistake, such a huge mistake, I never should have done it. Was I out of my mind? Oh man, I am in so much trouble...'

George listens to my rant patiently before saying, quietly, 'Shh.'

I stop and look at him.

'Was it a mistake?' he asks. 'Really? Nick is gone and no one knows it was you except Jesus and myself and for now that's nothing we can't handle. Don't think it was a mistake until you're sure of it. Because at this point in time it's looking like the right thing. Granted it's only been a couple of hours, but it never hurts to think positive, right?'

'But how did they find me so fast? It only happened last night and they were here the very next day...'

'The drunk,' George says. 'He went to Nick's house, saw the blood and called the police. The cops came and treated it as a murder investigation. They didn't only find you, they also found Jesus and Beau. And Jade. You were probably just one of the numbers in Nick's phone book. It doesn't mean anything so don't panic.'

George's words are registering but he's a long way from calming me down.

'I can't believe I actually killed him,' I mutter. I say it over and over, 'I can't believe it, I can't believe it.'

'You'd better stop saying that or someone's likely to hear you.' George sighs and says, 'Look, in the scheme of things, it's no big deal. One life doesn't amount to shit. Things die all the time and they just add to another thing's life. We can't live without death. Life is death. It's the whole circle of life thing; something dies which means something else can take its place. One thing feeds off something else to make it stronger. You fed off Nick, that's all. He was a smaller fish and he got in your way. It's all very Buddha-ish. He died to give you life. His death will make your life better. So don't sweat it.'

I snort a laugh. 'I don't know what to say to that.'

'Don't say anything. Just agree with it. Stop worrying. Keep your wits about you and try to spot any holes in the story. Plan ahead but don't panic.'

I think back to the social worker telling me that people who go the extra distance usually get what they want. People who put themselves on the line come out in front.

'What do you think the odds are of Jesus keeping his mouth closed?' George asks.

'I don't know. He made it through Jacobs' questions, and if he was as tough with Jesus as he was with me then I think Jesus is pretty reliable. As crazy as that is.'

'That's good. If Jesus keeps up his end of the story then you've got no problems at all. And now that he's talked to the police and denied any involvement he's in it almost as deep as you are. Do you think he'll change his mind?'

'I don't know.'

George nods. 'Keep an eye on him.'

'I will. I'll be fine, right?'

'Don't stress. You'll get through this.'

'I sure hope so.'

George smiles. 'Trust me.'

Jesus calls me later that night and suggests we meet up and discuss what has happened. I agree, feeling that I should remain on good terms with Jesus for as long as I can, despite how I may feel about him. I don't want to be alone with Jesus so I call Beau and tell him to meet us later, too. After some internal debate, I also make a call to Jade and, for once, she answers.

Beau says, 'We're dropping like flies.'

Beau, Jesus and I are sitting at a table in a bar. It's not a club this time; we needed to go somewhere quiet where we can talk. Jade has not yet arrived and I did not tell her what the purpose of this meeting was. The three of us nurse a beer each I know it's only a matter of time before we move onto something stronger.

'What the hell is going on?' Beau asks the table. 'I know Nick was a dickhead, but who would do something like this? What kind of fucked-up piece of shit would break into his house and cut him up?'

Jesus and I exchange a look.

'I don't think they broke in,' I say after a moment. 'Apparently Nick let them in.'

'Which just makes it worse,' Beau replies. 'It means Nick knew who it was. Which means, quite possibly, that we know them, too.'

'Don't jump to conclusions,' I say. 'We don't know anything yet. Let's just let the police do their work and they'll find whoever did it.'

Beau snorts. 'I hope they do. As if losing Mel wasn't bad enough, now we've lost Nick, too.' He takes a sip of beer. 'Fuck,' he says. 'I've got to hire another funeral suit.'

The door of the bar opens and Jade walks in. She scans the room and sees us sitting at our table. She smiles and walks over.

'Hey guys,' she says. 'How is everyone?' She sees our faces and her smile fades, replaced by a look of concern. 'What's wrong? What happened?'

'Sit down, Jade,' Beau says. 'Better yet, get a strong drink, then come sit down.'

There are no tears. As Beau relates the story Jade's face gets whiter and whiter but she doesn't cry and I find this tremendously relieving. The thought of sitting here watching her cry over Nick McCarr makes my stomach turn.

She doesn't say anything for a while. Shocked, she asks, 'Do you think the police will come see me?'

Beau says, 'I don't know. Hopefully not, but something tells me they will. Just, you know, be prepared.'

She shrugs and laughs nervously. 'What can I tell them? I mean, I don't know anything.'

'When was the last time you saw Nick?' Beau asks.

'What does that have to do with anything?' I interrupt.

'Just asking.'

'I saw him… Oh god, I saw him right before he died.' Her eyes go wide and she covers her mouth with her hands. 'Oh my god, the police think I did it, don't they?'

'No, they don't think anything,' I tell her quickly.

'I was the last person to see him,' she says. 'I must be a suspect.'

'If they thought you were a suspect, they would have visited you already,' I assure her.

'Do you think I did it?' she asks us. 'You do, don't you?'

'No, of course not.'

'Then why did you ask me when was the last time I saw him?' she asks Beau.

He replies, 'I'm not accusing you of anything, Jade. Believe me, you're the last person who I think did it.'

'So who do you think did it?'

'How can he know that?' I say.

'I don't know,' she says, her voice breaking. 'I don't know what to think. People are dying here. Everything is falling apart. First Mel, now this…' She stops and covers her eyes.

'Don't be upset,' I say reassuringly. 'It'll be okay.'

'No, it won't,' she says. 'Nick's dead. Mel's dead. Who's next?' She lets out a sob and says, 'I was the last person to see Nick alive.'

'Don't worry about the police. You didn't do it, so you've got nothing to worry about,' Jesus says.

'They'll find whoever did it,' Beau says. 'Don't worry about that. Then we can all sleep a little easier.'

I force a smile, nod, and take a drink.

I move from beer to bourbon and Coke and then to straight bourbon. No matter how much I drink, I can't seem to get drunk. My head starts to buzz and then I get sleepy but there is no drunk phase. This angers and disappoints me immensely so I have another drink to allay this mood.

Jade excuses herself, saying she doesn't much feel like being out right now and she needs to be alone. We tell her again not to worry about the police and we'll see her over the next couple of days. She nods and leaves.

Talk revolves mostly around our visits from detectives Jacobs and Abrahams. We take turns in relaying our tales and comparing the questions asked and I am greatly relieved to learn that the same questions were asked of the others, too. It seems they pressed Jesus quite hard for answers, which worries me, but he didn't let anything slip. He was the one who told them about Mel and Jade but the police seemed to figure out the Jade-Nick-Me triangle for themselves. I'm slightly comforted that this was all he told them, which is insignificant compared to what he could have, but it still worries me that they are leaning heavily on the one person that can bring the whole thing crashing down.

From what I gather, the detectives seem to have no real leads at this point and they are just clutching at straws; asking us various questions to see what kind of reaction they get. This is vaguely reassuring, and I know as long as Jesus and I stick to our stories there is nothing to worry about. As far as I'm concerned they may think I have a motive, but they have no evidence and no body, so for the time being I am safe on solid ground.

Twenty-one

I'm sitting at Beau's house watching television though neither of us seems to be paying it much attention. It's just supplying noise, which is better than silence under the circumstances.

'I was thinking about what Jade said,' Beau tells me.

'Yeah? What was that?'

'She said, first Mel, now Nick. Who will be next?'

'It was just an expression. I don't think she really believes any more of us are going to die.'

'It makes you wonder, though.'

'Death comes to everyone. A lot of the time it is unexpected.'

'True. But two people in the same group in a matter of weeks?'

I tell him, 'It probably wasn't anything to do with Nick, personally. It might have just been some random thing.'

'Oh, that makes me feel so much safer.' Beau pauses, then says, 'You can't be too careful, you know.'

'What does that mean?'

He watches the television for a moment more before standing

up and disappearing down the corridor. He returns carrying a shoebox.

I'm almost afraid to ask what's in it.

'It's my dad's,' he tells me. 'I've known about it since I was only small. He's had it hidden away for so long that I figure he's forgotten about it, so I went over the other day while he was out and took it from the cupboard.'

Beau opens the shoebox and reaches inside. He lifts out a gun.

'He hasn't noticed it's missing so far, so hopefully he won't, at least until all this has died down.'

'Don't you think you're overreacting?'

'Not at all. If someone could do that to Nick, what's to say they couldn't do it to me, too?'

'Maybe whoever did it had a grudge against Nick?'

'And what if someone has a grudge against me?'

We sit there, looking at the gun clenched in Beau's fist, shining in the light of the television.

'Is it loaded?' I ask.

'Yeah,' he says and I don't know if he's joking. 'Want to hold it?'

'No thanks,' I answer quickly, my mind jumping straight to the word fingerprints.

'Alright,' he says, and places it back in the box, closing the lid.

'What if the police find out you have it?'

'They won't.'

'It just seems like a risk, is all.'

'I know,' he says. 'But isn't that what life's all about?'

Jade calls me and asks if I want to meet for coffee.

At first I panic when the phone rings, worried it's going to be the police, and I am relieved then overjoyed when Jade speaks instead of a detective. We agree to meet at a local coffee shop and

I tell her I'll be there in half an hour. As soon as I hang up my hands begin to shake as my heartbeat increases tenfold and I almost lapse into hysteria over what I am going to wear.

I get there before she does and I stand in the little bathroom looking at myself in the mirror. I have trouble breathing and I know there is no point in hiding so I stand tall, inhale deeply and head back out into the café. I make my way over to a vacant table and sit down, forcing myself to sit still.

Jade walks in before I have time to leave. She looks around, sees me, and walks over.

'Hi,' she says, smiling as she sits down. 'How are you?'

'Alright,' I tell her.

'Thanks for meeting me, I just needed someone to talk to. I was suffocating and... well, thanks.'

'Of course. Any time.'

She lets out a long breath and scans the café. She looks at me and smiles and I can tell she's tired but trying not to let it show. She says, 'I haven't been out like this for a while. I mean, having a coffee, talking like a normal person. This is what normal people do, isn't it?'

'I assume so. I don't know how normal I am, so...'

She laughs and I relax slightly.

A waitress comes over and takes our orders. I ask for a flat white and Jade asks for a hot chocolate. The waitress nods, smiles, writes something down and walks away.

I turn my attention back to Jade. I ask, 'How are you, really?'

Her smile fades sadly. 'I'm okay. I'm handling it. We're all handling it, aren't we? We don't have much of a choice.'

'Did the police come and see you?'

She nods. 'They did. They asked me all sorts of weird questions.'

'Weird? Like what?'

She laughs. 'Like if you and I ever dated.'

This throws me. I have no idea what to say to this.

Mister... something...

I force a laugh. 'What did you say?'

'I said no. They also asked if Nick and I ever dated and I told them no to that, too.'

'It's been a while since it happened. If they had any leads you'd think they'd have acted by now.'

'It's been less than a week.'

'It seems a lot longer.'

'It does,' she agrees.

The waitress brings our cups. She places them in front of us then walks away again.

Jade looks down into her chocolate and stirs it with a spoon. 'Do you miss him?' she asks without looking up.

I pause for a moment, thinking of how to answer this. I finally say, 'I try not to think about it. Do you?'

'Sometimes. I hardly knew him.'

'I know. It's still hard, though.'

'Yeah.' She looks up, trying to brighten. 'So. Are you going back to uni?'

I shrug. 'It seems kinda pointless.'

She pauses then says, 'You miss Mel, don't you?'

'I guess so. I try not to think about that, either.'

'Don't forget her.'

'I won't forget. I'll always remember her, but... she's gone. If I dwell on her it's just going to lead to bad places. Things have to be kept in perspective.'

'That's easier said than done. When I first met you, you didn't seem very happy.'

'I wasn't.'

'But now you are?'

It's almost ten seconds before I answer. 'I don't know. I think now I can just hide it better. How can anyone be happy after what's happened?'

'I don't know. Come on, let's not discuss this. We're trying to get our minds off things. Be happy.'

I nod and smile. 'Okay. We're being happy.'

I take a sip of my coffee.

I tell her, 'When I was younger, my father once told me that you have to make your own happiness. That it isn't something that happens by accident.'

'That's fairly true, I guess.'

'He said paradise wasn't a place, it was somewhere in your mind. I didn't understand him at the time but it makes more sense now.'

'How long ago was this?'

'I don't know. A long time. I think he was right, though. That's maybe the only right thing he ever told me. Paradise is somewhere you find in yourself.'

'How do you think you get there?'

'I wish I knew.'

'We keep going,' she says. 'We don't give up. Things will get better. Keep walking the road and see where you end up. You'll find where you're going along the way.'

I nod slowly.

She says, 'I think we're here for a very short time so do with it the best you can. Try not to hurt anyone because they're just trying to make their way, same as you. Everyone is walking the road, which is sometimes very long and most of the time very lonely, so try and hold someone's hand to make the journey a little more pleasant and hopefully someone will hold yours, too. Maybe that's enough of a reason to keep going. Now and forever.'

I know now, more than ever before, that I am totally in love with Jade.

I tell her, 'That's a pretty good way of looking at things.'

She smiles. 'It makes sense to me.'

I look at her and ask her to tell me about herself. I don't know anything about her.

She smiles enigmatically. 'Wouldn't you prefer it that way? Keep the mystery alive?'

'Where were you born? Do you have any brothers or sisters? What do your parents do? What did you want to be when you were younger? Favourite actor? Favourite song? Book that has inspired you the most? What are you most proud of in your life, if anything? All those clichéd questions.'

She sits smiling at me as I recite this list. She says, 'Ask me again. Slowly.'

'Where were you born?'

'In a hospital.'

'Do you have any brothers or sisters?'

'I don't remember.'

'What do your parents do?'

'Whatever they want.'

'What did you want to be when you were younger?'

'Grown up.'

I look at her. 'We're not going to get anywhere with this, are we?'

She smiles. 'Are these things you really need to know? Is this going to help classify me in some way? You need these facts to make an opinion of me?'

'No, I just thought it'd help me get a better understanding of you.'

'Why do you need to understand me? Do you think I understand you?'

'No, but...'

'Does anyone really understand anyone else?'

'I guess not.'

'Of course not. We've known each other for a while and we've never needed to discuss this before. Why start now? Why ruin the mystery of each other?'

I can't help but smile. 'Alright, fair enough. No more stupid questions.'

'Good. The past is only a story. What matters is what lies ahead.'

'And what does lie ahead?'

She smiles in that way. 'Let's just wait and see.'

The thought of Dawson begins to invade my head with alarming regularity.

I find myself thinking about him when I wake up in the mornings; I wonder what he is having for breakfast, what sort of shampoo he uses, what his aftershave smells of.

He creeps into my thoughts throughout the day. I picture him sitting at a desk, typing words into a computer or filling out a form with an expensive pen. I see him having lunch in one of those posh cafés, then going out for drinks after work with his colleagues. I see him sitting in a brightly lit bar drinking Scotch on the rocks; no cheap beer in a dim sports bar for him.

In the evening I see him going to a restaurant and ordering whatever he feels like without needing to first consult the price. He orders wine by the year instead of the colour and his food comes with extravagant garnishes and the meat cut into attractive shapes. He will leave a large tip after charging the meal to his platinum credit card before going home and soaking in a large bath. He'll get out and put on a large fluffy robe before sitting in a plush recliner and watching a foreign film, the kind with subtitles instead of dubbing.

I think of all this while I go without breakfast and spend the day ambling around trying to think of what to do, of why I am so depressed. I think of this while I sit in a noisy club drinking warm beer or a weak B&C. I think of this while I eat my Big Mac then go home and sit on a lumpy couch while my gran watches reruns of old sitcoms.

Things should not have worked out this way.

Jesus calls me and asks if I want to go out clubbing.

'I dunno man,' I tell him. 'I don't know if I'm really in the mood.'

'Come on,' he says, 'it'll be great. We'll have a few drinks, do a bit of dancing, it'll be just what we need to take our minds off… you know.'

I don't like the way he drops Nick into the conversation.

I tell him, 'Okay. I'll see you there.'

'Great,' he says, 'Bye.'

I think I just need to keep him happy for as long as I can. Just until this whole thing blows over.

I get to the club and wait in line for about twenty minutes. I haven't been to Bassment before so it's all new to me; the music is of the typical club variety, in that there isn't much variety. It's all fairly repetitive, the thump thump of the bass, over and over. I know this is the sort of stuff Jesus likes so it explains why he wanted to come here. The club is filled with flashing lights and everyone is moving very quickly. It's obvious most people are on drugs of some sort, probably Ecstasy, and I fight my way over to the bar.

I tell the guy I'd like a beer.

'No beer,' he yells over the music, shaking his head.

'Oh. Okay. Bourbon and Coke then, thanks.'

He shakes his head again. 'Cocktails only. This is a cocktail lounge. We only do cocktails.'

'Fine. Give me a cocktail then.'

'What sort?'

'I dunno, anything. Something strong.' As he walks away to make it, I add, 'I think I'm gonna need it in this place.'

He brings me back a tall glass that is filled with green liquid. It has one of those little umbrellas.

'Thanks,' I mutter, and take a sip. It tastes like fruit juice so I finish it in a couple of mouthfuls. I don't want to know what was in it.

My phone goes off and I think it's Jesus but I can hardly hear him over the noise. I yell into the phone that I'm at the bar and hang up, not knowing if he heard me. I really don't want to be here, especially with Jesus, so if he doesn't arrive in five minutes I decide I'm going to leave.

I look into my empty glass and decide I want another one. I hold it up and the guy nods and begins to make another.

Someone taps my shoulder and it's Jesus.

'Hey,' he says. 'How are you? What do you think of this place?'

I tell him it's interesting. They don't serve beer.

'No, it's a cocktail lounge. Only cocktails.'

'Yeah, I got that.'

The guy brings another one of the green drinks over.

Jesus asks, 'What are you drinking?'

'One of these green things,' I tell him.

He nods. 'Right.'

'Is Beau coming?'

'No. I thought it could be just us tonight.'

I finish the drink in one single gulp.

'Another?' the bartender asks.

'Sure.'

'Want to dance?' Jesus asks.

'Not right now, thanks.'

The bartender brings my third drink over and Jesus tells him he'll have what I'm having.

'Why didn't you invite Beau?'

'I thought this would give us a chance to talk.'

'About what?'

'You know… about everything.'

'There's nothing to talk about.'

'What are we going to say to the police?'

'Nothing. We've already covered all that. We told them nothing and we're going to stick to our story.'

'What if they come back? I held them off once but I don't know if I can do it again.'

I'm not sure if this is some sort of vague threat so I say, 'Just do your best. We're both in this now. This is no time to be doubting yourself. We're in this together.'

'Yeah, we are, aren't we? Partners in crime.'

'Sure. Whatever. Just don't blow the game. We're almost out of the woods.'

'Don't worry,' he says. 'I won't blow it. I've helped you this far, I won't let you down.' He smiles.

I hate it how he makes it sound like I owe him, like he's got something hanging over my head and I will be forever in his debt. He doesn't realise that he is in it as deep as I am.

I force a smile back. I drink my green cocktail and it must be strong because the three I've had in the last few minutes are starting to affect me.

'I was thinking maybe next weekend we could go to that new dance club they've been advertising on the television, if you're not doing anything?' Jesus suggests.

'Oh, I dunno,' I say. 'I think I'm busy.'

'Yeah? What are you doing?'

'I'm... going out... with Jade.'

'Jade?' he says, eyebrows raised. 'That's cool.'

'Yeah,' I nod.

'You've been seeing a lot of her lately?'

'Sometimes.'

'Cool,' he nods, though not as enthusiastic as he was a minute ago, and for some reason this makes me feel better. 'I suppose you've seen more of her since Nick died.'

'I guess.'

'Yeah. They were pretty close, weren't they? And now that Nick's not around, she's found herself with a lot of free time. And now she also needs a shoulder to cry on.'

I turn to look at Jesus, who is staring hard.

'Would that be a safe assumption?' he asks.

'I dunno what you're talking about.'

'Don't you? It seems convenient that Nick died when he did.'

'What the fuck are you getting at?'

'You know what they say. There's nothing harder than watching the person you love love someone else.'

'That has nothing to do with anything. How the hell would you know anything about that?'

'I know,' he says, looking at the bar. 'Trust me, I know.'

I press my finger into Jesus' chest. 'Look, you already know what happened. Is a motive really that important at this time?'

He shakes his head. 'I guess not. We do crazy things for love.'

I laugh. 'Like go to stupid nightclubs and act like fuckheads?'

He smiles falsely. 'Like dispose of bodies,' he says, and walks off.

Mister Uh-oh.

I realise that I may have just fucked up this entire situation beyond repair.

The bartender walks over. 'You want another one?' he asks.

'What I want is a double bourbon and Coke.'

'Sorry, only cocktails,' he says.

I raise my voice and yell, 'Then get me a glass, put some bourbon in it, add some Coke and maybe a bit of ice and there you go, a fucking bourbon and Coke cocktail. Okay?'

He shakes his head at me and walks off.

'Fuck you,' I call after him. I close my eyes, take a deep breath, walk away.

Twenty-two

Jesus calls and asks if I want to go to the movies.

Jade and I are at another coffee shop and I excuse myself when my phone rings. I tell him I can't, I'm busy at the moment. He says okay and hangs up.

'Who was that?' Jade asks.

'No one important,' I tell her.

I do feel guilty over getting Jesus involved. The fact of the matter is I had no choice. As much as I hate to admit it, I could not have done it without him. If he had not come to Nick's, I would now surely be in prison. But this does not give him the right to force himself deeper into my life. He does not need to constantly hold it over my head, reminding me that he can break at any time and tell the police everything. The fact that he has this information infuriates me and I know there is nothing I can do; I simply have to put up with it.

Jesus calls and asks if I want to go out for a drink.

'Sorry,' I say. 'I have to feed my gran.'

The social worker comes the next day and the leftovers are out on the counter, ready. She asks how I'm doing and I tell her about the police coming.

'I know,' she says, nodding. 'They came to see me. They told me all about the murder.'

'They came to see you? Why? What did they want?'

'They wanted to know what you're like. Whether you'd told me anything that might help them in their investigation.'

'What did you tell them?'

'Nothing. I told them that anything we discussed was confidential, like it is with any of my other assignments. This pissed them off for a while but then I told them you hadn't said anything about murdering anyone; that's probably the sort of thing I'd remember, seeing as how it doesn't come up in conversation all that often.'

'What else did you say?'

'Very little. I told them we'd known each other for years and I didn't think you'd be the kind of guy to kill someone.'

It's good to see she knows me so well.

Jesus calls and asks if I want to go to a club.

I'm at Beau's so I tell him, I can't, sorry, I'm already out. Another time, though.

Beau has been getting rid of all his old furniture. First a couple of tables disappeared, then some chairs, and I didn't think very much of it. But now the couch has vanished and I ask him where everything is going.

'I've been giving it to charity,' he says. 'Doing some good.'

'But… what do you sit on?'

'I'm getting new stuff,' he says. 'I haven't been drinking as much, or doing as much drugs, so I've got all this spare money.

Plus my parents have been feeling sorry for me, with everything that's happened, so they've been paying me rather than talking to me. I thought it was time to get some nice stuff. I know it's pointless and very materialistic of me but I can't start acting like a better person until I feel like a better person.' He shrugs and says, 'Sitting on the floor gets really uncomfortable. I can't do the whole Buddha thing. I can be enlightened and still have good posture.'

'When does the new stuff get here?'

'A few days.'

'Cool. This sitting on the floor sucks.'

'Tell me.'

Jesus calls and asks if I want to go shopping.

I tell him I can't, I have no money.

He says that's okay, he just thought I'd like to go out somewhere.

'Thanks for the offer.' He starts to talk but I hang up.

Jade and I are out again. We go have a drink, then decide to see a movie. I don't know what movie it is or who's in it or what it's about and afterward I can hardly remember anything that happened. I'm too busy freaking out from sitting next to Jade in the dark for two hours. She laughs occasionally and I laugh along with her because I know something funny has just happened but I have no idea what. At one point our hands brush as we're reaching for the popcorn and my heart almost gives out.

Afterwards we get a coffee and Jade has a piece of cake and asks me what my favourite part of the movie was. I tell her I don't know, I liked all of it.

'But no favourite?'

I shrug and say, 'The end?'

She laughs and nods. 'Yeah. That was good. Very clever.'

'It was,' I agree.

'I like to see something with a happy ending for a change.'

'Yeah, it's nice. Doesn't happen very often.'

'No, it doesn't. Which is sad.'

I nod and pray things will have a happy ending.

I'm at home with George when my phone rings. The screen says it's Jesus so I don't answer.

'Tell him to fuck off,' George says.

'I can't. He knows too much. If I piss him off he'll go to the cops.'

'No, he won't. He would have done it by now if he was going to. It's like a for-real suicide attempt versus a cry-for-help one. The fake one stands on the ledge and waits to be talked down. The real one gets up there and jumps straight away.'

'He'll get the hint. I'll keep ignoring him and eventually he'll get the hint and stop bothering me.'

George says, 'He thinks because he helped you, you'll see how much he cares and realise some deeper feelings.'

'That sucks.'

'Yeah. But that's how his mind works. He's persistent, at least give him that.'

'I just want him to leave me alone. I didn't do it for him, I did it for Jade.'

'Don't say that,' George says. 'Don't ever say that. You did it for yourself.'

I scratch an ant that's running up my ribs.

*　*　*

Jade and I go to the beach.

It's the first time we've gone together and it's the first time we've been there in the daylight. It seems strange to be on the beach with her and not looking up at the stars.

We walk along the sand, watching the gulls sail around the sky.

George told me he'd teach me to fly one day.

Jade looks at me. 'Sorry? Did you say something?'

'No, sorry. Just talking to myself.'

She smiles. 'Okay.' We walk on in silence for a while before she says, 'Have you seen Jesus lately?'

I look at her, startled. 'Umm. I saw him a while ago. Why?'

'I haven't seen him much since Nick died. I just wanted to make sure he's okay.'

'I guess he is. He seems alright, from what I can tell. We're all handling it as best we can.'

'Beau seems to have changed a lot recently.'

'Yeah, he has. It's made him think a bit, reassess his life.'

'I admire him for that.'

'When did you see Beau?'

'The other night,' she says. 'Beau called Jesus, but he said you two already had plans.'

It must have been when we were at the cocktail place.

I say, 'Oh yeah. What did you do?'

She shrugs. 'We just hung out. Talked about everything. You know.'

I nod, warding off the pangs of jealousy.

'Thanks for coming out with me so much,' she says. 'It really helps.'

'It's no problem at all. I enjoy it.'

She smiles. 'Good, I'm glad. It's times like this when you realise how much you need people. Seriously,' she says, 'thank

KILLING RICHARD DAWSON 255

you. I couldn't have gotten through this without you. I know we're not through it yet but we've made a start. I'm holding up a lot better this way. So thanks.'

I'm about to tell her it's okay when she stops walking and hugs me.

I feel her arms dart around my neck and then she's pulling close to me. My heartbeat races and my lungs can't seem to get enough air. I slowly place my hands on her back and we stand there in the sunlight, listening to the waves break on the sand and we stay like that a while.

Driving home I replay our moment of contact in my head. The only thing that keeps pushing this thought away is her spending an evening with Beau. What infuriates me is I missed out on spending time with her because I was with Jesus instead.

I make up my mind, then and there, that I will tell Jesus to back off.

When I get home Jesus' car is parked outside my house. I groan as I see it and as I pull up he gets out and walks over to meet me.

'Hey,' he says.

'Hi.'

'You weren't home so I waited. I hope you don't mind.'

'Were you waiting long?'

He shrugs. 'I dunno.'

'Okay.' I walk away from the car towards the door to my house and he follows.

'Where were you?' he asks.

'At the beach.'

'With Jade?'

'Yes, with Jade. Is that okay with you?'

'Does it matter? It wouldn't change anything anyway, would it?'

I stop, sigh, turn to face him. 'Look, Jesus, I appreciate your helping me. I really do. But you've got to stop this.'

'Stop what?'

'This. This coming around, this calling me every day. I'll always be in your debt, but that doesn't mean you can hang over me all the time.'

'I didn't know I was.'

'Yeah, you were. So just, like, back off, okay?'

'Sorry. I just thought that, you know, seeing as how we're in this thing together...'

'I know. It's not that...'

'I mean, it's not like I'm risking anything for you. I haven't put my neck on the line at all. I wouldn't expect anything in return.'

'I don't know...'

'I wouldn't expect a little decency, a little friendship, because I'm dealing with all this really well. It doesn't bother me in the slightest that I helped get rid of the body of a good friend of mine, then lied to the cops about it. I'm not in the least bit bitter about being called to the rescue and then kicked to the sidelines.'

'I didn't kick you...'

'God forbid I should get looked after. Be nice to me? No way. He's only good for helping people out of tight situations. Other than that, fuck him. Let's treat him like shit because what's the worst he can do? Tell the police? No way, he'd never think of that.'

Jesus is breathing roughly. He looks straight at me.

He says, 'He'd never think of telling the police.'

I meet his eyes. 'You wouldn't.'

'Wouldn't I? Why not?'

'Because we're in this together.'

'I'm sure they'd give me a deal. I'll tell them exactly what happened, I'll even take them to the body, in exchange for immunity.'

'Maybe. But would you risk it?'

He shrugs. 'I don't need to tell the police. I could always tell someone else.'

'Who? What're you talking about?'

'I'm sure a certain lady friend of ours would love to hear what really happened to Nick. I wonder what she'd think of you after that piece of information came to light?'

I stare at him and ask, 'What do you want?'

'So now you're prepared to talk to me, huh?'

'What do you want?'

'Nothing much. Just to be treated civilly. Not to be forced out of the picture. You know.'

'Sure. I get it.'

He nods. 'Okay. Thanks.'

I grit my teeth and try to restrain myself.

He smiles. 'I knew you'd understand.'

I open the front door and he turns to walk away. 'By the way,' he says, and I reluctantly turn to face him. 'I was thinking of going out for a drink tonight. Interested?'

'Sure,' I growl.

He smiles again and I want to knock his fucking teeth out. 'Great,' he says. 'I'll pick you up at seven.'

Jesus starts calling me most days. He asks if I want to go out and I have to say yes. He drops lines about the police here and there, subtle enough to remind me. We go out for drinks, movies, coffee, everything.

Jade calls and asks me if I want to go out and I tell her I can't because I'm going somewhere with Jesus. Luckily she doesn't ask if she can come so I don't need to make an excuse as to why Jesus wants it just the two of us.

Beau calls and says he and Jade are going to the movies.

Jade calls and says she's going clubbing with Beau.

Jesus calls and tells me he'll pick me up at eight.

Jade calls and asks me to come out with her and Beau.

Beau calls. He's going out with Jade that night.

Jesus calls and tells me the plans for that evening.

Beau is going with Jade. And I'm stuck with Jesus.

One night, after Jesus and I go to a movie, we're walking around the streets and I look in a café.

Sitting inside is Dawson.

He's there with a beautiful woman, half his age, and they are smiling brightly at each other across the table, champagne glasses in hand.

'You okay?' Jesus asks when I stop walking.

'Fine,' I tell him.

I think of what Jade is doing tonight. She's probably out somewhere with Beau.

The chance I have been fighting for is passing me by. I've come this far and the whole thing is slipping through my fingers. I ask myself, what would George do?

'Let's go,' Jesus says and puts his hand on my shoulder.

This has pushed me too far.

Twenty-three

I lose sleep. My days blend together into one seemingly endless nightmare. I lie in bed, my thoughts haunted with images of Jade and Beau. Each morning I awake from my maximum forty-five minute sleep, wondering what day it is, wondering how long it will be before Jesus calls.

I lose track of what is imagined and what is real. My dreams creep over into my waking hours and I am no longer sure what I have actually seen and what my mind has conjured up.

The thought of losing Jade is unbearable. I am at risk of having her taken away just when we are starting to get really close.

I ask George what I should do.

He smiles. 'Fight fire with fire.'

He really is a bad influence.

I try to think of ways of bargaining with Jesus, ways of getting out of this fix he has me in. I try to come up with ways of getting to Jade without him finding out.

The social worker's voice comes back to me.

Go the extra distance. Get what you want.

I've come this far. In for a penny, in for a pound. There's no sense doing things by halves.

The whole time I'm driving, I keep telling myself how sorry I am. I tell myself he left me with no choice. I'm doing this because it's the only solution left.

I tell myself I'm sorry but I'm not sure if I believe me.

I wonder again if I'm doing the right thing.

It's better Jade hears it this way than from Jesus.

I realise that the right thing no longer matters; all that's left is the better thing, the lesser of the evils. Things really have sunk so low that I cannot differentiate between right and wrong, only what suits me better.

There is a touch of guilt at this thought but it fades quickly.

All you do is pull the trigger.

I walk into the police station.

The officer behind the counter looks up at me as I approach. She asks, 'Can I help you?'

I tell her I hope so. I'm here to see detectives Jacobs and Abrahams.

'Are they expecting you?'

'No.'

She picks up a telephone and punches in three numbers. After a moment she says, 'There's a gentleman at the front desk to see you.'

At first I don't know who she means.

'Hold on,' she says and cups the mouthpiece with her hand. 'What's it regarding?'

I look at her and tell her I have information concerning the murder of Nick McCarr.

* * *

'Hi,' Jacobs says. 'It's good to see you again.'

'Is it?'

'Sure,' he says. 'After our little chat last time, I was wondering if you'd come in and see us.'

I shrug and force a smile. 'Here I am.'

He nods. 'Here you are. So what can we do for you?'

We're sitting in a small grey room. I'm on one side of a table with Jacobs and Abrahams on the other. Jacobs sits close to the table and Abrahams sits further back, one leg crossed on top of the other.

I say, 'Before we get into anything, I need to know a few things.'

'Like what?'

'Like, if I give you information, I want to be safe.'

'From who?'

'Everything. You.'

'Us?' Jacobs says, raising an eyebrow.

'Yeah. I want it so you can't arrest me. What's it called? Immunity?'

Jacobs nods. 'That's what it's called. First we need to know that the information you've got is worth making a deal over.'

'I can tell you who did it. I can tell you where the murder weapon is.'

'How about the body?'

I shrug. 'Maybe. If it's still there.'

They exchange a look. 'So you've known all this time? Why are you only coming forward now?'

I look down, pretending to be conflicted. 'Guilt, I guess. Nick and I weren't that close and we had our problems, but he was still a friend. And no friend deserves to go through that.' I let out a long, tortured sigh before continuing, 'I just want this to be over. I haven't been sleeping lately and it's getting too much. I think it's time I came clean.'

'In exchange for immunity from prosecution?'

'Right.'

Jacobs says, 'We can't just give you full immunity. We need to run it by people higher up and we need to know that it'll be worth it. We'll discuss it afterwards, depending on what you give us. That's as good as you'll get, for now.'

I look back and forth between them. 'Alright,' I say. 'Deal.'

Jacobs nods and says, 'Good.' He presses a button on a tape recorder sitting on the table then introduces the three of us and gives the date and time. 'Okay,' he says. 'Let's have it.'

I let out a long breath. I say, 'Nick wasn't the most sensitive guy in the world. He knew I was interested in Jade yet he went after her anyway. With friends like him, who needs friends, right?'

Jacobs smiles but says nothing.

'Things got harder and harder between us. I asked him to stay away from her but he wouldn't. It led to one argument after another. He was completely insensitive to other people's feelings.'

I look around the room. 'Sorry,' I tell them. 'This is hard, you know, bringing all this stuff up again.'

'It's alright,' Jacobs says. 'Take your time.'

I watch the wheels spinning in the tape recorder and say, 'He wasn't just like this with me, either, but the whole group. It got to the point where everyone was mad at him. Then when he started blaming me for what happened to Mel, well, that pushed people too far.'

'Which people?'

I shrug. 'All of us. Myself, Jesus, Beau, all of us.'

'And one night it got too much,' he says. 'You snapped.'

I shake my head. 'No. I didn't.'

He leans forward over the table, staring intently. 'Then who did?'

I cover my eyes with my hands. I tell them, 'Jesus.'

He raises his eyebrows. 'Jesus?'

I nod. 'Yeah. It, uh, it was Jesus.'

'How do you know?'

'Because I was there.'

He leans back, surprised. 'Really? You were there? Tell me what happened.'

'I was asleep. It was about three o'clock in the morning. My phone rang and it was Jesus. He asked me to come to Nick's house. He didn't say why.'

'You're sure about this? We can check phone records, you know.'

'I know. Double check it. You'll find a call from Jesus' phone to mine.'

He looks at me for a moment, checking for signs of my lying. After a moment he says, 'Okay. Go on.'

'I went around there and parked in the drive. Jesus was there, and so was... Nick. Or what was left of him. There was blood all over the place. It was... disgusting.'

'What happened then?'

'We got rid of the body. We wrapped it in bags and took it to the dump.'

Jacobs and Abrahams exchange a look. They're both thinking the same thing I am: the murder was over two weeks ago. The chances of finding it in a dump, with all the new rubbish coming in all day every day, getting moved around and buried, are very slim. The chances of them finding my clothes, which I don't intend to mention, are even slimmer.

'What did you do with the weapon?'

'The knife? It's somewhere in the dump, too.'

It's hard for me to read Jacobs' expression.

'So you went around to Nick's house at three o'clock in the morning and helped clean up a murder?'

'Yes.'

'Why? Why did you help? Why didn't you call the police, or try to convince Jesus to?'

I sigh again, like this is very hard. 'Because I knew how Jesus felt.'

'What do you mean?'

'I empathised with him. We both know what it's like to lose someone we love. I was losing Jade to Nick. And Jesus was losing Nick to Jade.'

Jacobs' brow furrows. 'You might have to explain that a bit further.'

'I don't know if you know or not, but Jesus is gay.'

'Homosexual?'

'Yes. And he had, well, feelings for Nick.'

'So Jesus was angry that Nick was spending all his time with Jade?'

'Yeah. And like I said earlier, Nick wasn't very sensitive. When Jesus told him how he felt, Nick laughed in his face. He was really hard on him, taunting him all the time. Jesus tried to take it, but being humiliated by the person he loved, and seeing that person fall in love with somebody else, well, it was too much.'

'You knew how he felt. And, let's be honest, having Nick out of the picture benefited you, too, didn't it? Leaving Jade open.'

I shrug. 'Jade has her own mind. She can choose who she wants.'

'But it didn't hurt that he was gone.'

'I guess not.'

'So let's go through this one more time. Nick snubbed Jesus' advances, gave him a lot of shit and made his life hell. He then went and formed a relationship with someone else which pushed Jesus over the edge. He went to Nick's house to confront him over it and things got out of hand. He calls you and the pair of you get rid of the body. Does that sound about right?'

'Right.'

'Why didn't you tell us this straight away?'

'I don't know. Jesus made me promise to keep it between us. I thought I could live with it but I can't.'

Jacobs watches as I take a deep breath and let it out slowly. I look him in the eyes and tell him that Jade makes me want to be better. 'How can I deserve her if this is the sort of thing I do? She's worthy of someone better than me, so maybe by doing this, by doing the right thing, I can somehow atone for what I've done. I might lose her forever because of this but at least it'll be because I did the right thing. Isn't living honestly better than living a lie?'

'Maybe,' he says.

'I'm sorry for not telling you before and for dicking you around. I just… I just want it to be over.'

Jacobs nods and looks at Abrahams. Abrahams nods. Jacobs looks back at me and says, 'Understandable.'

'You said there was a witness at the scene. Did he not give you anything useful?'

Jacobs shakes his head. 'No. He was drunk, unfortunately. He remembers what happened but no details. He remembers going to Nick's house, letting himself in, then finding the house in a mess. Then he called us. That's it.'

'So he didn't see anything?'

'He saw a car parked in the driveway,' Jacobs says. 'He knows it wasn't Nick's but he doesn't remember the make, model or even the colour. We think the killer was still in the house when he arrived but managed to escape.'

I nod.

Jacobs says, 'We'll need to examine your car, of course. We'll contact you as soon as we get Jesus' statement.'

'Okay.'

Jacobs smiles and turns off the tape recorder. 'We'll see you real soon.'

I get a telephone call later that evening.

'You fucking bastard,' Jesus screams down the line and I have to hold the phone away from my ear. He continues yelling and I have a hard time understanding what he's saying.

'Jesus, calm down,' I tell him.

'Calm down? You're telling me to calm down? Do you know where I am? I'm in fucking prison. They arrested me for killing Nick. How can you do this? Do you have any idea what you're doing?'

'What makes you think I had anything to do with it?'

'Because you told them. I know you did, you asshole.'

'Did they tell you that?'

'They don't need to. Who else would have? Oh god, I can't believe you'd do this.'

'I didn't do anything.'

'Fuck you,' he screams and again I have to hold the phone away. 'I know you did and I'll expose you for this. I'll tell them everything. It'll be your word against mine.'

I don't know if anyone is listening in on this call.

'Jesus, I'm sorry,' I say. 'I couldn't live with the guilt of knowing what we'd done. I had to come clean. I'm sorry.'

'But I didn't do anything,' he screams, frantic. 'You're setting me up. I'm in here for something you did and you're going to let me take the fall for this, aren't you? Aren't you, you fuck?'

'Jesus, settle down. Come on, man, breathe.'

He screams hysterically, not even words this time, just a noise of pure rage and hopelessness. 'You can't do this to me. Please, come tell them what really happened. Please.'

'I'm sorry, Jesus, I can't.'

'Please, I'm begging you, please don't do this to me. I promise, I'll never bother you again, I'll leave you alone if that's what you want, I'll do anything you want me to, but please, please don't do this.'

'Jesus, I...'

'Goddammit, please. I'll leave the city if that's what you want. I'll move with my parents, we'll all go. God, my parents, my mother was hysterical when they took me away, you have no idea what you're doing to us. You're ripping all these people apart, you selfish prick, you're killing all these people. And for what? For a girl? You're destroying all these people for a girl?'

'Leave her out of this,' I tell him. 'That's none of your goddamn business.'

'This is all my business. You don't get much more involved than this. How can you do this? How can you live with yourself, knowing what you're doing?'

'What am I doing?'

'You're killing me.' He pauses, takes several deep breaths and his voice softens. 'You're killing me.'

'I'm not killing you. You did that yourself when you started blackmailing me.'

'I'm sorry, I really am, I had no idea it'd come to this.'

'Yes, you did. You threatened to tell the cops if I didn't do what you wanted. You knew exactly what you were doing.'

'So you got in first.'

I sigh. 'I didn't want this to happen.'

'Neither did I.'

'Yeah, well, it did, and you brought it on yourself. So deal with it.'

He screams again, his voice resuming its ear-splitting volume. 'How can you do this?' he asks again. 'Don't you have any fucking morals? Any decency? How can you watch an innocent person go down for what you did?'

'Innocent?' I yell back. 'Who's innocent here? You? You didn't wrap a corpse in plastic bags and take it to the dump? You haven't tried to blackmail me for the last few weeks?'

'That's because of you. I did it all for you.'

'You still did it.'

'I know.' He starts to sob. 'I did it and I regret it every moment. I'll regret it for the rest of my life.'

'I know. It's hard. But you'll get used to it.'

'I shouldn't have to,' he yells through his tears. 'I shouldn't have been put in that position in the first place. You're killing me here. How does that feel?' he hisses. 'How does it feel killing two people? How does it feel destroying two families?'

'I'm not sure,' I tell him and this is the truth.

'Please, just come get me out of here. We'll forget it all, put the past behind us. I'll leave you alone, I swear to God man, you'll never hear from me again.'

I think of Jade.

'I can't,' I tell him. 'I'm sorry. There's nothing I can do.'

'Fuck you. There's plenty you can do. How about telling the truth?'

'The truth is… very subjective.'

'Get me out of here,' he howls. 'I don't deserve this. I never hurt you, you asshole. Please, please, get me out of here. Help me.' More to himself, he says, 'Please, God, help me out of here. Make him get me out of here. Please, God.'

'Jesus,' I say softly.

'What?' he asks.

I tell him softly, 'There is no God.'

His sobs redouble. 'Fuck you,' he cries with his hitching breath, his voice thick with despair. 'Get me out of here, you fuck, get me out of here.'

'I'm going, Jesus.'

'Don't leave me,' he pleads, hysterical. 'I'm begging, please don't leave me.'

'Bye, Jesus.'

'Come get me out of here, please, I'm begging you, you fucking asshole.'

'I have to go,' I tell him.

'Don't, please, don't go…'

'I have to.'

'Don't you hang up this phone, you fucking…'

'Goodbye, Jesus.'

His screaming voice gets smaller and smaller as I lower the handpiece and it's cut off mid-yell as I hang up.

The house seems amazingly quiet. My ear is ringing from the exchange and there is a strange feeling in my chest. I sit for a while, staring at the phone, breathing deeply through my nose.

I pick up the phone, start to dial, then hang up.

I look at it for a while longer, then I pick it up once again, dial, then when she picks up, I ask Jade if she wants to go for coffee.

I get to the coffee shop and Jade is already there, and so is Beau.

'Hi,' I say, walking over. 'How are you?'

'Fine,' Jade says, smiling.

'Hey, man,' Beau says and we slap hands.

'Beau came along,' Jade says. 'I hope you don't mind.'

'No, of course not,' I say, sitting down, trying to look pleased.

'Haven't seen you around for a while,' he says. 'How's things?'

'Fine. Same as usual, you know.'

'We'll see you tomorrow?'

'Tomorrow? What's tomorrow?'

'Nick.'

It takes me a moment, but then I remember. The funeral. Nick's parents had been waiting for the police to find the body.

I tell them yeah, I'll be there. 'It's messed up, burying two friends in as many months.'

Jade nods. 'I pray this will be the last one.'

'For sure,' Beau says.

The waitress comes over and we order.

'I'll be glad when this is all over,' Jade says. 'I've cried enough this year already.'

'Not much longer now,' I tell her. 'We're almost at the end.'

She smiles at me. 'I hope so.'

'I hate this,' Beau says. 'Not knowing who did it. The feeling of things being unresolved. I just hope everything will come out at the end.'

'We might not have to wait that long,' Jade says. 'Look.'

We follow her gaze to a small television behind the counter. The newsreader is talking into the camera and there's a photo of

Nick McCarr superimposed on the background. He appears to be looking straight at me and I feel a shiver run up my back.

The vision cuts to footage of someone being led out of a police car with his shirt pulled up over his head.

'Oh my god,' Jade whispers. 'They've found him.'

'Who is it?' Beau asks. 'Do we know him?'

I pretend to squint at the television. I say, 'It looks like… Jesus?'

'Jesus?' they both ask.

'I dunno, it just looked like him. Hasn't he got a shirt like that?'

'Yeah, but… Jesus? It couldn't have been Jesus who killed Nick,' Jade says.

'Why not?'

'Because…,' she trails off.

I pretend to be as shocked as the other two.

The waitress brings our orders over.

'Excuse me,' Beau says. 'Did you hear any of that report?'

She looks back at the television and says, 'The murder? They got the guy who did it.'

'Did they say his name?'

'Yeah, though I don't remember what. It sounded Spanish.' She laughs.

Jade and Beau look at each other, stunned. I ask the waitress, 'Did they say how they caught him?'

'I didn't hear,' she says. 'Sorry.'

'Thank you,' I say, and she leaves.

'Oh god,' Jade says. 'It was him all along.'

'Wait, wait,' Beau says. 'We don't know that yet. Let's not jump to any conclusions.'

'The cops must have a pretty good idea,' I say, 'or else they wouldn't have arrested him.'

'Let's give him the benefit of the doubt, shall we?' Beau says. 'I just… I can't believe it was Jesus.'

Jade looks down at her drink. 'I don't think I want this anymore.'

Beau says, 'I just can't believe it.'

I get to the funeral and I'm wearing almost exactly the same clothes I wore to Mel's. I don't have much in the way of funeral attire so I have to make do with what I've got.

It feels strange being here, walking amongst Nick's sobbing relatives. I wonder what his mother would do if I walked over to her and said, 'Hi, I'm the guy who killed your son.'

I feel like an intruder, like I don't belong here. I look around and see all these people crying, knowing that I am responsible for their suffering, and it moves nothing in me. I feel detached, like they are in another world, or I am, and I am trying hard to blend in, to look upset. I raise my hand and wipe my eyes; not because of any tears, just because it seems like the appropriate thing to do, because maybe a fake emotion is better than nothing. The situation seems to call for some display so I go along with it.

A speaker walks to a lectern at the front of the room and the crowd falls silent. He says, 'Ladies and gentlemen, we are here to celebrate the life of Nick McCarr.'

It sounds very familiar.

The ceremony is similar to Mel's except that it's indoors and I'm paying less attention this time. I'm sitting by myself towards the back, scanning the crowd for Jade, but there's no sign of her.

People keep coming in and taking seats wherever they can. I look around and am relieved to notice I am not the only one who isn't crying.

The rear doors open and two people slink in and take seats on the opposite side of the aisle from me, a couple of rows further ahead.

Beau and Jade.

They haven't noticed me on their hurried search for a seat and quickly try to blend in without causing too much of a disturbance.

The speaker continues talking but I'm not listening. I'm just staring at the backs of Jade and Beau, with Jade occasionally wiping her eyes and Beau sitting calmly.

The place itself is fairly nondescript. Thinking back, I don't remember what the outside of this building looks like and I have a hard time remembering how I got here. The walls and carpet are some colour and there is a large photo of Nick on an easel beside the catafalque, where a coffin sits, closed and empty.

Jade places a hand over her eyes and leans forward slightly. I can't help but be angry; all this over Nick? My anger shifts to Nick and how he is putting her through this pain. He's still having an effect on her even after he's gone.

My heart stops as Beau puts his arm around Jade and she leans in to him, resting her head on his shoulder.

The first pricks of tears sting my eyes and I get up and leave the room.

I wait around in the condolence lounge and after a while the people start to file out, talking softly. Jade and Beau exit, his arm still around her shoulders.

She sees me and smiles and walks over. 'Hi,' she says. 'We didn't see you in there.'

'I was at the back.'

She nods. 'At least it's over now.'

Beau is looking around the room. 'Doesn't look like Jesus is here,' he says.

'The police must still have him.'

He shakes his head. 'I never would have guessed it. Not in a million years.'

I shrug. 'Strange things happen.'

'Yeah. Listen, we're going to get a coffee or something, want to come?'

'No, thanks,' I say, unable to stomach the sight of them together. 'Have fun though.'

Beau snorts at this. 'Fun after a funeral. Great.'

'See you,' Jade says, and they leave, his arm still around her.

I grit my teeth and also head towards the exit.

On my way I see the drunk from that evening, sober now, and our eyes lock briefly before I push through the doors and out into the sun.

Outside I turn on my phone and there is a missed call and one voice message waiting for me.

'Hi, this is Detective Jacobs,' the recorded message says. 'Please give us a call as soon as you get this, there are a few things we need to clear up. Thanks.'

He leaves a number and hangs up.

I delete the message and turn my phone off again.

Twenty-four

It feels like the walls are closing in.

There is a constant pressure in my head, a deep throbbing that will not subside, no matter how I try to escape it. There is a constant weight on my chest. I want to do nothing but sleep and this is one thing I cannot do. Whenever I begin to doze I am plagued by dreams that snap me back to full attention, making my heart race and my skin break out in a cold sweat. This lack of sleep causes my feelings of unease to multiply without my being able to resolve anything.

There is Jade and Beau.

There is Jacobs, Abrahams and Jesus.

And there is Dawson.

Everything else seems like a blur. I forget to eat. I misplace things and then spend hours looking for them, periodically forgetting what it is I am searching for. My gran sits on the couch for hours, staring at walls, and I find myself joining her. There is the constant presence of these thoughts, these three main issues, and I cannot escape them no matter where I hide.

I try to remember what Jade told me, about how we're all walking a road. Find someone's hand to hold and maybe someone will hold yours, too.

I tell George that Beau is my friend. I should be happy for him.

George says, 'Happy while he walks all over you. You're such a sucker.'

My mind keeps returning to Dawson. All the roads lead back to him. Dawson with his money, his comfortable life, his car and his clothes and me with nothing. Me starting out with nothing and losing by the day.

George says, 'Find him. You know where he is. Find him and do what you've been planning. It's time to end this.'

I know what needs to be done.

The sky starts out being fine but by the time I reach my destination clouds have covered the sun and the day has darkened. Birds call noisily to each other, warning of some approaching danger. The wind blows strongly through the overcast streets and I find myself standing outside a café.

It's an expensive café with no booths; instead there are fine wooden tables with flowers. There are ornamental lights and attractive waitresses.

I walk inside and there he is, sitting at table, reading something from a folder. He lifts his cup and takes a sip without looking up from the page.

My heart thumps painfully and I take a deep breath before starting over towards the table.

…And your life comes down to an action. Your past, present and future are decided by a single moment and sometimes what you do will shape the world. All you do is pull the trigger and it all changes.

I pull back a chair and sit down opposite him. He looks up at me, confused at first, but then recognition sweeps his face.

'Maybe you've seen me around?' I tell him.

He says, 'Hi', and the sound of his voice strikes a chord in me. He smiles hesitantly, unsure of what I want from him. 'How are you?'

'This is a nice café,' I say. 'I've never been here before.'

He closes the folder and places it on the floor next to his briefcase. 'I work around here. It's close.' He speaks quietly, considering his words before he answers.

'How long have you worked there?'

'About eight years,' he says.

'You like it? Lots of benefits? The salary is good?'

'Sure,' he says.

…And maybe everything has the right to life. Not just the physical aspects but true life. Living. Loving. Being loved. And if someone denies you of that then should they be punished? Or forgiven?

I sit staring at him and he is clearly uncomfortable but the enjoyment I was expecting from this moment does not come. Instead, I feel almost sorry for him. This whole thing feels like a dream, like I'm not even here. In a way, I guess I'm not.

'How's… everything?' he asks slowly.

'Do you really want to know?'

He shrugs. 'I guess so.'

'Well, to tell the truth, things are bad. Terrible, in fact.'

'I'm sorry to hear that,' he says in a carefully measured voice.

I tell him my mother died when I was eleven.

He looks down at the table and doesn't say anything for a long time. 'Where do you live?' he asks.

'With my gran.'

'How is she?'

'Not so good.'

'Oh,' he says, and reaches for his coffee, needing a prop to play with.

'My mother gassed herself,' I tell him.

He nods without saying anything, still looking at the table, anywhere but at me. 'What do you do?' Eager to change the subject.

'Nothing. I used to go to university but I forgot what the point was. I don't have any family except for my gran and she doesn't know who I am most of the time. I don't have any real friends; they all try and go behind my back and don't care about anything except themselves. I've been to two funerals in the last two months. I don't have a girlfriend or anyone who cares about me. I don't have a reason. I have nothing.'

Somewhere in this speech he has looked up and now watches me with a mixture of pity and guilt.

'I'm sorry,' he says.

'No, you're not. You're sorry I brought it up but you're not sorry it happened.'

'Don't be like this. Please.'

'How do you want me to be? Am I ruining your perfect world?'

…And maybe understanding is almost as good as forgiveness. Maybe that's all you can hope for.

'I don't know what to say,' he says.

'There's nothing you can say. What's done is done. I just wanted you to know the past is not easy to get away from. It follows you around. It stalks you and you can't forget it and hope it'll go away. Some things you can't walk away from,' I tell him.

'It was a long time ago.'

'That doesn't change anything. You're living this perfect life and here I am, suffering. How is that fair?'

'Life isn't fair,' he says, for the first time sitting up and sounding as though he means what he's saying. 'It sounds like you've learned that already. Nothing in this life is fair.'

'Now you're giving me life lessons? Isn't it a little late for that?'

'Some things you can't understand,' he says.

'My mother killed herself.'

'I know, and you have no idea how sorry I am for that but it has nothing to do with me.'

'It does,' I tell him. 'It has everything to do with you.'

'People always have a choice. She could have lived. She could have made changes.'

'She tried.'

'If you work for something hard enough, it'll happen,' he says.

'That's not true. You never get what you want. People never get to live their dreams. It doesn't matter how hard you try, this world will crap on you and force you down. No one ever gets what they really want, they just end up settling for less.'

'Anything worth having is worth fighting for.'

'I've been fighting. I've been fighting all my life, so hard, and look where I am. Look what I've got. I fight harder than I thought possible and I keep sinking. You beat one and five more come and take its place.'

He says, 'You think I got to where I am easily? You don't think I fought to get where I am today?'

'I think you stepped on everyone in your way. I think you threw away anything that slowed you down, any kind of responsibility at all.'

'Some things you don't understand.'

'I understand you're a selfish fuck who doesn't give a damn about anything except yourself.'

He starts to get angry but relents. He sighs and rubs his eyes with his hand. 'Listen,' he says. 'Some things are just complicated. Some things just don't work, no matter how hard you try.' He says, 'I tried. You have to believe me. I tried, but it just wasn't working. We wanted different things. We'd grown apart. There was too much fighting and that was no way to raise a child. I don't know what she said, but...'

'She told me you were dead.'

He doesn't say anything for a moment, then, 'I guess that explains a lot. Why you didn't call, or try to contact me. She was angry and I guess that's how she saw fit to punish me. To turn you away.'

'She didn't turn me away. You did that yourself when you walked out.'

'It wasn't that simple,' he says. 'It wasn't a spur of the moment decision. We agreed it was better for both of us that way.'

'Is that why she would cry herself to sleep every night? Did you agree it would be better for both of you if she killed herself?'

'What happened, happened. We wanted to go our separate ways.'

'No, you wanted to go your way.'

He nods. 'I guess I did. But that doesn't mean I wanted anything like this to happen. If I had known she'd do that, or you'd... you'd turn out feeling this way, then things might have happened differently.'

'Really? Would they?'

'I don't know. How would any of us know? Don't think I don't look back on it and not care. I do care. I can't say whether or not things would have happened differently if we could do it again. That doesn't mean I don't regret what happened. Don't ever let anyone tell you that you can't have any regrets. People say, "No regrets", but that's bullshit. You can have as many regrets as you want. Use them. Learn from them. If you're lying there on your deathbed and look back over your life and you have no regrets, it makes me wonder if you actually learned anything.'

'Do you feel bad about your life?' I ask.

'I feel bad for your life. Isn't that enough?'

I snort a laugh. 'No, it's not enough. You should have been a man and stood behind your responsibilities. You had a responsibility to me. You could have at least called me? Didn't I ever cross your mind once you walked out the door?'

'She told me not to. She said she wanted nothing to do with me. She said that, if I go, I stay gone. There was no going back. There's never any going back. We talked, we tried to get through things, but we couldn't. I couldn't. What happened was between your mother and me. It had nothing to do with you. I often wonder how you turned out. And now I know.'

'You could have contacted me if you really wanted to. If it really mattered, you would have done it.'

'I didn't want to intrude. I didn't know how you'd take to me showing up out of the blue. If she told you I was dead then that would have been even worse. I'm sorry. I should've...' He sighs. 'How did you find me?'

'I've seen you around a couple of times.'

'And you never approached me?'

'And say what?'

He shrugs. 'You're here now.'

I laugh bitterly. 'Yeah, I am.'

'Why? What changed your mind? Why now, why today?'

...And maybe the past has everything to do with what you are now or maybe it has nothing. Maybe we just are who we are and that's all.

'I came today because I had seen you before. I couldn't keep going on, knowing you were out there. I couldn't let you get away with what you've done. I had to show up here and remind you of what you lost. I wanted to tell you how much I hate you for what you did to me and my mother. I hate you for leaving us to die.'

'I didn't...'

'I hate you for having all the things I don't have and never will have. If you are at all responsible for my... state of mind, then I hate you all the more.'

'I'm sorry you feel that way.'

'Don't be. I don't want your pity.'

'I can understand you hating me. But is it my fault about your friends? Your girlfriend? That's not my doing. You did that yourself.'

'You know what they say about the sins of the father,' I tell him.

'You don't think people are responsible for their own lives? Who says exactly the same thing wouldn't have happened if I had stayed? I don't know. It's something we'll never know. You are who you are and you shouldn't apologise for that. But you shouldn't blame people either.'

He says, 'We all make our own way.'

...And maybe death is the only place you will ever find peace. Maybe being reborn is the only way to start again.

'What happens now?' he asks after a long pause.

I sigh. 'I don't know. I get up, walk out, and we resume our lives as normal.'

'Will I see you again?'

'Does it matter?'

'What does that mean? Of course it matters.'

I shake my head. 'Does it? You've come this far without seeing me and it doesn't seem to have bothered you. Does any of it matter? Does anything we do in this life really amount to anything? The only thing every person has in common is that, in one way or another, they will let you down. Everyone you love will leave you and everything you do will be forgotten. Everything in this world dies alone.'

He shrugs sadly. 'Everything in this world lives alone, too.'

I nod. 'You're right. That's the first time you've been right. Everything lives alone. The thing that draws us together is the fact that we're all alone.'

'Try to be happy,' he says. 'Whatever's happened, or whatever will happen, try to be happy.'

'You can't say that to me. You're a stranger. You don't know anything about me.'

'I'd like to know you.'

'It's too late for that now. It's too late for anything now,' I tell him.

Once certain plans are set into action there's no going back.

My body is crawling with ants.

I stand up. 'That's all I came here to say. I hope you enjoy the rest of your life, however long it may be.'

'See me again. Please. Let me call you.'

I shake my head. 'We're done. Goodbye, Dawson.'

I start to walk away and he calls after me. I stop and, without turning around, wait for him to speak.

'Call me Dad?' he asks.

I leave.

*   *   *

I make it back to the car before I start sobbing, shaking violently, and I feel like I may throw up. This has been the hardest thing I have ever done and I know the true impact will not be felt for days. There seem to be ants everywhere and my mind no longer recognises the barrier between my nightmares and my waking hours simply because the difference is negligible. There's a sharp pain in my stomach that flares up but fades as quickly as it appeared. This has been one of those life-changing moments and I barely remember what was said. I remember the table and the folder he held but not even the sound of his voice registers with me. I wonder how far out of it I really am; whether any of what just happened was actually real.

I get home and the house is silent. This is no big deal, it just means my gran has forgotten to turn on the television before she started watching it.

I walk through the house calling, 'Gran?' but she doesn't answer. I check the main room, the front room, her bedroom and the bathroom.

All empty.

There is one plate of leftovers sitting on the kitchen counter. The other is lying face down on the floor.

Gran is lying on the kitchen floor, food scattered around her.

She lies on her back, her face swollen and purple. Her eyes are rolled up to the eyelids and her chest is not moving. One hand is clenched around her throat and the other is reaching for the telephone, which lies just beyond her grasp.

I step into the kitchen, quietly asking, 'Gran?' She does not move. I kneel down beside her and, already knowing what I'll find,

I search for a pulse. I place my hand over her open mouth, feeling for any air being exhaled, but there is nothing. I lean forward and there, sitting in the back of her throat, is a chicken bone.

I yell into the empty house, 'I told you not to eat the leftovers. Now look what you've gone and done. Why couldn't you have waited?'

My voice echoes in the room. The silence following seems even more complete. It weighs down on me like a physical load. The house feels like a tomb.

I stare at her, lying amid the food, knowing she died alone on the kitchen floor, reaching for the telephone.

I lean over her and pick up the receiver.

'Hello?' a voice asks me. 'What is the nature of your emergency?'

I tell him my gran is dead.

He asks me what my address is and I tell him.

This is all so very déjà vu.

After a moment, he tells me an ambulance is on its way.

I tell him there is no need to rush, I don't think she'll be going anywhere.

I think of my gran as a young girl. She's working behind the counter in a general store, serving people. A young man comes in and buys a loaf of bread. He smiles at her and leaves.

He returns a while later for a bottle of milk. This time he speaks to her, asks her what her name is. She tells him and he smiles, saying what a beautiful name it is. She blushes and says thank you. The young man leaves the store, the bell jingling over his head as he pushes through the door.

Throughout the day she thinks of the boy, who she has seen in the store from time to time. They have never spoken before;

perhaps because he usually comes in with his mother. As the store closes she sweeps the floor and wipes down the bench tops, and her boss, a woman her family has known for years, tells the young girl to go around the back of the store and make sure the rubbish is ready for collection the following morning. The girl disappears around the back and examines the rubbish. Some boxes need tidying up and after a short while everything is in good order.

She tries the back door but discovers it is locked. She knocks on it but there is no answer; the boss must be busy elsewhere in the store.

The young girl begins to walk around towards the front entrance. Just as she reaches the door it swings open and the young man steps out. He smiles when he sees her approaching.

Hello, he says.

She is too shocked to reply at first. She soon overcomes this and finds herself smiling. *Hello*, she says bashfully.

I looked inside for you, but you weren't there, he tells her.

No, I was out the back. Did you want something?

He smiles. *I came to walk you home, if that's alright.*

I don't live far, she tells him.

That's alright, he says, undeterred.

I probably live in the opposite direction, she says, hoping he'll persist. He does.

I've got nowhere else to go.

She nods with a smile and gives in, allowing him to walk her home.

Throughout the next day she has kept an eye out for him, brimming with excitement as the day starts, but then it fades as the hours progress and he still has not arrived. At the close of the shop she lets the door swing shut behind her and there he is, standing under a tree. He waves as she sees him and she tentatively raises a hand in return.

This happens day after day until one evening, as he leaves her at her doorstep, he asks her if she would like to go with him to a dance at the local hall. She coyly accepts and from then they are never apart.

They get married a few years later and move into a modest house. They live comfortably for some years before she falls pregnant. Both parents are overjoyed but also concerned if they will be able to afford the new addition. The father-to-be takes on a night job and as much overtime as he can get, saving it all up for the arrival of the baby. It turns out to be in vain, however; the baby does not make it to full term. They are devastated but manage to pull through with each other's support. A year later, the young woman becomes pregnant once again. This time the baby is born in full health, a smiling baby daughter.

The family grows together and there are no more children. The marriage survives the baby's growth, her schooling, her teenage years. The parents never stray or have second thoughts about their marriage, they are committed to each other totally and completely. It survives the daughter's boyfriends and her troubled adolescence. It survives her anger at them and her moving out. They support each other through everything and the marriage withstands the toughest tests. It survives everything except the young man's cancer. They continue to love each other right up until his body gives out, his stomach having eaten itself away.

The daughter returns seeking forgiveness and the news of her father's death brings the mother and daughter closer together. The daughter has now experienced enough of the world and needs the support of her mother, and the mother needs her child to see her through the blackest time of her life. For the first time she can remember, she is without the man she loves, the boy who waited for her outside the store, day after day.

The mother and daughter live together while the daughter works and lives her life. The mother never gets over the loss of her husband and even with her daughter living with her, still feels the ache of loneliness and the onset of old age. One day the daughter tells the mother she has met a man, a man who loves her and they are planning on living together. The mother is saddened by this news but agrees to support her daughter and her decision.

The mother's loneliness grows and she turns deeper into herself, so much so that nothing can bring her out of her grief. She would never have believed a person could love so much, mean so much, that their absence would bring about the end of one's own will to live. Not even the daughter's news of her pregnancy can bring the mother out of her condition, which deteriorates by the day.

By the time the baby comes the new grandmother is so withdrawn it appears there is no hope she will return to the girl she once was. The grandson cannot bring the family together and in some ways, the old woman sees the new boy as a replacement for her lost love. The grandmother accepts the child as best she can and, as depression gives way to dementia, and after a sequence of events she will never fully understand, she finds the grandson living with her.

She told me the first half of this story more times than I can count. It was always repetitive and meaningless but now it makes sense. This story is what made her who she was. Now a story is all it is, and I am the only person who knows it. There are details I will never know and there are more stories that have died with her.

No matter how eventful a life, it all boils down to this.

No matter what we do, it all ends up the same for each of us.

Your entire life gets reduced to the dash between two dates on a tombstone.

The executor of Gran's will makes all the arrangements. There is no funeral because there isn't anyone to attend. Instead her body is cremated and the ashes are scattered, both without me being there. I have no tears left to cry. My inside is burning at the realisation that now, more than ever before, I really am completely alone.

Twenty-five

The social worker sits on the couch and I sit on my chair opposite her. Neither of us speaks.

My eyes keep returning to the photographs hanging on the wall. Baby pictures of me, of my mother, of someone else. Pictures of me sitting on my dad's lap. Pictures of me smiling.

The ghosts of who we once were.

These are the only real ghosts in the world. Ghosts exist only in memories and photographs, those captured instants in time. Ghosts exist within ourselves and the dreams we leave behind.

The wounds left behind from when we were happy.

All the memories of the people we've loved, the places we've been, the things that once meant something. We move along through this life and they fade away like stars in the dawn.

The social worker watches my eyes searching the photos and she asks quietly, 'How are you handling things?'

After a moment I shrug.

'I'm sorry I couldn't be here,' she says. 'I had another assignment who needed me. It was unavoidable. I am sorry.'

There's a long silence.

'Listen,' she says, 'there's something you need to know.'

I look at her, waiting.

'I got a call from the head office this morning. They think that… Well, they told me that now you're older. You're not as young as you used to be.'

'That's very observant of them.'

She forces a smile that only lasts a second. 'They told me that you're older and now that your gran isn't around, they think you can look after yourself.'

'What does that mean?'

'It means they're not sending me anymore. This will be my last visit.'

I nod, taking this in.

'I mean, I'll still see you. That is, if you want to. But it won't be like this. It won't be a fortnightly thing. It'll be as friends.' She sighs. 'As of today, you're no longer one of my assignments.'

There's a sense of things coming to an end.

It seems that everything is wrapping up. All the loose ends are being tied. It is a very strange feeling and it makes me suddenly very sad.

'I'm sorry. There was nothing I could do. It's out of my hands.'

'Do you have another assignment yet?'

She shakes her head. 'Not yet. They're sorting out some paperwork.' She laughs sadly. 'You know how it is with these bureaucrats. Everything by the book.'

I nod again.

'But we still have today. We still have now. So let's talk.' She strains a smile and opens her folder for the last time. 'So. How are you?'

I feel a tear roll down my cheek.

I tell her I'm sick. 'I'm really, really sick. I feel like everything is closing in on me. I have these dreams, these nightmares that I can't get away from. My mind is a mess. I don't know what's real, what's not; I can't tell the difference between what I think and what I do. I talk to myself without realising it, I just...' I wave my hand to show how useless it all is.

She looks at me, concerned. 'How long has this been happening?'

'I don't know. As long as I can remember. It's worse lately. The last few weeks have been bad. Oh god, I've done things, terrible, terrible things.'

'Like what?'

I shake my head. 'It doesn't matter. I don't want to get into it.'

'Why? What makes you do these things?'

I let out a sob. 'I don't know. Part of me wants to. George tells me to do them.'

'Your friend George? You don't have to listen to him.'

'It's not that simple. He's the only person who's always been there for me. I can't just ignore him.'

'You can. You do what you want. It's not too late to start saying no to him.'

'Believe me, it is. There's no going back now.'

'George doesn't sound like a good friend if he's telling you to do things you don't want to do. If he's making you feel this way, maybe you're better off without him.'

I tell her, 'He always gives me the answers. He knows things I don't.'

'But he makes you feel this way? Cut loose, before he makes you do anything else.'

'I can't, I can't...'

KILLING RICHARD DAWSON 293

She says, 'You deserve to be happy. Everyone does. But it sounds like George is stopping you from achieving that. Think about it, what has George ever done that made your life better?'

'He was there when I needed someone.'

'And that's all? You needed a friend and George was there. So you clung onto him, regardless of what he did, taking his every word as truth. Your attachment to George clouded your vision. You believed everything he told you, even when what he told you was wrong. So I'll ask you again: how is your life better? What has George done that has made you happy?'

I think back over the years. We played together. We kept each other company. He saw me through the breakdown of my family. But after that...

I hear him telling me how worthless life is. How people are replaceable. Expendable. How people are shit and can be used however I see fit to get my own way. I hear him telling me to sacrifice everyone I know in order to get what I want.

'Maybe you're right,' I say. 'Maybe he really hasn't done anything for me. Maybe he's just made things worse. Now it's too late.'

The social worker, she says, 'It's never too late.'

There's another long silence.

You don't need to die to destroy yourself.

I ask, 'Have you ever been in a situation where there seems to be only one way out, and that one way is... not the easiest solution.'

'Most of the time that's how it works.'

'See, there's someone I've seen around. Someone I knew a long time ago. Someone who did the wrong thing and has gotten away with it.'

'Do the police know?'

'It's not that sort of wrong thing. But... I can't get over it. He's trapped in my head like a bird in a cage.'

'Have you spoken to him?'

'Yeah. It didn't change the way I feel.'

She nods. 'Who is he? What happened?'

I ask, 'What do you know about my father?'

She shrugs. 'Not much.'

'What did they tell you at your office? When you first started on my case, what did they say?'

'They said you had been orphaned. They said your mother had recently passed away and your father... they didn't mention him.' She looks at me and asks, 'What are you saying?'

I'm all of a sudden very angry. I tell her I've seen him. 'I've seen him walking around, I've seen him in shops, in cafés, at his work. He's not dead. My mother lied. She hated him so much she told me he was dead. But he's not.'

'You're sure? You're sure it's him?'

'Positive. Don't you have notes or something? Can't you check?'

'Not here with me. I'd have to look in the archives at the office. You sure you're not clutching at straws? What do you remember from that time?'

'I came home, he was gone. His stuff was gone a few days later. That's all I remember. I asked my mother what happened to it all and she said it went to charity. He probably came around while I was at school and took it.'

'You didn't go to a funeral? You never visited his grave?'

'No. She said it would upset me. It was better to remember him the way he was...' I trail off, the tears returning. 'I can't believe she'd lie to me.'

'Are you sure?'

'Yes, I'm sure. I've thought over all of this a million times. I know. Trust me, I know.'

She sighs and nods. 'Okay. I believe you. What are you going to do?'

I almost say, Kill him. Instead I tell her, 'I don't know.'

'Do you want me to look into it for you? I can check on the computers at the office and see if there's any information.'

'I don't know. Let me think about it.'

She nods and looks at her watch. She closes the folder and smiles sadly at me. 'It's time.'

I let out a deep breath. 'Okay.'

We stand up.

She says, 'I'm glad you were assigned to me.'

'Me too. I hope I wasn't too much trouble.'

'You were,' she says, and laughs. 'But it was worth it.'

I smile back. 'So. I guess this is goodbye.'

'Only for a little while. I'll see you again. Maybe we'll go clubbing sometime. We don't have that social worker-patient barrier anymore, so who knows?'

We walk to the front door. She opens it and turns to hug me. I return the gesture, patting her gently on the back, trying to swat the ants that crawl over her.

'Listen,' she says, 'if I don't see you again for a while…'

'Yeah?'

There's an awkward pause. 'Have fun, okay?'

'Sure.'

'Bye,' she says, and starts to walk away.

'Hang on a second,' I say. 'Did you mean what you said? About looking in the computer and finding out some information?'

She nods. 'I guess.'

'Could you get his home address for me?'

'Oh, I don't know about that. That's a big ask.'

'I understand if you can't. But if you can…?'

She sighs. 'Maybe,' she says. 'I'll see what I can do.'

'Thanks. I appreciate it.'

She nods and starts to walk again.

I begin to close the door when she softly calls, 'Hey.'

I look around the door, waiting for her to speak.

She goes to say something, then stops. She says, 'Never mind.'

Twenty-six

The silence of my home becomes overwhelming and on the drive to Beau's I realise there is nowhere else to go.

I pull over to the kerb and recognise the car that is parked in the driveway. I get out and head towards his front door. As I get there it opens and Jade walks out. Beau is behind her and they're laughing.

'Hi,' she says, surprised to see me. 'How are you? I just came around to see his new stuff.'

'New stuff?'

'The furniture is here,' Beau tells me. 'Come in, take a look.'

'I've got to go,' Jade says. She starts to walk towards her car and turns to Beau. 'I'll call you later,' she says.

'Sure,' he says, and smiles.

She gets into her car. I follow Beau inside.

His house looks totally different. The chairs have all been replaced by new couches and the old television is gone; in its place stands a new top of the range widescreen.

He points and says, 'Have a seat.'

I sit down on his new expensive grey couch. He sits on an armchair opposite.

'How's your enlightenment going?' I ask him.

'Don't say it like that, man,' he says. 'You make it sound all religious. It's not like that at all. It's just… another way of looking at things. It's a new way that lets you see all the love in the world.' He smiles and I know he's thinking about Jade.

Mister Restraint.

'What's been happening with you?' he asks.

'My gran died.'

'Holy shit, seriously? When did this happen? Why didn't you tell me? How are you handling it?'

I shrug. 'I don't know. As well as can be expected.'

'You're welcome to stay here,' he says. 'I mean, if you want to.'

'Thanks. It's hard to get my mind around. Everything I had is gone.'

'I'm still here. Jade's still here.'

There's an ant crawling down my ear, making it itch inside.

'Is she?' I ask.

'Of course,' he says, looking confused.

'You two seem to be pretty friendly.'

He nods and smiles. 'Yeah. We are.'

'She's great, isn't she?'

He nods. 'You don't still… I mean, you're not still after her, are you? I thought you were over her.'

I shake my head.

'Oh man, I'm so sorry,' he says. 'If I had known, I never would have…'

'Never would have what?'

He lets out a long breath then smiles self-consciously, the first time I've ever seen Beau shy. 'I love her.'

'What? How can you? You're Beau. Beau doesn't fall in love. You don't love her.'

'I do, man, I honestly do. It's never been like this before, I mean… When I had the doll, everything was great, but it was all shallow. There was no attachment. There was no caring. But now… It's amazing.' He smiles brightly.

'I know. I've been there.'

'She's just something else, you know? Something very… exotic.'

'I know.' I say, 'Listen. You don't know what I've been through, but you have to let her go. You can't do this to me. Not after everything I've done.'

'What?'

'I've been through too much lose her. I've come so close, so many times, and every time something comes along and snatches her away from me. I can't let that happen again.'

'What are you talking about? Are you okay?'

'I'm sick,' I tell him. 'I'm trying to get over it, but…'

'What can I do?'

'Leave her alone,' I say. 'Don't call her, don't see her. Please.'

He sighs. 'I don't think I can do that.'

'Why the hell not?'

Beau says, 'Because I love her.'

'No. You don't. I do. I saw her first.'

'Don't do this.'

'Leave her alone. If you don't, I don't know what will happen.'

'What does that mean? Are you threatening me?'

'Goddammit,' I yell, standing up. 'Can't I have just one thing? Just one little thing?'

'Come on, man,' he says quietly. 'We're friends.'

'Don't give me that shit. Beau, please, I'm telling you, leave her the fuck alone.'

'Don't do this,' he says again, standing to face me. 'Don't go here. This is a one-way street.'

'Life's a one-way street. Isn't that what she says? And we're all just walking down it? She told you all that, too? My trip's been hard enough so far, please don't make it any harder. I need this. I need her. Please, I can't do this by myself.'

'You can, just…'

'I can't. Don't you see that, you fuckhead?'

'Hey, watch it,' he says. 'Don't start this shit with me. I understand you're having a hard time right now but don't attack the people who care about you.'

'Care about me?' I scream, exasperated. 'You care about me by going behind my back and stealing the girl I love?'

'You don't love her,' Beau says. 'You love the idea of her. You love what she represents. You think she's going to save you, to make you feel better somehow. Trust me, only you can do that. I've learned that recently. Save yourself.'

'She is your reward, is she? For changing your ways? Is that what you're telling me?'

Beau shakes his head. 'There are no rewards. Nobody is watching us, ready to give us a pat on the back for doing a good job. If we live a good life, no one cares. There's no prize for doing everything perfectly. But Jade is my reason for trying.'

He says, 'We all have our own Jade.'

I nod. 'I just wish you could have found a different one.'

'You're not getting what I'm saying…,' he starts, then trails off. 'Don't I deserve to be happy?' he asks finally.

I sigh. 'Yeah, you do. But at my expense?'

'I'm sorry,' he says. 'There's nothing I can do about the way I feel.'

'Don't fucking talk like that.'

'What the hell is wrong with you?' he yells. 'We're friends. We're best friends. And this is what's happened to us?'

'Shut the fuck up. Just because you're "enlightened" now? Just because you've stopped drinking and got new stuff... that makes you better than me?'

'I never said I was better than you.'

'No, but you wanted to become a better person. Isn't that right? Better than who? Nick? Jesus? Me?'

'That's not what I meant and you know it.'

'You haven't changed. You're just seeing thing differently because you feel bad about Mel.'

'Does it matter why? As long as I'm making an effort to change, isn't that the most important thing?'

'Let her go,' I tell him, my fury rising. 'Don't take her away from me again.'

'I'm sorry,' he says. 'I can't help it.'

'Yeah, you said that already. Just try. You want to be a better person? Then leave her alone. Help me out.'

'I can't do that.'

'Fuck you,' I yell, my temper breaking. 'You leave her alone. Don't you see her again. You see her again and I'll stab you in your fucking head.'

'You better leave,' he says.

'I'm serious, Beau,' I yell. 'If you see her once more I'll come back here and I'll kill you. Leave her alone, you motherfucker.'

He looks at me, realisation slowly dawning. 'Oh my god,' he says softly. 'It was you.'

'Shut the fuck up.'

'It wasn't Jesus at all, was it? You killed Nick. Oh, god,' he murmurs. 'How could you do that? And Jesus? What about him? You set him up? You're letting him take the fall for this?'

'I couldn't help it,' I scream. 'Nick wouldn't leave her alone, I didn't have a choice. I tried talking but he wouldn't listen. Beau, please, leave her or I don't know what I'll do.'

He backs away, shaking his head. 'You're sick,' he mutters.

'I know. I can't help it.' I begin to sob.

'Go home,' he says. 'We'll talk about this when you've calmed down.'

'Fuck you,' I cry, the strength fading from my voice. I double over, my stomach suddenly throbbing painfully.

'You okay?' he asks and steps forward.

'Leave me alone.'

Another cramp rips through me.

'Seriously man, you don't look so good.'

He lays his hand on my shoulder and before I know what's happening I see my fist uppercut into Beau's jaw. His head rocks backward and he stumbles, falling into his new grey sofa. He puts his hand to his jaw, checking for blood, then looks up at me, first shocked then angry.

'Get out,' he says.

'I'm sorry, I don't know what's happening to me...'

'Get the hell out. I'm calling the cops.'

'Beau, please, don't...'

'Get out. Now,' he bellows.

I move towards the door, one hand over my belly, the other pushing off the walls as I pass them.

'I'm sorry,' I call back but he doesn't answer.

I get in the car and begin to drive, tears blurring my vision.

Twenty-seven

As soon as I get home my phone starts to ring. I lift it to my ear without checking who it is and say, 'Hello?'

'This is Detective Jacobs,' the voice says. 'We need to talk. There are a few details we need cleared up. We'd like you to come in as soon as possible.'

'I don't know if I can,' I mutter, my voice still raspy from crying. 'Um...,' I sniff, 'I'm kinda busy today.'

Detective Jacobs says, 'I'm sure you can reschedule.'

'Is this really necessary? What's this about?'

'A couple of things Jesus told us. We'd like to hear more of your side of the story.'

'Alright.' I sigh. 'I'll try to come in this afternoon.'

'Within the hour,' he says, 'or we'll send someone to pick you up.'

I hang up before he can say anything else.

'Who was that?' George asks, walking in from the other room.

'I didn't know you were here.'

He nods. 'The cops again?'

'Yeah.' I walk through to the bathroom and run the faucet, splashing cold water onto my face.

'What are you going to do?' he asks.

'I dunno. I might go see them. Turn myself in.'

'What?' he says. 'Why? Don't do that. Jesus has told them his side, that's all. It'll be the same story you told but the other way around. That doesn't mean they think it's you.'

'What's the point? I may as well turn myself in. There's nothing left out here.'

He looks at me for a moment. 'Why?' he says quietly. 'What happened?'

I tell him about Beau and Jade. As I relate the story his face gets angrier and angrier.

'What's the plan?' he asks.

'I'm going to go to the police station. Take my chances.'

'Don't do that,' George says. 'You're almost there.'

'Almost where?'

'At the end,' he says. 'There's only one obstacle left.'

'That's what I thought about Nick.'

'Seriously, think about it. Beau is the only thing standing in your way. After him, it's just you and Jade.'

'Don't you think that'll look a bit suspicious?'

'Maybe,' he shrugs. 'But you got away with it once.'

'George,' I say. 'Shut up. I'm not going to kill Beau.'

'I'm not telling you to do anything you don't want to do. It's always been up to you. You've always made the decisions yourself.'

'George,' I say, thinking of the social worker. 'Please. You'd better leave. I don't need this right now. I think... I think it'd be best if we didn't talk for a while.'

He looks shocked, confused. 'Why?'

'Because you keep filling my head with all this shit. I can't keep living like this. Listen, Beau is happy. He's in love. More importantly, Jade is happy. They're happy, George. Let's leave them alone. Let them walk together.'

He snorts. 'Don't give me that "life is a road" shit. It may be a road but it's a fucking dead end.'

'At least they'll be happy while they can. Isn't that what it's all about?'

'No, it's not. Come on, you don't really believe any of that shit, do you? The only people who believe in fate are the ones that don't have the balls to make their own decisions. Life isn't a game because games are meant to be fun and at the end there's a winner. Neither of those are applicable here.'

'Beau is my friend.'

'So am I.'

'A real friend wouldn't encourage me to think like this.'

'Haven't I always been there for you?' George asks. 'Haven't I stuck by you through thick and thin? Didn't I pick you up off the schoolroom floor when you were sobbing like a fucking baby? I've carried you all the way from that day. And now you're pulling this shit. What is the matter with you?'

'This is not Beau's fault. It's not Dawson's fault. It's mine.'

'It's arguable they put you in this position.'

'And I wasn't strong enough to get out. Beau saw his chance to change and he took it. I didn't. That's why he got what he wanted. Because he tried.'

'Now it's your turn. Go the extra distance. Get what you want. Put yourself on the line.'

'And kill Beau?'

He shakes his head. 'Did I say that? I've never made you do anything. I've just presented you with options, with ways of thinking. It's always been you who made the call. Don't blame any of this on me. None of this is my doing.'

'George,' I say softly. 'I'm through listening to you. Go away.'

George laughs and says, 'No.'

'Why the hell not?'

'Because you need me. You're not strong enough to do this by yourself.'

My stomach starts to throb again, the deep grinding pain returning.

'I am. Leave me alone. Leave Beau alone. They're happy, can't you see that?'

I push past him and walk into the front room. He follows me, staying close.

'I can see you're miserable. You need to fix that.'

'I need to stop hurting people and get on with my life. Now go. I don't want to see you again.'

He stops and looks at me, smiling. 'Yeah, you do.'

I feel the tears returning. 'George, stop,' I say, my voice breaking. 'Please.'

'Aw, what's wrong?' he says in a mock soothing voice.

'You're what's wrong with me,' I yell at him. 'I can't sleep, I can't function, I can't even tell what's real anymore.'

'Reality is very subjective,' he tells me. 'What's real to someone may not be real to someone else.'

'Shut up.'

'I'll help you out, as always. What's the problem? What don't you think is real?'

'It feels like there are ants everywhere…'

'If you can feel them they must be real. To you, at least.'

'What about you? Are you real?'

He raises his eyebrows. 'Me?'

'Yes. I knew, I used to know, but now I don't, I don't remember…'

'You don't know if I'm real?' He laughs. 'That's, like, insulting.'

'George, just tell me, are you real?'

'What do you think?'

'I don't know,' I roar.

'You're not sure if I'm even standing here? How do you know if anything else is real? Was the social worker real? Your gran? Nick? Jade? You? Has any of it been real?' He steps towards me and hits me hard across the face with his open palm. The crack rings out in the empty house. 'Was that real enough for you?' he asks.

I start to laugh, notes of hysteria creeping in.

He shakes his head. 'This is getting ridiculous. I think it's time to wrap things up now, don't you? This has gone on long enough.'

'You're right. Now get out.'

'No. You need to deal with Beau.'

I'm shaking my head. 'No, no, no…'

'Then we can take care of Daddy dearest.'

'Leave him alone…'

'What? You're not going to kill him anymore? Wasn't that the point of this whole thing? What turned the tables there?'

'I've fucked up too many lives.'

'Like he did to yours?'

'He didn't. We all make our own way.'

'That's bullshit. We're born, we get shit on, we die. That's life.'

'It's not. There's more to it than that. There has to be.'

'Like what? And don't say love.'

'Jade,' I say. 'Everyone has their own.'

And I realise Beau is right. Everyone does have their own Jade. Their own reason. The hard part is finding it.

'That's it. I'm not killing Beau. I'm not killing Dawson. That's the end of it.'

'We're not at the end yet,' George says.

'Just let them go, George,' I say. 'Don't touch them.'

The pain in my stomach is ripping, tearing, eating.

'Not even dear old Dad? We can't mess around with Daddy's perfect existence?'

'No. We're done with him.'

'We know where he works. We know where he eats.'

'No, I know where he works.'

George laughs. 'Are you sure there's a difference?'

Mister Frustrated Aggression.

I yell, 'Dawson is out of it. He has a new life now. I don't care anymore.'

'So that's it? You're giving up just like that? You're almost out of it. There are only two things left.' He holds up two fingers. 'One: Beau Branson. Two: Ralph Dawson. Then, you're home free.'

'Beau is happy. He's making someone else happy. And Ralph Dawson is my father. He's moved on. If he can then so can I.'

'Can you?'

'Yes. Now leave me alone.'

I push past him again and head towards the front door.

'Where do you think you're going?' George says, still following me.

'Out,' I say. 'I don't want you to be here when I get back. We're through, George.'

'Don't you dare leave this house,' George screams. 'Richard,' he yells. 'Don't you take another step. We're not through. I'm not through with you yet.'

I know he's angry. He only calls me by my name when he's angry.

'Goodbye, George,' I say.

'Goddamn you,' he screams as I slam the front door.

I get into the car and start the ignition, backing onto the road. I'm halfway down the street when I see George's car race up behind mine. In the rear-view mirror I can see him fuming, slamming the steering wheel with one hand.

I make a turn, then another, but he stays right behind me.

I speed up, weaving back and forth through the traffic, horns blaring.

George pulls up beside me and edges closer, closer, trying to force my car off the road. He sits behind the wheel like a devil, pointing at the side of the road, wanting me to pull over. I slow down, causing him to sail off in front of me. He changes into my lane, hoping to box me in, but I pull out around him, cutting off the car behind me. Other drivers give me the finger.

Can they see the car pursuing me? Or is it something only I can see? Are they blowing their horns at both of us or just one car that is driving erratically for no apparent reason?

I swerve off to a side road across two lanes of traffic and the oncoming cars skid to a halt, more horns wailing. George follows and I curse.

Up ahead is a set of traffic lights. I press down on the accelerator, forcing the car to speed up. George gains on me, bit by bit.

Ahead, the lights turn amber.

I floor the pedal and the car reaches the intersection just after the lights turn red. I blow through as the waiting cars begin to cross.

Behind me, George slams on his brakes and I lose sight of his car behind a wall of traffic.

I pull up outside Beau's house, wanting to warn him about George, and Jade's car is there once again.

I get out and slam the door, heading for the house. I cross the lawn and push the front door open, calling, 'Beau? Jade?'

I walk into the main room and they are standing together, Jade behind Beau, looking at me warily. Beau stands in the middle of the room, trying to remain calm.

He's holding his father's gun.

'Beau,' I say. 'I'm sorry, man. I'm sorry about before, I'm sorry about everything.'

'What are you doing here?' he asks.

'I'm apologising. I know I did the wrong thing. I know I've done many wrong things, over and over, and I'm sorry. I know it doesn't change anything, but…'

'I called the police,' he says. 'After you left. They're sending a car here in case you came back.'

'You were right,' I tell him. 'About everything. I should've listened to you. Things may have been different.'

A tear rolls down Jade's cheek.

'I'm sorry,' I tell them. 'I'm sorry for all the things I've done.'

I hear a car pull up outside.

I take a step towards Beau. He steps back and raises the gun.

'Don't move,' he says. 'You stay where you are.'

'Please, Beau, I just…'

'I mean it, Richard. Don't come any closer.'

'Please,' Jade says. 'Stay over there. They'll be here soon. Everything will be okay.'

I turn my attention to Jade. 'I'm sorry,' I tell her. 'I thought this was the right way to do things. Go the extra distance. Get what you want. But it wasn't, was it? I should have tried harder, done different things...'

'Shh,' she says, her tears increasing.

'Calm down,' Beau says. 'Let's not anyone panic.'

There's a bang at the front door. I turn around, startled.

'Don't move,' Beau says.

'Beau, don't, I'm not going to...'

There's another bang.

I say, 'You have to get out of here.'

'Why?' Jade asks. 'What's going on?'

'It's not safe for you to stay here.'

Bang.

'What are you talking about?' Beau asks.

'Richard, please, just sit down. We can end all this,' Jade pleads.

'You'll die if you stay here.'

Beau raises the gun slightly. 'Don't you move,' he says.

There's another bang and I can hear the door swing open.

'Go, Beau. Now.'

'Richard, what the fuck is going on?'

I don't need to look to know it's George coming up the hallway. 'Get out,' I yell as I quickly move to block the corridor, moving to shield Beau, hoping it's not too late.

'Richard,' Jade screams.

And then the gun goes off.

TWENTY-EIGHT

Let me tell you something.

I'm sitting here on this expensive couch and it feels like I'm sinking. I have no idea how they're going to get all this blood out.

George asks, 'What the fuck happened?'

There are things I don't remember. Big blank patches. Parts of my life are gone. The last year seems like a haze. Even parts of today are missing.

I remember the gun going off. I don't remember how many times.

I remember Jade crying and Beau looking shocked.

I remember them saying they're going to get help.

'They're not coming back, are they?' George asks me.

I shake my head. 'I don't think so. Would you?'

George's coughing tears through his chest.

'Your guts aren't going to, like, fall out or anything, are they?' I ask.

George snorts and says, 'Dude.'

I tell him I'm sorry. For everything. I know that's not the best thing to say to someone who's just been shot in the stomach but it's all I can think of.

He speaks in a rush, holding his breath against the pain. 'Have you called an ambulance?' he asks.

I shake my head, no. I ask, 'George?'

'Yeah?' he whispers.

'Do you think people really can have a second chance?'

He thinks about this. 'I don't know.'

Maybe the person you are can die. Maybe you can be reborn. Maybe you can try again. Maybe sickness can be cured.

I look around at all the blood. Is it really there? Is it George's?

Did the gun go off once or twice?

That pain in my stomach is back.

All you do is pull the trigger. The smallest action changes everything.

Would any of us change anything, given the opportunity?

'George,' I say again.

'Mm?' he asks, weaker now.

'You never taught me how to fly.'

He tries to laugh, fails. 'Yes, I did,' he says. 'I finally did.'

'What does that mean? George? What do you mean?'

'I'm going now, Richard,' he says.

'Don't. Don't, George,' I say, trying to swallow the lump in my throat, my voice breaking. 'Please don't go, stay for a little while longer.'

'No. I'm free. And so are you.'

'George?' I say. 'George?'

And then, just like that, George is gone.

I lean my head back against the sofa and cry. It hurts me to do this, it hurts in every way, but I simply cannot help it.

Can a person be reborn?

I clench my hands over my belly against the fire that is spreading there.

Can the sickness be cured?

There is so much that remains unsaid. How can life ever be summarised? There has been no mention of so many things, so many people and events. So many stories remain untold. I've left out so much; how I got the scar on my left elbow; the loss of my first tooth; my high school graduation; the years and the memories that have taken us to who we are now. All those wounds left behind from when we were happy.

I close my eyes and I see myself on the beach. The stars are hanging in the sky like pinpricks of fire and the roar of the waves breaking against the land is all encompassing.

There are gulls dancing in the wind, calling out, singing, and the sky is turning orange in the east.

It is the dawn of a new day.

And then I'm running, running across the sand, the cool breeze on my face, the spray of the sea wet against my cheeks like tears.

I look up at the stars fading in the light and then I push off, kicking against the world, lifting higher and higher, passing through the clouds. The air is getting cooler and as I break out of the blue and soar into the black there is a sense of peace, of wonder, as the stars regain their former glory. Eternity stretches out in every direction and I know I am a part of it, and no matter how small, every part contributes to the whole, and I am a part of it, swimming in the nothing, and I know if I had a big enough telescope I could see to the beginning of time.

I feel at peace at the start of this new day and I soar higher and higher until the black becomes infinite, stretching out forever.

Maybe I can start this new day with hope and maybe this is the first step to changing the world. The road is sometimes very long and most of the time very lonely, so try and hold someone's hand to make the journey a little more pleasant and hopefully someone will hold yours, too.

Maybe that's enough of a reason.

Now and forever.

If you like *Killing Richard Dawson*
then look out for
Robin Baker's next novel (coming in 2011)

Chasing the Sun

A dark coming-of-age comedy about
Feng Shui, vampires, exorcism,
pet psychiatry, genocide, belief
and mortality.

For more information, please visit:
www.PanteraPress.com

ABOUT ROBIN BAKER:
A young former English teacher, turned
funeral director. Knows death.
Lives in Perth, Australia.
This is his debut novel.

What they're saying about
Killing Richard Dawson

'...somehow doesn't miss a beat, all the way to an
ending that'll knock you sideways.'

Nick Earls, award-winning author

'Killing Richard Dawson takes the reader on an
unsettling journey...A truly gripping read.'

Bookseller + Publisher magazine

'*Catcher in the Rye* meets *Dexter*...a coming-of-age
tale injected with black humour.'

Reader's comment